The ice threatened to shatter under our mass.

If we fell into the water, having the extra burden of the chains on our wrists and ankles would certainly pull us down. But, as the unsavory fear of drowning settled heavily on my mind, the tall ship that had mysteriously appeared out of the blue, began to hoist her sails.

Men scurried about her yardarms in the processes of tying her sheets into place. I saw men hurrying to get into a longboat, and with their oars dipping into the water, they stroked in synchronicity toward us. It was a race against time. Even as our apparent rescue was near, the ice began to crack in protest. Any sharp or sudden movement was the end. I held my breath and waited, hoping the longboat might arrive in time.

"I will show you something different from either
your shadow at morning striding behind you
or your shadow at evening rising to meet you;
I will show you fear in a handful of dust."
-T.S. Elliot, *The Waste Land.*

Carl Lakeland

The
LOST
ONES

First published in Australia by Carl Lakeland 2019

Copyright © Carl Lakeland 2019 https://carllakeland.com
Typesetting: Carl Lakeland
Cover design: damonza.com
Editing: Trent Maier and Ingrid Fry
Proof reading: Ann Parry

ISBN numbers:9780987619877 (paperback) 9780987619884 (hardback)

Distributed by:
Ingram Content: https://www.ingramcontent.com/
Australia: Phone +613 9765 4800 |Email: lsiaustralia@ingramcotent.com

Milton Keynes UK: Phone +44 (0)845 121 4567
Email:enquiies@ingramcontent.com

La Vergne, TN USA: Phone 1-800-509-4156 |
Email: inquiry@lightningsource.com

Gardners UK: https://www.gardners.com/
Phone: +44 (0)1323 521555 Email: sales@gardners.com

Bertrams UK: https://www.bertrams.com/BertWeb/index.jsp
Phone: +44 (0)1603 648400 Email: sales@bertrams.com

A Catalogue record for this book is available from the National Library of Australia

For my friend and fellow writer, Ingrid Fry.

TABLE OF CONTENTS

ONE

THE WINDS OF CHANGE

CHAPTER ONE

The Marooned USS John Steinbeck

Ross Ice Shelf, Antarctica, 2157

Through the cutting glare that reflected off ice and snow, I could make out the line of individuals curling around Emert's Turn in a long S-shape. Trailing behind them, tied in a sled, was the body of that asshole, Chad Lucifer. Good riddance. The seal skins wrapped around his body were such a misuse of resources. They should've taken him away naked. Good seal skins. What a waste. Now he was getting something reserved for those who *deserved* a funeral. If it were up to me, I'd have had him dragged down to the coast; chained him on an ice floater and watched those killer whales out there rip him to pieces. But no. They decided to give him that funeral. I huffed my disgust and, head down, I walked on. Seeing that funeral procession was like seeing something filthy and not worth my trouble. Maybe I'd get to forget the bastard if I just kept walking.

My eyes followed the yellow line as I walked the metal and cracked bitumen surface of the flight deck. Trying hard to get Chad Lucifer's image out of my head, I cast my gaze around the place and focused, but no matter what I did, his memory infected my mind. How would I ever get over it?

After giving my face a good whack with my fur mitted hands, I began to wonder what it must've been like on the USS *John Steinbeck* during the Pre-Fall. I imagined it must've been buzzing with activity. Jet fighters everywhere. Maybe the smell of kerosene. Cold, salty sea spray. Shouting, yelling voices. Guys in colorful shirts sprinting here and there, each with their own job to get done. I imagined the deafening sound of the catapult shooting down the middle of the strip. The ear-splitting roar of afterburners. Orders bellowed over the PA. I imagined it must've been one heck of a show. But the visions I had in my head were, in reality, nothing more than a bunch of tattered and tarnished photographs that hung on walls where we all got together to mess.

After the bombs fell, they'd dumped all those aircraft over the sides. Sometimes we shared movies in cine-hall showing history as it was back then. But showing movies used up electricity. It was one of the luxuries that had to go.

"Hey, Ditch," my brother said over his shoulder as he clicked his big steel cleats past me. "Not surprised you wouldn't be part of Chad Lucifer's send-off, huh?"

Ditch. He'll never let me live it down. Not Richard. Not even Dick, even though I hated that name even more than Ditch.

"Hey . . . Quit calling me Ditch!" I said through my teeth.

"Well you did fall down that crevasse," Jason said eyeing me curiously. "Well, crevasse equals ditch . . . Ditch. Not to mention the major pain in the ass job it was to get you out. You're lucky. I'm just saying."

"Son-of-a-bitch!" I yelled after Jason as he turned and stepped away. But I had other things on my mind. "It seems you're the same as me or you wouldn't be here. You'd be part of that freaking waste-of-a-funeral they've got going for that asshole, Lucifer."

Jason spun and gave me that look again as I caught up with him. "Yeah, Ditch. I *am* like you. I'm just not so vocal about it. What Chad Lucifer did was horrible. If I had a hand in it, he wouldn't be taken off to no cemetery. I hate to think about his body being buried in the same ground as our clan. But he *has* the right to share the same ground as his, don't you think? Especially after the *good* stuff he's done. We remember the good, not the bad. And I have to keep reminding myself, all that's going on down there right now is, after all, his human right. Something you need to think about, Ditch. In the end it's *our* choice to pay, or not pay our last respects to a man who murdered his wife and kids then opted out by taking his own."

In my mind, I thought about what Chad Lucifer had done. We were *all* in danger of losing it. Losing grip on reality was as horrifying as just thinking about it. It made me shudder as I stood there. The fact was, the blackout was coming. Another stretch of months with nothing but the cold and the black. But this time it was different. This time, with *Steinbeck's* reactor dying out, the horror of the blackout was made worse. We'd not have enough electricity to see it through. Maybe Chad Lucifer's deed was done out of empathy for his family. Maybe he didn't want to be alive during the black nights and days, as one by one, people turned into psychopaths with an intent to murder anyone. How I hated this place. How I wanted to be away. How I wanted to get in a boat and get to Australia. It was a chance to start a new life. A chance to survive. A chance to have night after a day, and a day after night. No blackouts. No whiteouts. How would that feel? Everyone talked about it.

Jason dragged me back from my thoughts. "Where are you, Ditch?"

"Jase. We need to get away. Before the blackout. Before the reactor is dead and everyone is . . ."

Jason reached and pushed his hand up to my face. "Hey, quieten down," he whispered. "Haven't you noticed how Skipper didn't go to the funeral either? And that man's got ears all over this place. I agree. But how? Don't you think that's been worked over already? If it were possible, we'd *all* already be there."

Jason put his hand down and looked at me. I didn't know what it was that was sitting there behind his bluish-pink eyes. For a second, I thought it looked like sadness. Jason was never sad about anything. But as he blinked and looked down, it was there. For some reason, I felt a smile coming on. Maybe it was because I'd seen him in a light I've never seen before. It told me Jason was human and he feels things. But, as I caught his gaze again, I put that smile away. Fast. Knowing Jason, he'd never admit to having feelings. Jason and feelings? That seemed so odd. But there was no denying it. It was the same hopelessness sitting there in his eyes that we all shared knowing, blackout was coming, and coming fast. After the reactor dies, there'd be no electricity for heating. There'd be none for lighting. There'd be no desalination, which meant no fresh water. And harvesting fresh-water-ice in blackout was a suicide mission. As soon as I thought about it, I realized it was going to be the last stretch of black months for everyone. Without the reactor, nobody on *Steinbeck* would ever emerge into the daylight again.

"Jason. Listen to me." I brought Jason back from wherever he went. As he looked up at me with a set of red-rimmed eyes, almost childlike, peering directly at me through his pure white fringe, I knew I only had a moment to confess everything. Jason the hard was gone. This Jason was somebody else. I came out and said it. "Chloe is pregnant." I took a half step back and held my breath. Jason didn't react. I expected him to swing a punch. I expected his abuse. But there was nothing. He turned his back. I thought for a second, he might step away and not respond at all. After a long pause, he spun and faced me again; his expression was much different than before. Harder. Nastier. Jason the hard was back. I stood and braced.

"How far along?" Jason said in his normal unforgiving tone. I looked down at his hands that seemed as though they'd be used at any second to put me on my ass.

"Not sure. Fourteen weeks, I think." By now, maybe covering my face with both fur mitten-clad hands was a great idea. I didn't. I just stood there waiting for the worst. My fault. I'd take whatever was coming.

"You idiot! How did this happen, Ditch?"

I shot my brother a stare, telling him with my eyes what was the obvious scenario.

"Skipper will know soon enough," Jason said after a couple of seconds. "You can't hide from this for too much longer."

"Chloe is going full term, Jase. Nobody's going to take our baby away. We need to get away from here and get to Australia. It's the only hope we have left."

I saw Jason's shoulders drop slightly. Then he stepped up and got into my face. "You need a plan, little brother."

"I've got one, but I need your help."

"You've already thought about this?" Jason was surprised. He stepped a pace back and looked at me, scanning me up and down as if he thought his little brother was all grown up. Of course, I was all grown up. Maybe older brothers never change.

"I've had nothing else in my head, Jase. I've thought about everything. But so far, I don't have all the things I need to make it work. Are you with me on this?"

I told Jason about what I had planned. It'd start with collecting enough ice to thaw for fresh drinking water. We'd stash blocks of ice at the edge of the coast. The next stage was to repair a lifeboat.

Jason's eyes compressed into slits, looking at me as though I'd already lost my mind. "Repair a lifeboat? Those boats have got holes in them the size of basketballs; put there to make sure no one will ever leave here. Guess what? That was a hundred and fifty years ago. No one's ever going to leave. Forget about everything."

As soon as he said it, I realized it for the first time. I often wondered why the Oudarretians sabotaged the lifeboats. They could've simply dropped them into the seas as they did with the entire squadron of returning aircraft. Maybe it was a visual reminder to our ancestors they'd become prisoners to the elements. Jason was right. But I was about to change his mind or die trying.

Just when Jason turned and clicked away, I managed to grab his arm and spin him around. "The boats can be repaired. Believe me. We have seal skins. We can mend the holes."

"Oh, you think no-one has thought of that? And if what you're thinking is plausible, how do we get to keep the seal skins in place? So that nothing leaks?"

There it was. Jason said the word 'we.' Now I knew he was on board. I smiled briefly before saying, "We'll paint the seal skins into place with glue."

Jason looked at me, his eyes wide open. In an instant, the surprise was sitting there glistening at the edge of his eyelids. But he didn't know I'd already done some playing around. The gelatin I'd got from boiling seal' flippers. They always threw flippers away. There was no use for them. But I had other ideas. Then there was the glycerin I got from penguin fat. It took a while before I managed to extract the stuff. Once I had it down, I ended up with the glycerin I needed. The final piece to the puzzle was vinegar. I was vigilant, always watching for the opportunity to gather vegetable castoffs from ship's garden deck. I took little by little, sticking small bits of castoff into my pockets when nobody was looking. Once I had enough, I squished down the castoffs and waited for it to go off. In the subzero temperatures, it was a challenge. After I had all three things, I was able to come up with a glue that would do the job nicely.

Jason stood agog in front of me as I described my invention. It was the first time in my life I might've genuinely impressed him. But he'd never tell me. It was all in his expression, and that was good enough for me.

"How did you?"

"Ship's library," I cut him off. "I've read every book there is."

I saw the edge of a brief smile. I had him! "Okay. So, you've got glue," he said. "Now. Tell me how we're going to get the boat down to the water. And if they float, how're we ever going to stop from floating around in circles?"

"I haven't worked that part out yet. That's why I need your help. I can't do this on my own."

Jason eyed me intensely with a hand up to his chin. "We'll need to make sails."

"Not sails. We'll use the life boat's diesel engines."

Jason smiled, but this time it wasn't out of anything cheerful. He looked at me briefly, shaking his head, and then turned to step away. I grabbed him by the arm and spun him again. "C'mon, Jase. We can do this!"

"You know no-one has ever cranked those diesel motors. And even if they *did* crank, where's the fuel?"

"Biodiesel. All that seal and penguin fat we've used for cooking. It's all still there buried in drums out past Emert's Turn. If we don't do this, we'll die with the rest of them. All our clans. Lucifers, Michaels, Gabriels, Raphaels. The blackout is coming.

We have a month at the most. Chloe *will* be showing. What do you think is going to happen to her?"

"You still haven't given me an answer about navigation," Jason said. But the fact he wasn't walking away in disgust meant he was more in the moment than I thought. "And, you haven't told me who you've got planned to join us." This time, Jason grabbed my arm and spun me around, while at the same time checking over his shoulder. We both sat at the edge of *Steinbeck's* flight deck with our legs dangling over the edge, both silent, looking out at the pure white snow from roughly eighty hands up. Several moments passed before Jason finally broke the silence. "Tell me who's in on this," he whispered, checking again over his shoulder, swinging his head around just to make sure no-one was around.

"So far it's just you and me who know. I'll be letting Chloe know later."

"Our mother will join us," Jason put in.

"Our mother? Jase. Our mother left us a long time ago. I don't know who she is now."

"She's still our mother."

"She won't make the journey. She's not strong enough." Yeah, I was going to say it out loud for the first time. The words sat at the edge of my tongue and lingered there as though the words themselves had tiny hooks that screamed, *'no . . . you're not gonna say it!'* But out they came. "She's already dead, Jase. Her body lives. That's all there is."

As I said it, I held my gaze and saw the glisten in Jason's eyes. Something told me he'd finally conceded with the topic of our mother's health. He put his head down and sighed.

After a couple of moments held in silence with nothing but the low howl of the cutting ice wind, I asked my brother, "Is she still doing that London Bridge thing?"

"Yeah." Jason's sniffles broke into light sobs he seemed desperate to hide. The very first time I'd seen him like that. He tried to say something. It came out garbled. Even though his words seemed to curl around his sadness, somehow, I knew what he was trying to say. Now, it was my turn to take this idea home. "Jase. I'm about to tell you something that's gonna be hard. But before we leave here, our mother will be at rest. We'll not leave her to the blackout. We'll not leave her to a slow and painful . . ." As I realized it, it went whizzing around in my brain. If I take my own mother's life, am I not as bad as Chad Lucifer? All the hate. All the anger I had for him. I'm now about to commit the same offense. It was an epiphany that went pinballing around inside my head. There was no escaping it. I was going to murder my mother! I was another Lucifer.

"How?" Jason cut into my thoughts, dragging me back. He wasn't angry like I expected. He was exactly the opposite. It seemed so surreal, and it was as though a stranger had stepped into his body. Cautiously, I put my arm around my brother's shoulder. "I've got sleeping meds stashed away. It's supposed to be a most pleasant passing."

"How'd ya get it?" Jason pushed my arm away from his shoulder. "The sleeping meds. How'd ya get it?"

He was back to being Jason. *Jason the hard.* I paused a little, then answered. "Moonie."

"MOONIE!"

"Hey, shut up, will you!"

"You've signed your death warrant, you idiot! Moonie's a Lucifer. Did you think you could trust him? One—our sleeping meds are all we have in case somebody needs an appendix taken out. Two—they'll float you when they find out. And they *will* find out."

"We'll be gone."

"You hope!"

"Hey, drop your voice, Jason. Jeez . . ."

"I can't believe the risks you've taken!"

"I know, but I've thought everything out. Ever since Skipper told us about the reactor." I didn't say anything else. I let my brother sit there and mull things over. But I *did* have everything planned in my mind. Who'd know if my escape strategy was possible, much less plausible? We had to try. Or enter the darkness and perish in unspeakable ways. Everyone sound of mind would see their demise. And those already mad would be the last to die. Nobody could ever last months of blackout when the lights went out, and the cold entered, collapsing over everything with its icy claws of death. The only thing that lifted my spirits was the thought of one-day stepping onto dry land and doing away with the cleated boots. Doing away with the furs and feeling the sun burn my skin. But we're albinos. We'd need to learn coping strategies all over again.

Jason broke through my thoughts as we sat there at the edge of the flight deck, staring out toward the Ross Ice Shelf that held us captive. "You've had this in your head for how long?"

"Don't you listen? Since the time Skipper told us about the reactor. After that, I worked on coming up with a solution for fixing a lifeboat."

"And how are we ever going to repair it without being noticed?"

"I've thought of that too. We'll need to paste the skins over the holes from the inside."

Jason immediately shook his head and attempted to get up. I grabbed his arm and pulled him back down. "I know it's crazy. It's the only way."

"I dunno, little brother. Those skins will come off if you fix them from the inside. Imagine that happening while we're motoring, sailing, or even paddling halfway across the South Pacific!"

"Two things," I said. "If we fix them from the inside, we can do it without the fear of getting busted. And the glue will harden quicker because it's not open to the elements. But we need to paint the skin black so from the outside; the holes still look like holes."

"We need navigation equipment," Jason said, quickly changing the subject. "Charts and compass! A sextant as well!"

"For that, I have a plan."

CHAPTER TWO

Time to Go

The pipework running *Steinbeck's* lengthy corridors drew shimmering shadows on the walls as I stepped past a single lit oil lantern. Oddly, I wondered what might happen when *Steinbeck's* last lantern drew its last breath and went out. I'd be long gone. *We'd* be long gone. But it didn't stop me from wondering. Black. Not just black, but true black. Silent. Cold. That old ship smell; leather, grease, and fish oil filling the cold Antarctic air. And out of the cold and silence, the crying voices of those trapped would arise. The cackles and wallows of the insane. Then the happenings. The rampage. The random, indiscriminate slaying would begin. But it'd be much worse than anything I could imagine. So much worse. Death would come for every last being.

I shuddered in my spot as I thrust those horrible inevitabilities to the back of my mind. There was no point filling my brain with a weight I had no control over. Turning on my heel, I put my hand up and knocked on my mother's cold, steel stateroom hatch. The corridor around me echoed as I knocked. I smiled briefly, wondering why I bothered to knock at all. Old memories, probably. At a time long ago when my mother was lucid, she'd give me a mouthful of abuse if I didn't knock before entering. Old habits, I thought. Some things never change. I pushed the big steel hatch open and stepped inside. I could already hear her doing that London Bridge thing.

"London-bridge-is fall-ing-down . . ."

"London-bridge-is-fall-ing-down . . ."

She sang the first line, repeating it over after a slight pause. The same as she always did. Nothing had changed even though I hoped. From under a single dim light bulb that hung, slightly swinging from a long cord, she rocked herself forward and back while sitting at the edge of her bed. Singing. Rocking. Singing. The sight of her doing that brought me to the edge of tears, and it was as though someone had thrown a rock on my heart. There was a time this woman was one of the hardest individuals living among us. A true Gabriel. Hard, but at the same time compassionate. Caring. Considerate. Now, my mother was awake but gone. And she'd gone without telling anybody.

"London-bridge-is-fall-ing-down . . ."

I sat beside my mother; a bowl of warm broth made from the meat of emperor penguin resting in the palm of my hand. I swept her hair from her face, then; placed a spoonful of the broth next to the corner of her mouth. She wouldn't take it.

"London-bridge-is-fall-ing-down . . ."

"Mom. Please. You know you have to eat something."

"London-bridge-is-falli . . ."

"Mom!"

"London-Bridge . . ."

"MOM!"

I loved my mother, and it was so painful to see her trapped behind this thin membrane of insanity. At times I wished hard to be given the power to reach inside her body and pull her back to the surface. This thing that has taken her; it made me feel anger and frustration in a whole new way.

Just as I thought I could scream out my frustrations, my mother stopped with the singing. She rocked forward and back as though singing those words inside her mind. It occurred to me then; had she noticed my anger? Was she more lucid than I realized? If that was so, was she playing games? Maybe she wasn't insane at all. Maybe, just maybe, she was doing all these things as a means of escape. A way to hide from the others. A sort of evasion and deception. What if she had a plan to escape *Steinbeck* all to herself? What if she was playing us all, and at any second she might come clean, laugh her lungs out, and 'fess up? My mind began to spin knowing what I had stashed away. Nine vials of highly concentrated sleeping medication. Probably the last in existence. I'd locked them away in a place they were safe. They were ready whenever I was ready. But now this. Doubt. Uncertainty. It made me want to cancel all of my plans and start over.

"Mom? Are you faking this?"

There was no response. My mother kept up the same rocking tempo without so much as a slight change. Then I realized I was clinging to hope. And hope makes things appear to be what they are not. Hope is an emotion that can cloud logic and sensibility. I had no room for hope in my escape strategies. Then, as I realized it, I felt as though somebody dropped me from an awful height.

Again, I attempted to feed her. Now it was like I wasn't there at all. She didn't attempt taking her once favorite soup. "Mom, it's emp. You like it. Remember?" I placed a hand on her back, so she'd be still. I held up the spoon. There was no recognition that it was ever there. She'd retreated even further into her darkness than I realized. There was nothing further I could do.

* * *

My mother's stateroom hatch squealed opened, and Jason stepped inside. He went straight for the metal chair in the corner and dragged it over, sitting himself down heavily as if he'd spent the entire day harvesting blocks of ice and stowing them away in secrecy.

"Did you stash them with no trouble?" I said over my shoulder as I tried again with feeding my mother.

"Yeah. We've got enough freshwater ice in reserve for a couple of weeks. It's safe. I think it's stored close enough to the McMurdo ruins without it becoming radioactive. But you still haven't told me how we're gonna store it before we leave. You can't drink ice, Ditch."

"I've got it covered. We'll cut the blocks into sizable chunks first then tie seal skins around them. As the ice melts, they'll be like water inside skin canteens."

I'd already made seven canteens that were ready to go. But seven wasn't going to be enough. I estimated we'd need around thirty canteens to last us the trip safely across to Australia. And that was being conservative. Forty was a good round number with a buffer in case there was trouble. But fifty was the goal I had in my head. We'd not leave without having fifty canteens full of freshwater ice. Or as close to it as possible.

Jason suddenly seemed a little brighter. "You and your seal skins, huh? How's our mother doing?"

I handed my brother the bowl of emp broth. "Here. Your turn. See what you can do."

Immediately after he took the bowl off me, my mother again began to sing her tune, rocking back and forth as she'd previously done. "London-bridge-is-fall-ing-down . . ."

Before my blood had the opportunity to boil up all over again, there was a polite tap on the hatch. The hatch swung open, and Chloe delicately stepped inside. It never stopped amazing me how the Raphael clan were inherently light on their feet, and Chloe possessed the ability to slink around the place with the prowess of a puma. She stepped past Jason and me while grabbing the other metal chair, sliding it over. "Hope I'm not too late." Chloe sat slowly, eyeing my mother as she lowered herself into her chair. "How is she?"

"She's in la-la land," I said. "No change."

Then, all of a sudden,

"Chloe? Is that you? Come here, dear." My mother said it as though it was of no nuisance. No bother. Jason and I exchanged our shocked glances.

Lucid.

"Mom? It's Ricky. How're you feeling?"

"Richard? Richard? I . . . It's the bridge, Richard. It's the bridge."

"Mom?"

"It's falling . . ."

Shit!

"London-bridge-is . . ."

"MOM!"

"Leave her," Chloe took the bowl of broth from my brother and began the same task with which we'd had no success. I watched Chloe go through the same steps I'd worked with, and with the same result. No good. She turned and placed the bowl out of the way. Somehow, I knew the broth had already gotten cold, and emp broth that went cold always had a gritty texture with an aftertaste that wasn't pleasant. If I knew my mother, she would've complained bitterly had she been lucid.

The hatch opened. Immediately, Jason shot me a look that told me he wasn't impressed. Moonie stumbled, almost tripping through the opening. He was intoxicated again, but with all of his faults, we needed him. Jason would have to get over it.

Not able to grab a seat in time for gravity to take over, Moonie sat heavily on the floor with crossed legs as though a little kid at school time. He looked up with a grin as though he'd accomplished something impossible. Getting the meds that I needed *was* a feat by itself. Being a Lucifer, however, Moonie's greatest gift was at night. He saw things with the clarity of a nocturnal creature. The other reason he had to be with us was for the need of a sextant. Skipper had one locked away on the bridge. Moonie was Skipper's son. How simple could it be? Not only did we have access to a sextant, but we also had someone with us who could use it. Moonie was far too important. I knew he *had* to be part of the plan and now, I only hoped Jason knew it as well.

Chapter Three

Convicts

The Raphael clan shared the same auburn hair, blue eyes, and the same sporadic dusting of freckles as each other. But each time I looked into Chloe's crystal eyes that reflected the same blue as glacial ice, I never stopped enjoying the one thing I loved to do the most. I'd linger there in the reflection of her gaze where sometimes her eyes were so liquid, I swear I could swim in them. Trance-like, there'd be no words, and I'd stay there. Chloe seemed to know it was something that made me feel contented. She never looked away. She always smiled. "I love you," she'd say, breaking the silence by words louder in volume than they truly were. I'd look away from her smile. I'd rest my head on her chest and listen to her heart, feeling the muscles in my cheeks. I was happy.

Life's realities can invade even the happiest of thoughts and the most peaceful of moments. Earlier, I'd told Chloe about our plans to escape. At first, Chloe was like Jason. She was disbelieving of the whole affair. She couldn't picture in her mind how such an audacious plan could ever succeed. But after she'd had the time to think it over, she conceded. For the sake of our unborn child, it was the only option we had left. But I omitted one important detail. I held back on telling Chloe about my mother. I didn't tell her about the nine vials of sleeping meds I'd kept stashed away in my footlocker. I didn't know why I couldn't bring myself to say it. It appeared I was having a bout of indecision. I was having second thoughts.

Deep in my mind, the decision to end my mother's life was in utter turmoil. It was as though some dark force was throwing me in one direction, then back to the other. How could I sit there at my mother's side and watch her take her last breath? Was it evil of me to do such a thing, even if it were out of compassion? I kept repeating in my mind, the steps I needed to take. But it never made anything easier. I was still a murderer. It didn't matter which angle I looked at it. I was going to commit a murder, and not only that, I was going to commit an appalling crime; matricide.

"I can feel your brain ticking over." Chloe's words were loud through her chest as I laid my head there. At that moment I decided she must know everything.

"My mother . . ." I took a huge gulp of air. I was about to continue.

"You're going to euthanize her, aren't you?"

Chloe knew me so well; there wasn't a thing I could keep from her. She knew my unspoken words as plainly as any spoken words. It was another trait of the Raphaels. They all seemed to possess this strange ability. I'd gotten so used to it, it never surprised me, but this time it did.

"You've got meds to send her to sleep?"

Not able to answer her question outright, I nodded. I hoped Chloe could feel my nod on her breasts. It was then I felt her arms pull me in and I cried openly. Oddly at the same time, a voice inside told me there's no shame for a man to shed tears if he shares them with his wife. I'd never wept so hard. So uncontrollably. I don't think there was a time, ever, in my life where such sadness trapped me. I was overwhelmed and broken. The reality of what was to come hurt so bad; I felt every bit of it. With every pulse around my heart. With every breath of air in my lungs.

"Ricky, this sadness inside you is hard. But you'll take care of this."

After I was able to regain my composure, nothing more needed to be said, but at least now, I knew it in my heart, Chloe was right.

* * *

I opened my eyes to the sounds of commotion coming from somewhere at the end of the corridor. From down there, someone screamed out obscenities and other nonsense. I recognized it as Moonie. His outbursts instantly made me chill to the bone. My skin prickled on my forearms. I realized through his cries; they were beating him with terrible blows.

I responded, sitting upright in my hammock, cocking my head in the direction of the uproar. With the flat of my hand, I carefully attempted to awaken Chloe, taking extra care not to alarm her. As though reading my gesture, I felt her move in closer toward me. I was sending the wrong signal.

"Chloe," I whispered. "It's Moonie."

"What?" Chloe rolled over and raised herself on her elbow, listening with the same awareness as I'd done a moment before. "My goodness. What's happening?" At the same time, Moonie yelled out chillingly after another round of fleshy thuds. I flew from my hammock. Before I made it to the hatch, someone pounded at it with what I thought were bare fists. "Open up! Open-the-fuck-up. Now!"

The sound of his voice made me recoil on the spot. *Shit. It's Skipper!*

Somewhere in the back of my mind, I knew what was happening. All our plans. All our strategies. Everything. It was all over. Jason was right. They're going to float us.

I moved to open the hatch but stopped. I looked at Chloe. She pointed with a quivering finger to the footlocker. The vials of sleeping medicine. Panic went rocketing through my brain. Chloe knew where I'd stashed them. How? It didn't matter. But what was I supposed to do with them now? *Make them disappear.* My eyes went to the porthole. They'd land softly on the snow outside. Maybe nobody would notice them. And if there was no evidence, there'd be no floating. Maybe, just maybe, everything might not be lost after all. Maybe, after everything had died down, we could pick up where we left off.

I leaped across to the footlocker and opened it, at the same time signaling to Chloe. I whispered loud enough for her to hear, "Open the porthole, Chloe. Quickly." I rummaged through the footlocker and my fingers curled around the small metal box with the sleeping meds inside. Then I realized it for the first time. I might be able to get rid of the vials of death. But what about all the seal skins? What about the big containers of glue? What about the charts and compass Moonie had stolen from the ship's bridge? My head was about to explode in panic.

"Open the hatch, seaman Gabriel! That's an order!"

Chloe was at the porthole. She opened it just in time. I held the metal box up in the same way as I'd read in books about football. In my mind, I tried to work out how to make it spin after I hurled it.

"Seaman Gabriel! Open this hatch! Immediately!"

More footfalls arrived outside the bunkroom. Maybe there were seven sets!

I wound up my shot, aiming the box for the tiny opening that let in the daylight.

My life depended on it. *All* our lives depended on it. Getting busted with the seal skins and glue was bad enough. The stolen charts and compass was a long-term in the brig. If I didn't make the sleeping meds disappear, *holy shit* . . . It most certainly was death by floating. That small porthole wasn't much bigger than the metal box in my hands. Could I do it? From around thirty hands away?

I wound up my shot but before I threw it . . .

The hatch swung open. Skipper burst in and stood there with his master key dangling from his grip. His black as black pupils fixed on me. The word 'busted' whipped around my brain like a headless snake. I stood there and his pupils grew to cover the whites in his eyes. He looked as evil as ever. His voice lowered to some dark place, "Give-it-to-me!" He moved toward me with speed. I quickly glanced sideways to Chloe. She held her hands to her face and mouthed the word 'no,' but it was too late.

I got that metal box and raised it above my head. As soon as Skipper was within range, I brought the metal box down with my full weight, smashing it between his ebony-black eyes.

"No Ricky, NO!" Chloe screamed.

As Skipper collapsed to the floor, I caught sight of the heavily armed security detail who were with him. Two men moved swiftly toward me, metal batons extended. I gritted my teeth. Hard. As soon as one got close enough, I aimed and kicked. He spiraled away cupping his testicles, yelling out in pain, falling backward over Skipper's unconscious body.

In the next second, a loud *CRACK*, and the agonizing pain went straight to my head. Just as the horror of being kneecapped became real, my leg folded under my weight and I went down. Another crack on the collarbone and instantly, a wrecking ball of severe agony shot through my body.

Somewhere in the background, Chloe screamed out more chillingly than before, and I knew from that second, no amount of fighting and struggling could ever change anything. It was over. There was no hope and no chance of getting away to Australia. No hope to escape from the inevitable blackout. We'd all perish. And my execution would come sooner than lights out. There was no doubt in my mind that my fate was sealed. They'd have us chained on an ice floater, where I'd meet up with an orca, and my body would cease to exist.

* * *

A security guard yelled as I was dragged with speed down the corridor toward the ship's brig. "Make way! Make way!"

My feet skidded past Jason's bunkroom and I noticed his hatch was left open. The fear of it all struck me as I felt a hard lump form at the base of my throat. I was just able to fleetingly peer through the aperture of his hatch as they dragged my body past.

Jason wasn't there. My mind tried to hide from the reality, but there was no hiding. They had Jason and had taken him away.

Betrayal settled heavy in my mind. And the worst part of the realization was Jason's words, telling me I'd signed my death warrant by letting Moonie in. I thought I had it sorted. I thought Moonie would be a valuable asset when it came to navigation. I knew the risks. I knew the dangers. And I always thought Moonie never had it in him to turn. I was wrong. I took it for granted. Now I was pulling everybody I ever cared about down into this pit of despair I'd created.

They threw me to the floor in the brig and the loud echo of the brig hatch clanged behind me. Jason eyed me from one corner of the big space with his gaze of death. As I lifted my head, still dazed and dizzy, I expected him to say something. Anything. But instead, Jason got up from his awkward crouched position, and within a couple of seconds, I was feeling myself reeling back from an immense thump to my left eye socket. As I shook away more daze and came to, I noticed we weren't alone. Sitting right behind me in the opposite corner was Moonie.

Break Out

We exchanged no words. Outside the brig, the voices and foot-falls of souls going about their business, padded up and down the corridor as though it was the same day as any other.

I sat on the edge of a metal sprung bunk bed, swallowing back biting pain in my shoulder and left knee. The amount of damage I'd received from the end of a metal baton was immense, and I wondered how in the heck I could ever recover from such injuries. Somehow, I knew from beneath my swollen knee that was the size of a small melon; the bone had shattered into a million tiny shards. I knew my collar bone would never heal normally if nobody put it right. Then I thought, why would anyone bother fixing it? Our execution was probably only a matter of days away.

Jason finally broke the silence. "Little brother. What's your plan now, Ditch?"

I would've *shrugged* my response if it was possible. The thing was, I had no clue. But Jason's folded arms and pushed down brow told me he was demanding an answer. Who was I to deny him? "There's no plan, Jase. You and I both know what'll happen next."

"Orca teeth." Jason said it not as a question but as a realization. He was thinking out loud. I nodded my response even though he didn't need it. But in my mind, I thought there must be a way to get out of this mess.

I looked around the place. Everything was solid metal and cracked green-grey paint with the same pattern of intricate rivet-work as everywhere else. I'd watched movies of prison escapes back when there was the electricity supply to show them. The first thing I did was to look up, and there it was. But the air ventilation system was minuscule, and it wasn't big enough for anybody to use as an escape route. To my left, there was the porthole to the outside. No good. It was too small for any human to get through and they'd covered it with metal bars. Maybe they put the bars there to make the place look like a brig. The only way we were ever going to leave was through the hatch. So that left only one option.

Leaving my bunk bed, I scooted sideways over to Jason's side, grimacing with pain. "We'll need to overwhelm and disarm any-one coming through," I said.

Jason looked over his shoulder toward me, not bothering to change his seated posture. His body language said everything. "And judging by *your* condition, you'd be wanting *me* to take care of it."

"Who else? It's what you're good at. You're a natural born killer."

"You and your movies."

"Yeah, and I read too."

But just as I said it, I noticed something on the floor. I left Jason's side to go and take a closer look. I put my hand down and felt it to make sure I wasn't dreaming. Jason came over to my side in a hurry. "Well, will you look at that."

"Yeah. But how . . .?"

There was a metal plate on the floor that screws held into place. It wasn't riveted down. That said the plate was covering something that needed maintenance. The plate was roughly four hands by four hands.

"A crawl space?" Jason asked.

"The main electricity supply conduit," I answered him. "But maybe big enough to *use* as a crawl space. I think we can use it to get out of here."

"Only if we could undo the screws, Ditch."

Jason was right. How would it be possible to undo them? I sat back and thought it over. I wasn't satisfied leaving the morsel of hope alone. There must be a way, I kept telling myself. There must be a way, damn it! But even if we *did* escape the rusty steel confines of the brig, where could we go? We were on a ship. It didn't matter which way I looked at it; we were rats in a trap. In or out, it didn't matter. As soon as I thought it, my spirits melted away, and I was at the same place I started.

The big hand-screw on the hatch spun anticlockwise, and it swung open. We madly scurried to our bunks and made like a couple of guys who were up to nothing. Before the guard slammed the hatch closed and locked it into place, he'd hastily tossed another prisoner to the center of the brig. As I focused, it was as though my mind was playing tricks. Looking up from his half seated, half kneeling position in the middle of the floor was the ship's medical officer, Eli Raphael.

Jason put a hand up to his face. "You gotta be kidding,"

Out of my mouth came the obvious. "Why are *you* here?"

Eli looked up and his face contorted into something I thought was out of embarrassment. It was obvious he'd screwed up, but how?

"It seems a breach of security in the medical stores falls on my shoulders. The buck stops with me if things go missing, especially things like vials of sleeping medication." Eli shot a hard look to Moonie. He got up and raced toward him; hands clenched into fists. I grabbed Eli before he could do any damage to Moonie's physical appearance. "There'll be a time for that," I said as I somehow stopped him from getting any closer. "More important things need doing first. How would you like to come on a trip?"

"Ditch!" Jason yelled. But before Jason could protest further, Eli's mood appeared to brighten up. "Trip? Where?"

"Ditch, we have to get out of *here* first."

"So, what's your plan?" Jason asked again. Now I felt the pressure to come up with something. Anything. I began by looking around the place, taking stock of what we had available – things that could help us. We had a couple of steel sprung beds with cotton bedding. That was about it. I squinted my eyes and looked at those things closer. I looked beyond what they truly were and imagined what they could become. Parts. I needed items to; one – stop anybody from getting inside the brig, and two – to use as screwdrivers.

I closed my eyes.

I thought things over.

How could I get this done?

And then everything fell into place. I had all the pieces put together. And better than that, I knew it would work.

I said to Jason, "When was the last time you saw any metal cutting equipment on *Steinbeck*? I'll answer that for you. You haven't because there isn't any. Why? Because they'd destroyed all that stuff after The Fall."

Jason folded his arms tighter. "Your point?"

"If we block the hatch by jamming the hand-screw, nobody can get in. And even if they did find something to break in, it'd be too late. We'd be far away."

"And how do we block the hatch?" Eli asked.

"How? Like this." Managing to get to my feet, I cast my eyes on the steel frame bunk bed. I grabbed one of its steel legs and tugged. After a tug, I fell back to the wall and pain instantly shot up my spine and into my head.

"You'd better let me look at that," Eli said as he began to examine my injuries. My knee wasn't broken after all but severely bruised. My collarbone had broken, and from one of the bed sheets, Eli made a sling and placed my arm into it. After he'd set it up, the pain melted away and I could finally breathe.

Turning my attention to the job at hand, "I need one of those bed legs," I said and started pulling at it again, but the bastard wasn't coming off as easy as I thought. It was as though Jason caught on to my idea. He had his hands all over it, and I saw it was only a matter of time before he ripped the thing from the frame. With Eli stepping in to help, the steel leg made a snap, and it came away in one solid piece.

I pointed with my available hand, and Eli knew what to do. He took it and placed one end of the leg through the spokes in the hand-screw; the other end rested on the floor. Nobody was ever going to get in without cutting equipment. That's all there was to it.

"Now how do we get away?" Eli asked. I looked over to Jason who was again sitting on his bunk with his arms firmly locked in a fold. It was as though he was daring me to sort this out. He didn't know that I *had* it sorted out and I was almost thrilled to show him. I smiled as I reached and pulled a small spring from the side of the bunk frame. I got myself to the steel plate in the floor. The tip of the spring fitted snugly into the screw heads that were holding the plate down. I began undoing the screws.

Jason laughed as he got himself over to my side.

"Go and grab another spring, Jase. You can work on getting more screws out. The more, the better."

Eli grabbed another spring from the bunk frame. He came back to the plate and went at the screws with vigor. As several minutes slipped past and then turned into roughly twenty without so much as a single screw loosened, we all sat back out of breath.

I wiped the sweat from my face as I realized, all the screws were corroded and frozen into place and maybe frozen for over a hundred years. I wasn't prepared to give up that easily. I grabbed a sheet from the bed and stuck a corner of it in my mouth. With my good arm, I ripped off a strip. Eli, as though reading my mind, grabbed the sheet from me and ripped a strip away. "What do you want to do with it?"

"Put it around the spring so we can get more leverage."

Eli wound a strip of bed sheet around the spring and handed it over. At the same time, Jason ripped a strip of bed sheet and did the same. I placed the tip of the spring in the screw and put my weight behind it. Then something I didn't expect. The head of the screw snapped off.

"Shit!" Jason said.

"It's okay, Jase. If they break, we'll still be able to get the plate off."

Another screw head snapped off at the same time someone unlocked the hatch from the other side. The big hand-screw on the hatch moved a fraction and with the bed leg stuck in it; it became jammed into place.

Here we go.

We all held still and watched the hand-screw jiggle back and forth. Then it jiggled violently. We were only minutes from getting away to our new freedom.

"Open the hatch!" The voice yelled from the other side. The hand-screw jiggled back and forth more violently than before. "Open the hatch! Now!"

"Shit!" Jason said more urgently than before.

"Get your head into it, Jase. They can't get in. Concentrate. You too, Eli."

We bent down and went at the screws. Some screw heads broke off as expected. That was good. But others refused to break. And a couple of the screws just would not budge. If there was a time this needed to go smoothly, it was now. I counted them. Ten screws were busted. We'd loosened three. Two screws refused to do anything. Their heads became burred over. The slots were beginning to disappear. If the screws were located closer together, it wouldn't have mattered. But as Murphy's law would have it, they were far apart which meant levering up the plate to break them was impossible.

More booted feet came thumping down the corridor and stopped outside the hatch. Whoever it was this time worked the hand-screw over again. We watched as it jiggled back and forth. Then the voice spoke loudly on the other side, and I knew it was Skipper. "You have two minutes! That's all you've got! It's up to you!" There was an inaudible conversation between Skipper and others who were out there; then they sprinted away.

Jason shouted, "SHIT!"

"Jason. It's like I said. They can't get in. Just get that damn plate off!"

With only two screws to go, I tried hard to stem the rise in my frustration. I was beginning to feel sick. My hand ran around the edge of the plate, and I could almost get a finger under it. "We're almost there!" But something made me instantly stop. The breeze of someone rushing past me. Moonie scampered to the hatch and began tugging at the metal bar. I reached out and grabbed his jeans leg and tried to drag him back. Pain screamed into my head, and I couldn't move.

Just as I thought it, Jason sprang up and rushed past me. He grabbed Moonie and pulled him back. He pulled a sleeper hold on Moonie. Within a moment, Moonie went still and collapsed to the floor.

The danger was over. I went back to the screws.

Then, the sound of something rushing in. For some reason, my eyes went to the air vent above, and the horror struck me. "Eli. Can you rip off a couple more strips from that sheet?"

He nodded without question and went to it. After handing me a strip, I pointed to the vent. "Tear gas. The bastards are trying to gas us out!"

For the first time in my life, I saw terror in Jason's eyes. Eli handed him a piece of rag which he took and used to take cover from the rushing gas.

I pointed with a finger to the air vent and motioned to Eli. Without words, he took the rest of the bed sheet and pushed it up to the vent.

"SHIT!" Jason yelled.

"Jason get it together!"

Then, the last two screws gave way with an audible snap. I shot a stare at Jason and smiled as I lifted the plate away. The happiness of getting away was shortlived by mere seconds. What I thought would most certainly be a crawl space, turned out to be nothing more than a pit going down roughly five hands, filled with pipework and valve handles. We weren't going anywhere. We were done.

Jason stood and as though without thinking about it, took the bed leg away from the hand-screw. The hatch sprung open. In ran the booted feet of armed guys in gas masks. The butt of a rifle rushed at me. Blackness came.

Chapter Five

Ice Floater

I opened my eyes, and I was welcomed by the cold crispness of the Antarctic outdoors. Vapor shot from my breath, and somehow, I knew I was closer to the floating than I could ever realize. When they wanted to get rid of a prisoner condemned to death, these guys wasted no time. Why waste time on a guy who was about to commit murder by killing his own mother? Why waste time on a guy who was behind the theft of valuable medical resources? A guy who planned to initiate an audacious escape strategy? A guy who made his woman pregnant? I was fast-tracked. No fuss. No bother. I was on my way. I could almost feel a set of cold orca teeth puncture my body and rip me apart. And I'd be alive to feel every bit of the pain.

I tried to jiggle my wrists free and I realized with a heavy heart I wasn't alone. Eli's voice protested profusely at what was happening. Then there were Jason's words in his standard tone telling

Eli to *shut-the-fuck-up*. From behind me, someone was sprouting off garbled nonsense, and I knew it was Moonie.

"CHLOE!" I shouted.

"Ditch! It's no good, Ditch! They're floating us today, Ditch!"

"Richard . . ." Eli's voice from somewhere in the front. "Don't waste your breath, Richard. You'll need all your strength."

Is this really happening?

"CHLOE!"

"Ricky . . . Don't die, Ricky."

Chloe's voice was faint from somewhere far behind. I realized she was still on-board *Steinbeck*, probably the flight deck. She was probably being made to watch.

"CHLOE . . . I'LL COME FOR YOU!"

"Ricky . . . I love you . . ."

Some big guy stepped over me. Blackness came.

* * *

I opened my eyes to find myself chained on the ice right by the water's edge. From what I could tell, Eli, Jason, and Moonie were close by. They'd chained all of us within easy reach of the orcas that roamed the freezing Antarctic seas. There were no words between us as the bastards who put us there got busy with finishing things up. Skipper's words came slicing through the subzero stillness, sounding every bit as cold. He spoke as though reading aloud from some official paper, the numerous charges and a quick, emotionless verdict of guilty; then, he imposed the death sentence with the same blasé as making a morning brew. Our deaths would arrive through the teeth of an orca, or worse, through the gut pinching distress of dehydration.

In the next moment, a series of vibrations through the slab of ice confirmed they'd cut us from the ice shelf and cast us adrift. The cold Antarctic wind took over, and it wasn't long before we were well out to sea.

* * *

I had no idea how long we'd been out floating. The ice had already partly melted beneath us, and for the first time, I felt water splashing and lapping at my boots. I oddly thought how amazing it was that they'd tied us fully clothed. We were dead anyway. Why waste good clothing?

I jiggled my right wrist at the end of the chain and checked if the ice had melted around the poles that held us captive. The poles wiggled a little but not enough to make any difference. I no longer felt any sensation in my back, or pain in my knee and shoulder. I assumed the ice had anesthetized my body as I lay there.

"You guys okay?" I asked with my voice lightly crackling; my throat so dry.

No answer. I might as well have said it to the fish out there. But even so, how could I not be in awe of the scenery. The water so calm. The clouds hung low enough for me to reach out and grab them had I not been chained. Seabirds spiraled and cried out to each other. The sun cast visible rays of light across the water's reflection. If my head told me I was in a dream, I'd have believed it.

"Ditch! Wake up! Don't sleep or you'll die!"

What would it matter? I was dead anyway.

"Richard! Open your eyes, damn it!"

I immediately opened my eyes and pain racked my body. I just wanted to curl up and get away from it. Looking around the place, I was in exactly the same scene I'd been dreaming about. But this time I knew I was well in the stages of dehydration. I thought by the way I was feeling, I'd live another twelve hours. Maybe. Nausea came in waves, and if there was something in my gut to throw up, maybe I'd have done it. If an orca didn't take me soon, my eyeballs would become nothing but food for seabirds. We'd all end up that way. Then the ice would melt, and we'd become history.

As I lay there and listened to yet another bout of Moonie's nonsense, I attempted to get my head away and think of Chloe. I felt a big vibration strike the ice from underneath and my heart sank. Here we go.

Chloe . . .

In that split second, a killer whale breached the water right at my feet. All of a sudden, I was sweating needles. I wanted to kick it away. The orca stared, surveying the area with one huge eye before slowly sinking back into the water.

"Oh . . . This is it, guys," Eli said. But just as he said it, the huge mammal breached the water with its full length, then fell back down, causing a wave of salty sea to crash over us. For a few seconds, I became fully submerged. Not properly prepared, I swallowed back a big mouthful of seawater, and after breaking the surface again, I coughed hard before I could finally take another breath.

As though in a mad panic, Moonie started to sound off. The huge sea beast breached the water and came down belly first, wrapping its teeth around Moonie's abdomen. Moonie yelped, and before any other noise escaped him, a snap, a rip, a spray of blood, then Moonie was gone. I gazed out on the blue water where I'd last seen Moonie and the sea bubbled, became tinged with red, and I knew he could never survive.

"Hey, Ditch. Today is a good day to die. Die easy, my brother."

I closed my eyes. I always thought when death came, I'd meet it head on. But this was something else. I closed my eyes to concentrate. I wanted to know for sure. The sensation was no lie. We were moving; there was no denying it. I felt the unmistakable awareness of movement. Something was under the slab, pushing us through the waters. The question was what, and how? As I realized it, we were moving through the water and picking up speed. The entire slab tilted at a steep angle and a bow wave began to form. An orca's tail broke through the water's surface. Then there were two. Then another. And another orca of no color at all. White as an albino. The same as me. The same as Jason. The same as any Gabriel.

"Ditch . . . What's happening!"

"We're being rescued." I didn't know how I knew it. I just knew it.

"Rescued, my ass. We're going further out to sea!"

"And we're going north," Eli worked out. "North into warmer waters!"

"Warmer waters! The ice will melt!"

I wondered briefly why the pod of orcas seemed to be helping rather than killing. Jason was right; the ice would melt in in the warmer waters. Then what? Logic told me, the only way to go was down. There'd be no chance for survival at all. The weight of having the chains on our wrists and ankles would pull us under. Even as my logical brain expressed these thoughts, there was the gut. And my gut told me there was something else.

After what seemed hours, skipping over the crests of waves, being pushed north, all of a sudden, nothing. No more forward momentum. No more speed. Rushing to a stop, I was horrified to see that the ice under us was minuscule in dimension and the fact we remained above the water's surface was nothing less than a miracle. The poles that held us chained had completely fallen out of the ice and disappeared. And out there; there was nothing. There was nothing but the sea, horizon, and blue-blue sky.

Eli pointed into the distance. "Over there. Look."

I adjusted my gaze in the direction Eli pointed. Jason jiggled his chain and cupped a hand over his brow. At first, I was hard-pressed making out anything. But as I looked harder, a container surrounded with some old rags bobbed up and down with the motion of the sea. When the object finally got close enough, for some reason, all I wanted to do was kick it away. A person's skeletal remains in bedraggled clothing floated with its arms outstretched; one boney hand still grasping a handle of what looked like an old military footlocker.

"There's a box," Jason said as he tried to reach for it. "A plastic box, I think."

"Yeah, military footlocker but don't touch it, Jason. If you bring it up on the ice, it might sink us."

"It appears we won't have to worry about drowning after all," Eli said from behind me. "There's a ship out there. See it?" He pointed. I gazed into the direction, and I saw a silhouette backlit from the sunlight. The silhouette of a tall ship.

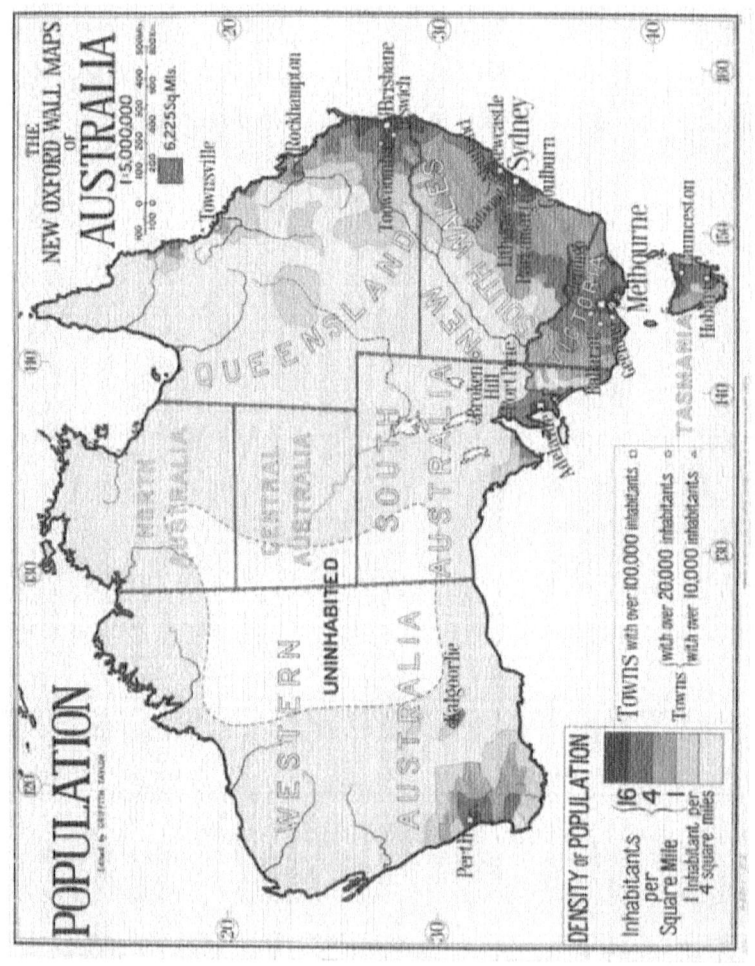

Chapter Six

Victory

The ice threatened to shatter under our mass. If we fell into the water, having the extra burden of the chains on our wrists and ankles would certainly pull us down. But, as the unsavory fear of drowning settled heavily in my mind, the tall ship that had mysteriously appeared out of the blue, began to hoist her sails.

Men scurried about her yardarms in the processes of tying her sheets into place. I saw men hurrying to get into a longboat, and with their oars dipping into the water, they stroked in synchronicity toward us. It was a race against time. Even as our apparent rescue was near, the ice began to crack in protest. Any sharp or sudden movement was the end. I held my breath and waited, hoping the longboat might arrive in time.

When at last the longboat drew alongside us, the danger was still not completely over. Getting into the longboat was a three-way coordinated exercise. Tricky maneuvering and a whole lot of luck was required. My injuries made moving around difficult and even more dangerous. But in the end, all three of us managed to get to safety.

The last item to be dragged into the longboat was the foot-locker, which a sailor clad in tattered clothes immediately dubbed as 'dead man's chest.' "We'll take that dead man's chest wiv us. There might be treasures to be 'ad in there. We don't take dead blokes either, mate. Leave 'im in the water."

Finding a spot in the longboat, I quickly looked sideways to Jason. "This guy talks strange. What's a bloke?" I whispered.

Jason shrugged. "Maybe it's just another way of saying dead guy."

Approaching the tall ship, I could see the figurehead mounted below the tall ship's bowsprit. I rubbed my eyes a few times. I thought maybe smacking my face a few times would bring me back to reality because, of course, I was dreaming. I'd seen the figurehead before. I'd seen it in books. I'd read the history. I was well acquainted. As soon as I realized it, it was without a doubt. But how was it possible? With her colorful English coat of arms, embellished in gold leaf, being in her presence was just as much surreal as it was awe-inspiring.

The men in the longboat pulled up oars as we came to rest alongside the huge timber and wrought iron ship. I looked up and counted them. Three levels of portholes where I knew the barrels of cannon were only inches from the apertures — a host of deck guns above that. Oddly, I wondered if it was true what they claimed. I'd read that if they fired all her cannon at once, there might be enough energy to tip her on her side. I was humbled in her presence. I fought through the urge to jump out of the long-boat and swim to the stern if only to see her name in all its glory. Eli and Jason appeared just as much awestruck. At that moment, several ropes were flung down from the quarterdeck. The cumbersome climb aboard this both magical and infamous vessel had begun.

* * *

At last, we were relieved of our chains. A couple of young sailors not much older than twelve gave us fresh dry clothes, and for the first time in a long while, I felt as though there wasn't any immediate danger around the next corner. I found myself relaxing a little as I checked out the surroundings. Below decks was the same as I'd learned in *Steinbeck's* library. The place was dark and lit up with oil lanterns in much the same way as I'd already become accustomed. Long shadows danced around the place with the aroma of what I assumed was whale oil in the air. I wasn't familiar with the smell of old timbers, however. I found it pungent – smelling of a mix of mildew, animal waste and what I thought might be gunpowder, saltpeter, and charcoal. Maybe it was just a case of getting used to it. Every now and again, loud cracking sounds erupted from the timbers as the ship rocked in time with the motion of the seas. It was somewhat unsettling as though this ship was alive and breathing.

With my arm in a sling that Eli had made from what they called 'calico gone spare,' the ship's Master, by the name of William Fletcher, ushered the three of us to a series of hammocks they'd slung between huge, ominous looking cannon. They'd given us instructions, and we were to refer to these hammocks as our allotted spaces. "We all work for our keep 'round 'ere," Master William Fletcher told us in an accent I'd not heard before. "There ain't no free lunch on this lady. You blokes are on swabbin' detail after first light. 'Cept you," he pointed at me with a gnarled knuckled finger. "Dunno what cappy wants wiv you just yet. It'll be at 'is pleasure, I'm supposin'. Nigh-nigh, yous lot."

It took a bit of an effort climbing up and into my hammock. But once I got in, my thoughts returned to Chloe. I hoped she was safe. Deep in my heart, I knew I'd have the opportunity to embark upon her rescue. In the morning, I'd lobby the Captain for his help. But I was tired. My eyelids had the weight of a barbell, and they almost instantly slammed shut.

* * *

Early in the morning and after mess, the three of us were invited above decks to meet the captain for the first time. My heartbeat quickened in anticipation but after we were face to face, I was completely taken by surprise. Dressed in the navy-blue woolens of a bygone era, he looked eerily, almost the spitting image of the pictures I'd seen of Horatio Nelson. The same Nelson who died during the battle of Trafalgar. This captain standing in front of us wore the same hat and all.

I was about the exchange my first words.

We have to go back . . . Chloe . . .

The words I had in my head never got the chance to form in my mouth.

"Welcome aboard His Majesty's Ship of the Line, *Victory!* I'm Captain Henry Bass. At your service," the captain said, then stepped back a pace and did this odd bow thing. It was so surreal, and I felt as though I'd gone back in time by a few hundred years. It looked as though all these guys were stuck in some weird time warp. But I couldn't ignore what was in front of me. What I was seeing was authentic. Everything down to the last stitch. Was I dreaming? Was this all for real?

Still not quite sure, I caught myself laughing a little under my breath as I asked my question, and Captain Bass answered with refreshing vigor. "Is she the real *Victory?* That she is, young lad, to be sure. I've known this ship both man and boy. We found her adrift. Albeit without masts, mind you. We fitted her with new masts and new rigging. We brought her back to her former glory. But we also added a few little . . . err. . . modifications to make her the very fine ship she is today. There isn't a vessel out on the high seas which can put a scratch on her paint, truth be told."

"You certainly dress for the occasion," Eli put in.

Captain Bass appeared to shrug off the irony, instantly changing the subject. "On the morrow, we shall set sail for the colonies."

"Colonies?" I butted in. "We need to head south. Back to where we came from."

"You came from the south? Are you sure? There's nothing south beyond this point, young lad; nothing but the ice and the wind. If you came from there as you say, I find it hard to comprehend how any man could feasibly endure such bitter conditions. It's quite impossible."

Eli stepped forward with a hand outstretched. For some reason, Captain Bass took a step backward, and I saw him place a hand on his sword. Eli immediately raised his hands and stepped back. "I'm sorry. I never meant any harm. I'm a doctor and wanted to offer my services if there's a need."

"Good to have another doctor aboard, Mister Raphael," Captain Bass said almost without pause. "I will make haste and acquaint you with our surgeon Doctor Hamell. I run a tight ship, and good morale among my men is my utmost priority. However, there are always the temptations to mutiny among those who may become, for whatever reason, discontented. For that reason, we do not move around below decks with abruptness unless it's required to do so. Mind you take heed of those terms during your stay. That way you shall keep all of your limbs intact by the time we reach the colonies."

I couldn't stand it any longer. "What colonies? We need to head south to Antarctica."

"Why should we, Mister Gabriel? What could be so important that I must abandon my business with the colonies and go on this gallivant extraordinaire of yours? Hmm?"

"There're people there who are trapped. My wife is one of them."

"Trapped? How?"

"They're aboard the *USS John Steinbeck* which was wr . . ."

"*Steinbeck,* did you say? Do I hear you correctly? Did you say *Steinbeck*, Mister Gabriel?"

I nodded. "We don't have much time. Everyone there will perish if we . . ."

"Legend has it; *The USS John Steinbeck* was lost with all hands. In the Sea of Japan. Why, that was over a hundred years ago."

"One hundred and fifty years ago," I corrected the captain. "Those who still live there are the descendants of the original crew. *Steinbeck* was never lost at sea. She became marooned on the Ross Ice Shelf, near McMurdo."

Captain Bass immediately put a hand to his chin as though I had him puzzled. Maybe I succeeded in my lobby. He turned his back slightly, then looking over his left shoulder, he asked, "How many souls, Mister Gabriel?"

In my mind, I didn't know how to answer. Only now I realized things might be different from what I originally planned. I answered the best way I knew how. "5,775 souls on *Steinbeck* at this time. Give or take."

"Good heavens! It would take a small armada to rescue them all. It's quite impossible, Mister Gabriel. However, in the port of Perthland, you may find sufficient help there. We shall make sail to Perthland when the winds allow. There you shall disembark. There you shall raise your inquiry."

"We could at least return and rescue a few. That way they'll all know there's hope."

The captain spun and walked little circles as though deep thought. "So, tell me, young lad. After we collect those whom you hope to collect, what then?"

"Then north to Australia. That was our original plan. We hoped Australia would be the best place for us to settle."

"Australia!"

"We know we could thrive there," Eli put in.

"Why, Mister Raphael, Australia is no longer. It hasn't been Australia since The Fall.

"Australia is gone?"

"Not gone. Just . . . err. . . changed. It is now known as The Province of Australee. The coastlines are not as you might think. The province consists of some islands. No longer is it the large land mass of yesteryear. The great seep destroyed most everything."

"The great seep?"

"The Great Seep, Mister Gabriel. The oceans from the north after The Fall. The entire length and breadth of what was once Australia became inundated. What is left are the islands of today. If you decide to venture there, you must take care. Australee is not a place for the unwary. There are many dangers. Much animal life has been changed forever due to the effects of radiation. Some aggressive animals have increased in their aggressive nature. Some have mutated into great beasts. And that, my dear fellow, is just the beginning."

I took a breath and sat down. I didn't know what to make of it. I'd set my heart on a vision. Now the vision was fading away. The hard truth of the matter became clear. It wasn't the paradise I originally thought. But one thing was for sure. We had to return to the south. Chloe. After that, we'd adapt and change to anything.

It was as though Captain Bass knew the news of Australee had an adverse effect on me. "Incidentally, we opened dead man's chest," Captain Bass said, changing the subject. "Inside, we found items of most interest. And some of great value. One of the items we found is a journal. Perhaps you might enjoy some light reading, Mister Gabriel. Over a tot of rum? Or porter wine if rum isn't to your taste."

"And about going south? You haven't given a straight yes or no answer."

I became short with our captain. But I needed to know, one way or another. I needed an answer. Right now.

"I will need some more time to ponder this whole affair. However, read to me the dead man's journal, and I promise you shall have your answer."

And just like that, it occurred to me. Our captain didn't read.

Chapter Seven

Picking up the Trail

In the morning, after a full night of uninterrupted sleep, I arrived at Captain Bass's great cabin. I was safe on *Victory*. I felt as though, after Chloe's rescue, I could've easily stayed on board to be part of *Victory's* crew. It was a tantalizing prospect. However, I couldn't swim. But I also knew most sailors during the days of old regarded the ability to swim as a bad omen. Maybe I wasn't far from the sea-dogs who were on-board, considering my upbringing.

Taking the opportunity for another breath, I knocked on the great cabin door.

Captain Bass's voice immediately responded, "Enter . . ."

On entering, a silhouette outlined Captain Bass against the early morning sunlight entering through several lavishly decorated windows. There was the sweet smell of lavender in the air, and I thought it was an attempt to cover up the much more horrible odors emanating from other parts of the ship.

"Welcome," Captain Bass said as he stepped from behind his desk and met me in the middle of the floor. For some reason I felt I needed to salute. Before I could, Captain Bass's hand was held out, and I took it and shook. Before I knew it, I was seated in an almost worn out old-style chair. It smelt of the same plush leather that was on *Steinbeck*, and when I sat, the chair almost wrapped around me.

On a side table to my left, under an electric lamp, were a pile of tattered pages, some in different dimensions, most with rips and dog-ears; all had smudging and discolorations in various shapes and sizes. I was also quite certain at least a few pages were bloodstained. I wondered what to do with it. But I wondered even more about the electric lamp.

"Electricity?" I asked, then became lost for words.

"We have a small wind turbine installed on the poop deck. Yes, I know. But we adhere to the tradition whenever possible. The small amount of electricity is for emergencies. Now, back to the task at hand, shall we?"

It wasn't easy to shrug off, but I reached and picked up the stack of papers. Closer inspection revealed no page numbers at all. It was as though the journal was nothing more than a collection of writing, where the writer used scraps of paper whenever and wherever he could find them. But then I looked at it from a different angle. Maybe it wasn't penned out of laziness. Maybe the writer wrote his entries on any piece of paper he could find, purely because there simply *was* nothing else. Looking at it in that light changed everything. I now felt the *need* to read it.

I picked up the unruly wad of papers and placed them in my lap.

"What do you make of this, Mister Gabriel?" The Captain's words interrupted me. "Do you think the dead man who was in the water could be the author of this journal?"

I lifted my eyes to find the captain standing, gazing down at me with a childlike eagerness in his eyes.

"Almost certainly," I said. "If it was in the dead guy's possession, then he must be the writer."

After a long silent pause, it seemed as though the captain's eagerness that was once there abruptly abandoned him. He spun, placed his hands behind his back and peered out of great cabin window. "Then I'm afraid we have . . . fucked it up, as it were."

"How do you mean?"

"The eagle figurine," he said, facing me again. "When you read the journal, you shall find reference to it."

"I'm sorry, Captain Bass. I assumed you couldn't read. I assumed that's why you asked me to . . ."

"There's an old saying," Captain Bass laughed. "Never assume anything. It'll make an ass out of you. I need a powerful mind. I need your help. After I read the first few pages of the journal, it became clear to me; we are missing this eagle figurine. It was missing from dead man's chest. So, the question remains. Where it is?"

After thinking about it, "Maybe it was in the dead guy's pocket?"

"My assumption also. But now this fellow has gone to the deep. There isn't a man on this ship who can swim much less dive into the depths without the proper equipment. If the figurine is down there, the only way to reach it is with the appropriate apparatus, which we do not have. We are quite literally between the devil and the deep blue sea. If we set sail to Perthland to procure the diving equipment we need, we'll lose our position. But if we don't, we're not able to dive."

"Why is the figurine so important?"

"Read on, Mister Gabriel. Read on."

* * *

Entry 722.

A spear of light sometimes rushes through it, casting a rainbow of colours. It's so refreshing to see colours again. Sometimes I find myself staring at it for hours. Sometimes it flashes. Sometimes it glints. Sometimes it sparkles, depending on the time of day. But it never moves. It sits there, frozen in time, sunrise after sunrise, nightfall after nightfall.

I pick it up occasionally. I dust it down. I polish it up. Then, I set it back down and stare at it all over again. The crystal figurine of an eagle, static, yet mesmerising in its beauty eats up my attention until the next time I get the chance to spruce it up. When my folks were alive, they said it was probably the most valuable find ever. They said it was even more valuable than its weight in crackle. More priceless than the Crown Jewels of England before the bombs fell. Those jewels are now gone. Under the waters somewhere, so they said . . .

"What's crackle? And I've never seen this kind of spelling before. Is it a dialect?"

"My dear fellow. Crackle is essentially super hard glass formed in the immense compression of a nuclear explosion. Its hardness makes it perfect for making tools and weapons. Its rarity gives it value. Therefore, they use it as currency between the colonies. They use crackle for the purchase of most anything. Oh, and your second question. I'm afraid I don't know what you're talking about. This person appears to be highly educated because most dwellers outside the colonies can't read, much less spell. But, read on, if you please."

. . . When my folks were alive, they said they could only guess from where the eagle figurine came. There were stories, but no one knew for sure. The scrounger who sold it to me showed me there were bones to go with it. Bones, with a significance. She even expressed an urgency that the eagle figurine and bones must stay together. Whatever the cost . . .

"A scrounger?"

"Good god, man! Just read, will you?"

. . . She introduced herself as Charlotte, and she was eager to offer her name. It was rare for a female scrounger to turn up, and the first in my experience. Having the pleasure of owning something so delicate, so beautiful, is something to fight over. Something to cheat death over. I'll guard it forever, bones and all. I still wonder to this day, why she offered those things to someone like me.

"You're Michael the Protector," she told me. One-how did she know my name? And two-I've never been a protector of anything except my own skin. But anyway. The bones and eagle figurine only cost me nine shards of crackle and a half measure of water. A bargain.

I never stop wondering about the scroungers. They only live short lives from what I can imagine. Out there in the waste, due to the radiation, they'd spend their time mostly in pain. But doing what they do, they're probably the richest individuals still walking. Only those knowing their fate would ever consider going into Fool's Desert. And the odd thing is this. Most scroungers don't usually survive long enough to see where their wealth will take them. They're mad. They're all mad. The lot of them. But without them, there'd be no crackle and no way to purchase supplies. But Charlotte; her face so fresh. Her complexion so perfect. No scratches. No lesions. No sign of discomfort or pain as though she'd never spent any time in the waste at all. I ask myself, how is this possible? And how was it possible to evade the Takers?

I rested the journal in my lap. I looked across the great cabin to a captain who was completely comfortable in his chair, tot of rum - as he called it - in his grip, even though it was early in the morning. "Anything the matter?" the captain asked.

"There's something that comes to mind."

"Go on."

"Charlotte. She had some human bones with the figurine and wanted them to stay together. Why? Also, she appeared to be without the signs of radiation sickness that others share. How?"

"Both valid questions, Mister Gabriel. I am as uncertain how to answer these as you are, I'm afraid. But we have the bones. They were in dead man's chest. Now you're beginning to understand how important it is that we have the figurine."

"And what about these so-called Takers?"

Captain Bass raised himself from his chair and once again stood at the window. He peered out at the same time taking a swig from his glass. "Let me bring you into the light, as it were," Captain Bass said as he took a sidestep and returned to his delicately crafted decanter. "Takers are quite simply our enemy. They will kill anyone to get anything. And due to this, the meek are usually the ones who go without and are the ones who fight for their survival.

"Many decades ago, an ad-hoc government was formed. It was the first attempt at bringing order to the people. During those years, the Takers were mere tax collectors. But, the habit of 'taking' became their prime directive. The juvenile government collapsed as a result. Now, the Takers will take anything at all.

They will slit the throat of anybody and do their damnedest to get anything they deem valuable. If you thought you could find a place to settle on the land far away from the Takers, you would be wrong, Mister Gabriel. They are everywhere. Including the high seas. Mark my words. There shall come the day when you shall see this enemy up close and personal."

Before continuing to read, I let Captain Bass's words linger in my mind for a while. He certainly painted a picture which had a profound effect. Even though I didn't know my enemy up close and personal, as Captain Bass put it, I felt as though I was now familiar with them. I wanted to know more, and somehow, I knew what was coming in the next few pages.

. . . They take everything from the corpses they leave behind. Guns are rare. Bullets are even rarer. The Takers had them and no one else. They're out there lurking. They settle among the dust and colourless landscape. They're among the blackened tree trunks and the blackened branches. Blackened branches that forever point up to an endlessly greyed out sky. The fact that I'm alive today is only through the death of the other. And now, those Takers have me on their blood list. They won't stop until they find me. One day they will. One day my body will be split apart and dismembered. They'll use their crackle encrusted bludgeons to do it. They'll save their bullets for killing scroungers. So, I hide. I shelter. Forever peering, forever looking over my shoulder, never looking straight on, never staying too long, traveling only at night and never, ever, on a full moon . . .

Suddenly, an interruption to my reading. The sounds of rushed footfalls thumped down the staircase and stopped at the great cabin door. Then an urgent knock.

"Enter!" Captain Bass yelled as though he was most annoyed.

"Pardon Captain," William Fletcher said as he was halfway through the door. "Enemy man o' war sighted. She flies *Excelsior's* colors."

Captain Bass immediately clasped both hands behind his back and turned his attention through the great cabin window. "Damn them. Damn their hides," Captain Bass said before spinning and locking his eyes with mine. "The Takers are here for the flesh from our bones, Mister Gabriel. If we engage them, we'll lose our standing position, and we'll lose the prospect of recovering that eagle figurine. If we don't engage them, we're a duck shoot."

With his tot of rum still grasped tightly in his hand, Captain Bass spun on his heel and faced his first officer. "Where away, Mister Fletcher?"

"She's comin' from the nor-east."

"And the weather gauge?"

"It's not in our favor, Captain. *Excelsior's* got the 'eadwind to which we ain't."

It was as though the captain needed to think fast and weigh up his options. Find the eagle or go to war. I could almost see the words on his facial expression as he paced around his great cabin, eyes down tracing the long oak floorboards. I thought a hard choice needed to be made. Much was at stake. Oddly, I found myself in a sort of relief that it wasn't a choice that I had to make. I wasn't a captain and *Victory* wasn't my ship.

"Very well, Mister Fletcher," Captain Bass said almost under his breath. "Beat to quarters, if you please."

"Aye, aye, Captain." Then just as quick as he arrived, William Fletcher was gone.

Captain Bass spun and faced me. There was an enormous disappointment in his expression, and I knew it in my heart what he was thinking. We will never retrieve the eagle figurine from the depths.

"It appears, Mister Gabriel, you're about to meet our enemy for the very first time. Let's give them hell, shall we?"

Chapter Eight

The Seven

From his great cabin, I followed Captain Bass up the steep flight of mahogany stairs. As we approached the commotion that was churning up top, my mind returned to Jason and Eli. I realized for the first time I hadn't seen them since daybreak. With all the urgency going on, I wondered where they were and in what jobs they'd found themselves. As I thought it, I heard the snare drums rattling away, calling men to their battle stations. I imagined the sea-dogs I'd once thought about were in the midst of being transformed from the unruly mob of liquor drinking sailors, into finely tuned men at arms. I realized war changes men in ways only soldiers and sailors could understand. Somewhere in my gut, I knew I was about to find out how.

"Captain Bass," I called out after him. "Captain Bass, sir."

"Come, come, Mister Gabriel. No time to waste. This way if you please."

Stepping out onto the quarter-deck, it was a scene straight out of a classic maritime novel. Huge sails were already deployed and were with the wind. Men were running here and there, but at the same time, they scurried with purpose, not panic. It was a cleverly put together choreography of movements. Everyone knew their place. Everyone jumped to their posts and stood fast. At the same time, Captain Bass strutted up and down the quarter-deck as though to make a final inspection. With a set of steely eyes hard-set against an expression of determination, he settled at his post next to the ship's helm and the coxswain who had the task of pointing the bowsprit to where *Victory* needed to be. After all hands were at their posts, Captain Bass bellowed out his orders.

"Lieutenant Bradley! Sharpshooters aloft, if you will!"

"Aye, aye, Captain!"

Moments later, red-coated marines hurried themselves up masts with muskets in hand. It was then I saw the outline of my brother disappear with them. He'd found his place among the men, and I had to be honest; it suited him. I smiled a little to myself as I saw him almost with seasoned ability climb the rigging up the main mast. One of the marines extended a telescope and after placing it back in its pouch yelled, "*Excelsior* ahoy!"

The captain smiled briefly and looked at me over his left shoulder. "She's a fine ship, Mister Gabriel, but she must be dealt with."

Immediately, Captain Bass turned and faced Master's Mate, "Raise our colors, Mister Tennant, if you please."

In the same breath without a pause, "Mister Finch! Run out the starboard battery. Aim chain and nail to flesh above decks. Eighteen pounders low on her hull. Make it so."

"Aye, aye, sir."

"Come up on the wind," the captain ordered his coxswain. "Lay us alongside the bastards, Mister Brice. With one broadside, we shall put her alongside Davey Jones' locker."

I looked up to the crow's nest; to a marine who had his telescope trained on *Excelsior*. His next shouted words changed everything. "Torpedo in the water! Tor-pe-do-in-the-wa-ter!"

In an instant without appearing to think about it, the captain responded. "Hard to starboard Mister Brice! Hard to starboard!"

As the ship took its time responding to the helm, I ran to the starboard rail and looked out. I saw it with my own eyes, the telltale trail in the water that was bearing down, heading straight toward us. I knew in my heart what Captain Bass was doing. I hoped *Victory* would narrow her target footprint in time. As she turned at a screaming slow pace, someone behind me yelled out, "All hands! Brace for impact!"

I needed to get myself to another part of the ship. I needed to get myself away from the blast zone as far as I could get. My legs betrayed me, and I couldn't move. I heard the torpedo drilling through the water with its bow wave forming in front of its warhead like a hammer. I watched on thinking at the same time; this is the end.

The torpedo came drilling through the water, so close I heard the sound of its electric motor. It barely skimmed *Victory's* starboard timbers with a touch so light; it was just a mere kiss. Without exploding as I'd expected, the torpedo passed harmlessly away.

The men roared their happiness at the same time the captain screamed from his post. "If they feel the need to fight with twentieth-century weapons, we'll answer it, by god! We'll answer it and send them to their deaths!"

Looking out to sea, I saw several small waves forming and dipping as though a pod of porpoises were at play beneath the surface. They moved with great speed toward the Takers Ship *Excelsior,* and I knew, these dolphin-like creatures weren't even close to what I at first assumed.

In an arrowhead formation with the albino leading, the group of orcas breached the water and crashed down in what I assumed was intimidation. Then they appeared to dive down deep, and I could no longer see the outlines of their huge bodies. Looking on, I could see the silhouettes of men on *Excelsior* begin to scurry in all directions. It was like seeing an old-fashioned silent movie; the ones I'd watched back on *Steinbeck.*

From where I stood, I saw the water near *Excelsior* rise slightly. Then a huge white Killer Whale slammed into *Excelsior's* larboard hull with enough energy to tip her briefly on her side.

As the Takers Ship righted herself, the booms of guns erupted from her decks in answer to the onslaught. Two orcas at the exact same time struck *Excelsior* amidships and again sent her over on her side. This time men on deck were brutally cast off and flung out into the water.

As *Excelsior* righted herself once more, the sea around her hull frothed with screaming, yelling men. Four Killer Whales as though in synchronicity to each other breached the surface and crashed down on them. After several repeated bombings, the boiling white water became a ghastly tinge of red. The urgent screams of men died slowly as three orcas, albino at the head, crashed with an almighty blow into Excelsior's hull, sending her capsized. The water bubbled and gurgled momentarily before *Excelsior's* stern raised high and she slowly disappeared beneath the surface.

Excelsior was gone. She was laid beside Davey Jones' locker, as Captain Bass had predicted. The water where she was last seen became still and silent. The seven orcas had vanished. And all the while, there was not a single peep from anyone on-board *Victory*. All were as silent as the day itself, including the captain. They were as though stunned, not able to move.

I thought it was up to me to break the silence. "Shit!"

Saying that one word had the same effect of a dozen. Behind me, a little snicker broke into laughter before the entire crew began to rejoice and celebrate the fact no one had lost limbs.

* * *

After the battle, I again found myself with Captain Bass's company in his great cabin. I winced with the pain in my broken shoulder as I lowered myself into the same old leather chair where I'd sat down before things went awry.

"Is it any better?" The captain said pointing his finger while holding his glass of rum both at the same time.

"It's coming along, I think. Still hurts like a bitch if I make sudden moves." As soon as I said it, I knew the captain mostly ignored what I said. His expression told me he was elsewhere. "What say you of those Killer Whales, Mister Gabriel?" Captain Bass asked as he returned to his chair and sat heavily down.

"I don't know what to tell you, Captain."

"Henry," the captain put in. "Please call me Henry. You're no longer on detail here. You and your brother are guests on board *Victory* as from this moment. I'd very much like to consider you as a friend."

"And Eli?"

"He's chosen to spend his time with our surgeon Doctor Hamell."

Just then, it occurred to me. "Oh? You think *I* had something to do with the orcas?"

"Well if you didn't, it does seem quite the coincidence, wouldn't you agree?"

For some reason, I left the conversation there. Maybe I thought it wouldn't hurt for the captain to believe what he was already believing. Maybe it would also bring better negotiating power to the table when we get to talking more about heading south for Chloe. It seemed whenever I brought up the subject, Captain Bass danced away from it. If I was a friend, as he said I was, perhaps he'd be more willing. I decided I'd cement the relationship first by giving him more reading time with dead man's journal. After which, there'd be no more dancing around the subject. I'd go at it full force until Captain Bass relented and took us back to Antarctica.

After taking some rum, I placed the glass to the side and picked up the wad of unruly papers. Captain Bass looked at me with eyes, eager to know what was written next. His expression said something almost childlike. It was as though this hardened man at arms had a soft spot for what might well turn out to be a treasure hunt. Then I realized this whole scenario was getting to be similar to any classic pirate story. Sometimes I wish I hadn't read so many books.

Entry 722 Supplemental

Last evening, a scrounger turned up with a book. After handing it over, I took it and pushed the dust away from the jacket. The Holy Bible was etched into the cover in what I thought could be real silver . . .

I put the papers in my lap and looked away.

"What is it, Richard?"

"What's a *Holy Bible*? Is it some kind of old classic?"

There was silence. I noticed the shock over the captain's expression as he pointed with a trembling finger toward the bookcase. There it was. *The Holy Bible* with all its embellishment on the spine was right there. But the silence ensued. I thought about asking my question again. I had no need.

"Richard. I'm both flabbergasted and staggered at the same time. This isn't a joke, is it? You truly have not read the good book on the holy scriptures?"

"I'm afraid I don't know what that is." It seemed as though the captain wasn't listening to me. To get that kind of reaction, however, I realized this *Holy Bible* must've been somewhat important. I decided I'd pursue this at a later time. But for now, a tactful ignorance was required, and it was back to the unruly pages to continue with the reading.

.

Chapter Nine

The Lost Ones

. . . At first, I thought the book was an offering, and I handed the old guy a few shards of crackle for his trouble. He pushed my hand away and then gave me two shards to have me read it to him. So, I read it, passing the entire night under my last few sticks of wax. As the first rays of sunlight pierced the horizon, the old scrounger got to his feet, nodded with thanks, and left. I found him a day later just down the hill. He'd taken a shard of crackle to his own throat. What could I do? The man was dead, and his flesh was too far gone. I couldn't use it. The flies were having a feast on his bloated body, so I turned my attention to the flies. In my mind, they were protein, but the bastards were too bloody fast. Then I thought about the scrounger's stuff. No point in not using it, so I took it. I now have a few extra shards of crackle I can use for trade, plus a skin of water, a fresh pair of boots that, tomorrow, I will modify slightly to fit my feet. Some other things; a dingo skin, salted red-belly-black meat, and a couple of old tins

containing what might be either corned beef or dog food. Rare as rare. In any case, there'd be a good time to crack it open; in an emergency when things get hard, and I know they will. What a surprise; the old bastard had candles and not told me. Prick!

I put the papers in my lap, and I was compelled to again look away. The man's story was starting to get to me.

"Richard. Whatever could be the matter?"

"I never knew about those hardships. I thought things were tough where I came from. These people are eating each other to survive?"

"Some do. Most don't. Those who live in the colonies will never stoop to such abomination. But the Takers . . . My boy, they are different humans to the civilized. As you've seen with your own eyes, out on the oceans, Takers have ships bent on taking souls for their meat."

"They're *all* cannibals?"

"Every last one of them, yes. Horrible to think about, wouldn't you say?"

So, there it was. If we'd lost against *Excelsior*, we'd all be meat for the eating. I shuddered in my spot thinking about it. But somehow, I cast that aside and kept going.

. . . I remember the old man telling me the waste was given other names to begin with. The Big Empty. The Hole. The Black Death, Fool's Desert, among others. Now, it's 'the waste.' It best describes what's out there. Nothing. Wind. Dust. Emptiness.

I learned to survive by perfecting the art of boiling my own urine to purify it a little. It doesn't matter how much I try; the stuff never tastes like real water. It always has that aftertaste that stays at the back of the throat and never leaves. I dream of a scrounger turning up one day with a condenser I can use. I'd pay whatever the asking. We used to have one when I was a kid. I knocked it off the table by accident, and it fell to the floor, smashing into little pieces. The old man broke my arm for my troubles. That broken arm never healed straight. It serves as a reminder to this day not to fuck up.

Real water I only ever drink if I don't make enough urine. It's a science knowing when to drink water or boil up a kettle of piss.

Lucky for the rain we get, even though you can't drink it straight away. When it rains, it comes down grey as the clouds it comes from. At night, rainwater has a strange glow. I save some of it in a container to see at night if I decide it's better to save on wax sticks. I still don't know how I'll get along once my supply of water purifiers run out. If I don't drink water, I won't piss. What happens after that, I don't know. That bloody condenser again. Wish I never smashed it.

Entry 723.

Gonna make this one quick. Running out of paper. Gonna have to find some from somewhere. And new pens too, else I'll be writing with charcoal. Hate that shit.

Another scrounger came through last evening. This guy with some kind of tribal facial tattoos and he appeared to be much younger than most. I was really hoping he had something I could use. I'd give my left nut for a new shifter. I bloody hate rust. After I asked him inside so I could start a barter, I noticed how bad his clothes reeked of diesel and the smell immediately took me back to a time when I was a kid. That said one thing. He must've come from somewhere that had diesel-powered electricity. I asked him from where did he come. He said east. Nothing more, like it was some kind of secret. I wasn't gonna let this guy get away without telling me the whole of the truth. I thought the place he came from couldn't have been far. Diesel fumes don't stick around on clothes for long. Not unless he was drenched in the stuff. If he was drenched in it, that said he obviously came from somewhere that had lots of it. So, me being me, I pressed him for the rest of his story.

After I gave this guy a palm full of pumpkin seeds which I never had any success with, I saw him loosen up a bit. Even so, I had to work harder. I had to do something that went against everything I believed in. I told him my name, hoping he would do the same. It worked. Michael, I said sticking out my hand. He took it and shook with one word. Temothy.

I thought he doesn't know how to pronounce his own name. "Don't you mean Timothy?"

"That's what I said, bro. Temothy."

I shook my head and thought maybe he had some kind of speaking impairment going on.

From there, things started to come and he finally 'fessed up.

Timothy claimed he came fourteen nights' stride from the east. A place called Newman. He said his clan had been there since Pre-Fall. Already, my mind went into bullshit alert mode. I said to Timothy, "Fourteen nights to the east is under the waters." I knew that from info I got from past scroungers. Then I pulled out my blade and flashed it about so he could see I was in no mood for the bullshit. Then he did something I wasn't expecting. From a back pocket, he pulled a wad of something I'd never seen before, only heard about. The old man once told me about *pho-to-graphs. So, imagine my surprise when I finally saw them. He passed them over and sure enough, ten or so pictures showing people at Pre-Fall, prepping for the coming of the bombs. Imagine my surprise when I could see what they were living in. A big area of buildings and sheds of different shapes and sizes. One picture showed someone up high on a mill, driven by the winds apparently, which Timothy reckoned helped make electricity and also pumped up waters from the ground. Imagine my surprise to see things of colour. Trees, plants, flowers—and animals that they called horses and cows.*

Sceptical, I asked, "Those animals still there?" knowing he'd have to be spinning the bullshit if he said they were still alive. He shook his head and said no. Then he added, "Gran and Pop were the last to see thim. But their mit is stell in our dip friz." He looked down and I could see the tears come to his eyes. I prompted further and he went on to explain about the generators. It seems Timothy's clan were on their last generator when it quit. Timothy reckoned it must've been a fuel blockage. He took the fuel lines apart, but he didn't have the nous to get all the lines sorted so the engine could restart. Now I know why he was drenched in diesel. It all made sense.

"Did you bleed the fuel system?" I asked him. "Diesel engines won't fire if there's air in there."

He looked up at me with these pleading eyes that almost made me sick. "You know how to fex et?"

"We have one of those generators here," I said. "But there's no fuel. There hasn't been for as long as I can remember. We had oil and used it to light up at night. But that ran dry too." I went on. "That old generator doesn't even crank anymore. Even if I had oil and diesel fuel, it'd make no difference now."

"But do you know how to fex et?" He repeated it again, looking up at me with his glossy, fucking pleading bullshit eyes.

"Yeah. Bleed the fuel system and it'll work," I told him. Then it struck me to what he was getting at. Timothy was hinting at the propect for me to go with him back to his place to repair it. For some reason, I looked at his hands, and I remembered the handshake. Timothy's hands were smooth and no rough bits at all. Suddenly, Timothy stood up and asked me properly. "I'll give you anything you want," he said. "If you fex et, you can stay with us for as long as you like. We have food and supplies—everytheng you nid."

I must admit—the prospect of leaving this place was very tempting. After all, what's left for me here? And I've never been fourteen nights east. If anything, if the guy was bullshitting, I'd finally get to see the edge of the waters. From there, I'd make up my own mind where to head, and leave this fucker in the dust where he belongs. There was only one thing stopping me from committing to anything. Takers. Then the thought really hit home.

Three nights east is a Takers' garrison. That's as far as I've ever gone. Even then it was too close for comfort. Too close to getting my head swiped clean from my shoulders. It was while I was out there, I encountered that lone Taker and killed the bastard outright. So, I asked Timothy how he got past the garrison undetected. If he did come from that far east, highly unlikely he'd gotten past The Takers alive. Now I'm thinking the bullshit was laid on thick as that rare sweet stuff they call honey. Yeah, just the thought of honey makes my eyes water. I'm just saying.

"Underground," he said. "Them up top. Me below."

It was a surprise just as much as it was a warning in my head. It made me cough and laugh, both at the same time. Yeah, I *thought. Now the bullshit tap was turned fully on. We were on first name basis. I stuffed up again. Now I'm thinking I'll have to kill the bastard before he gets away.*

So straight away I lunged forward at him. I put a hand around his throat and the tip of my blade just above his left kidney. Immediately his hands went up and he started to shake. Really fucking scared I thought this guy was. I looked into his eyes, pausing for a second, deciding whether or not to push the blade into his back. There was no bullshit there I could see. After a moment or two with no words, I relaxed a little and I sat down again, but my crackle blade was still ready to make a strike if I had to use it. "Underground?" I said. "Never heard of anything underground. And the Takers would know about it. They know everything out there."

"Not thes," Timothy said. "We've cammoed et so they can't find et." A stunted smile curled on his lips before he added, "We heaped all our toilet business there, so the Takers stay away."

I narrowed my eyes at him, willing him to speak more.

"Et's an old silver mine," he told me. "It goes right under the Takers place and et goes out the other ind to the gully."

"Go on," I said. "You're not convincing me yet and I don't much take to bull-shitters."

"Et's true. If you come, our place will sit you up for life. I just nid the generators to work."

I narrowed my eyes a bit more. "You just said, I."

He looked blankly, said nothing.

"You said, I. Not we. So, you're implying you're by yourself. You said we, before." I got up and charged at him, stopping so the tip of my nose just touched his.

He shrunk back. "No, I mint to say, wi. Just said I because I am here by myself. But we're numbers back at Newman."

"How many?" I shouted. He said two hundred and twenty-two without hesitation. It was the fact he said it without hesitation that made me wonder if there was truth to his words. Surely no one could drag a number from the sky so quick. And certainly, not a number such as two hundred and twenty-two. A hundred? A hundred and fifty? If he'd said that number, I'd have thought it was made up. But the two hundred and twenty-two said truth. So, I sat back again and tapped the tip of my razor-sharp crackle blade on the toe of my boot while I thought things over. Already, my mind had other questions to ask, if only to bring about some kind of clarity—if only to settle my mind. So far, there were things that didn't add up. Like the part about Newman being fourteen nights to the east when the silver mine was only three. If there was truth there, that meant they'd dragged their shit to the mine to keep away Takers. That meant at least eleven nights trudging the stuff. That was far beyond any belief. It was his last chance to set things straight. He'd better have a good answer, or he's stuffed. Plain and simple.

"We camp there sometimes," he said after I asked him.

"So, you've got food stores there?"

Timothy nodded sharply. Fair enough I thought. If there's food stores there, I'd have a supply if things went to shit. One down, one to go. Then, there was the question of the diesel fuel. How could they have enough of it to last all this time? I reckoned they'd need an endless supply. That's something unheard of. Then, the oil. They'd need that too. I asked him where he got it. As far as I was concerned, this answer was his life or death.

"We trade diesel fuel and oil for mit," he said. "From trad-ers, from up north."

"North! No-one's up there," I yelled at him. "That's all ra-dioactive. Up there, you'd melt before you get to glow green." This time Timothy was right out at the ragged edge of my pa-tience. I held up my blade again and twisted it in the candlelight so he could see I was losing it.

"You're wrong," Timothy said. "They've trucks and all sorts up there. They truck in our fuel and take mit away." Then he dropped his gaze. "That's how it was. We haven't heard from the Northerners in ages and our fuel is running low. That's why I'm out here. I've bin looking for new trade and seeing about getting ourselves back on our fit. Without the generators going, our mit stores will turn and we won't last long."

"Trucks," I said. "Never seen one. Stories. Just bloody sto-ries."

"Not stories. They're real."

"How long has it been since these northerners last came?"

"About two hundred days."

I got up and walked away. I left him there to stew for a bit. No one up north could survive. Every scrounger I ever met had the same thing to say about the place. Now I'm thinking if there were northerners, they'd had to have a way of surviving. I couldn't help it. The thought of people actually living up there drilled into my logical brain. It wasn't possible and it didn't make any sense. So, I asked Timothy what made them so different that they could survive the radiation sickness. Timothy replied by say-ing he didn't know why they were able to survive. He went on by explaining the northerners all had one thing in common. Orange hair. White skin. Lots of freckles. And they all looked the same.

As soon as he said it, my body shook from the inside out. Timothy's orange-headed friends exactly resembled a story my Pop once told me before he passed. Ambers. Some called them 'The Lost Ones.' People who were genetically altered to survive radioactivity. I asked Timothy if he'd heard about The Lost Ones. He said no he never. My mouth went suddenly dry and I said nothing more on it, at the same time thinking I might investigate the so-called northerners that could turn out to be The Lost Ones that my Pop described. It all depends on what happens after I fix his bloody generator.

So, I sat there and I ogled him a little. I wanted to make him feel uncomfortable. Maybe he'll spill some more, I kept thinking. I wasn't going to commit to going back with him until I had everything sorted in my head. No room for mistakes around here. Then he said something that made perfect sense. It was his words that finally made my mind up.

"Hell is an empty place. The devil and his demons are all here."

Chapter Ten

A Box of Stuff

Entry 723 Supplemental.

Almost packed. Timothy sleeps. The guy's knackered I reckon. A fourteen-night trek across the waste does things to the man, and I'm not talking about exhaustion, although that's something else to consider on top of everything else. There's things out there that'd make a man's blood freeze, over and I've only ever been three nights across. Looking at Timothy still makes me wonder how he managed to trek so far and still be alive. Luck is so rare, and he must possess a heap of the stuff to get him out here unscathed.

I've fashioned what I call a bug-out-sleigh that I can drag along. I reckon we'll take turns dragging it. I've had many a scrounger come through. Not one of them had a set of wheels on offer. Sad, isn't it? Not even wheels out there. So, the plan is for one to drag our stuff, the other goes behind and rubs out the tracks in the dust so if there's Takers they can't find us. Fourteen nights' trek will turn into twenty, I'm sure of it. Paper. Need more bloody paper. We'll wait for next sundown before we get going.

Entry 724.

Dawn. We're hunkered at the silver mine Timothy talked about. Thought I'd take the opportunity to pen a while as he busies himself answering nature's call. It's appropriate considering the huge pile of human waste dumped here. What he said was true. The stench by itself is enormous and enough to keep anything living away, not just the Takers.

Our travels across the waste were for the most part without any incident. I must admit—I'm relieved. There were lots of bones from many small animals that were already picked clean. That doesn't mean we didn't try because we did. Any small scrap left over is a blessing and any tiny morsel meant going further or perish. I saw bull ants for the first time in years. Not many. Just a dozen or so. And at night. Miraculous just by itself. Needless to say, we weren't about to pass up the opportunity for a protein boost. Timothy was about to put one in his mouth that was still alive. I said, "Timothy, you bloody idiot. At least pop the head first." He gave me that blank stare of his. It seems he's never ate one before. Then I went on and told him about bull ant bites inside the mouth. That's one nasty fucked up pain if you've never felt it. He smiled politely. I heard the bull ant head go 'pop', then it was gone. "Thanks," he said. Just like that. Simple and without any emotion. Then he did something that really got up my nose. I saw *his eyes compress, and he spat it back out in his hand. The fuck-wit. "Tastes awful," he said. I said, "We're not doing it for the taste. You wanna survive, don't you?" He shrugged a pause and licked it back up, at the same time wincing from the bitterness. After a few moments spent scrounging for more, and none were around, it was time to move on.*

While trudging, dragging the bug-out-sleigh behind me, Timothy in the rear kicked our drag tracks into non-existence, my head got to think about those bloody Takers. We were in prime territory for their numbers. We have weapons to take on close-up foes but we don't have any capability at all to answer the ranged weapons they'd have. But through the darkness, throughout the night, no-one was out and about. The old man's training came in handy. I still surprise myself sometimes.

We cracked open a tin after we got here. I broke the tip of my crackle blade. Jeez that made me angry. It took forever to find enough crackle and ages for me to make. What made matters worse was the discovery of cat food in the tin. Not dog food. Bloody cat food. That stuff stinks and the fish taste will stay in my mouth even after drinking a few gulps of boiled piss. I hope the rest of the day doesn't turn out crap. What a start so far.

I can't see the opening to the mine just yet. Timothy reckons we need to move all the human excrement to one side. The opening is underneath apparently. Lovely! Something I'm hugely looking forward to. Just saying.

Check back with a supplemental in a few. Timothy's decided to wipe his arse with a sheet of my writing paper! I reckon this day will have its hazards. I've already decided.

Entry 724. Supplemental.

We're inside. About five thousand strides down the horizontal shaft, we came to a large open area where there're other shafts heading off. It's a junction where all the other mineshafts connect. And, there's daylight here. A shaft goes straight up and reaches the surface letting light through. When we were on approach to this area, Timothy put a finger to his lips and gestured for silence. We had to pick up the bug-out-sleigh and carry it. Then he pointed up top indicating something. I figured out we were right under an area the Takers used to dispose of their rubbish. We had to remain silent; else they'd hear us messing about without any trouble. It was both amazing and disheartening at the same time. Directly under the shaft going up is a great pile of stinking Takers scraps and rubbish. It suddenly occurred to me this is the food supply Timothy was talking about. For some reason, I pictured something else in my mind. I pictured stacks of stored clean water. Shelves of tinned non-perishable food. Racks of packets and so on. Even knives and forks to eat it with. But this? Jesus Christ!

A closer inspection of the rubbish heap in the centre of the large area reveals something else about the Takers. They didn't eat everything. They chucked away stuff that, if it was me, I'd have microscopically cleaned. This pile of rubbish has stuff in it that can keep a man on his feet forever.

I quietly moved over to the heap and started to poke around a bit. Timothy moved silently beside me and pushed his mouth up

to my ear. My mind went, "Hey mate, don't even think about it."
But then he whispered into my ear, so softly that I'm sure no one
would hear even if they were standing right next to us. "Fresh
stuff coming," he said. "Just wait a bit." I froze. The word fresh
isn't in my vocabulary, but the tantalising prospect of something
fresh couldn't be ignored. So I waited. We both did. We hunkered
down without a peep. I looked up into the light and waited as
though some God was about to send something down through the
hole. My mouth began to water. I sucked back saliva and waited.

Sure enough, it wasn't long. Something came through the
hole. Whatever it was, it landed on the heap and rolled down the
side. Timothy smiled and moved forward at the same time as ges-
turing for me to stay still. I realised if he made a noise, it was bad
enough. If we both made noises, we'd end up in a state. He came
back a little bit later holding something in his hands and offered
it. Some small animal, half eaten. Lots of meat still left on the
bones--and it was cooked. My heart beat hard in my chest and my
mouth watered like the tides out past fourteen nights' stride. I took
it from Timothy and I took a bite of the purest, softest, sweetest,
most delicious meat I'd ever tasted. My eyes filled with tears. I
sat back and enjoyed it with a delight I'd never known.

More came through from up top. Timothy was right. We
could've easily stayed forever, and it was hard to consider the
fact we'd have to get going pretty soon. With my mouth, full of the
wonderful tastes that danced around for a while and melted away,
I happened to ask in a whisper right down low, "What is this?"

"Checkin," whispered Timothy with a smile beaming across
his greasy face.

"What? Is it like some kind of small roo? Like wallaby?" My mind traced back to when there were some around that the old man caught for us kids. Those were the days all right. Timothy looked at me with some kind of expression that said I must've been on Mars. "Et's Checkin. Haven't you had et before?"

"No," I said. It didn't bloody matter. I was ever so grateful. Now I know a place where the risks are so high, but the payoff is worth it. Funny, after I had that thought, anger raged inside me. Takers had this stuff while the rest of us go begging. It wasn't right.

I'd eaten until I was full up and couldn't eat anymore. I can't remember the last time my belly felt heavy and bloated. Now, all I want to do is sleep. Even now, as I sit and write under the dim light, I can see Timothy fighting his drowsiness. It's not an option. We must at least find ourselves a good part of the way down the end of the shaft. If we sleep here and snore, those up top would know. That would end up as a major shit fight.

Entry 725.

It was at least another five thousand strides away from the location that gave us our last meal. I have to add that five thousand or so of those strides were made with an almost crippling cramp under my ribcage, made worse by having to carry the bug-out-sleigh. Thank god we don't have to do that anymore.

We didn't talk much on the way down the shaft. I was quite content with my own thoughts. But Timothy said something that brought me back to the reality.

"Wanna see my treasures?" he asked.

It was the word 'treasures' that sparked my interest. Of course.

He pointed just up ahead of where we were. "Just up there. Wanna see?"

Then it occurred to me how lucky this guy was. Timothy had all the luck of the Gods on his side. However, I was immediately thinking what an idiot. If he had treasures, surely, he'd have the need to keep it to himself. What made him so sure I wouldn't rip him across the throat? Of course, I wouldn't, having come this far. But what if it was someone else other than me? He'd be dead, and the treasure somewhere else. So, I answered him. "Treasure huh? Okay, let's see what you got."

There was a slight depression in the side of the tunnel where we stopped after another thirty odd strides. It didn't look out of the ordinary and perhaps that's why Timothy's treasures were still there. Timothy reached into the depression and cleared away a few loose rocks. Then, he cleared some larger rocks that showed the opening to a small chamber that was cut into the wall. Probably some kind of exploration tunnel started there and then became abandoned for some reason. Further into the chamber and Timothy cleared dust and debris away from what looked like a large plastic container. When he pulled it away from a micro landslide, I recognised it as a military footlocker. I had one exactly the same back at my hometown, Kumarina. My Pop once told me they were used by the local militia and were big enough to store several changes of uniforms, a blanket or two and other things.

After Timothy opened the military footlocker, I was absolutely, positively, without a doubt, gobsmacked. The first thing Timothy retrieved was something tiny. Something wrapped in what looked like a faded yellow wrapper. It had writing on it and I could just make out the words Juicy Fruit. Timothy said it was chewing gum. He placed it in my hand and I ran my fingers over what felt like a ribcage of some sort.

"There's pieces in the packet. You put et in your mouth and chew on et," he said.

"Why?"

Then he looked at me oddly. "Dunno why. Et just es. People used to do et. But I reckon et'd be more like chewing on sandstone by now."

"So why keep it?"

"Because et's worth sometheng. And anytheng thet's worth sometheng you kip."

He reached into the trunk and pulled out something else. A small box that looked like it was at one time made from wood. The writing on the box said 'Flor De Tobacos, Habana.' He opened it and handed it over. "These are for smoking,"

"Like cigarettes? They're bloody huge."

Timothy nodded at the same time quickly closing the box and putting it back in the footlocker, adding, "I've smoked one and et made me seck for a day. Trust me Michael, you don't want to smoke thim."

What he said made sense. If we got ourselves captured by the Takers, the big cigarettes by themselves could save our lives in barter. Maybe. The next thing he pulled out was a huge slab of crackle, measuring five hands wide and four hands deep. So big, it took effort to retrieve. I reckoned there was enough of the stuff to buy supplies for a thousand days. But under the slab of crackle was the biggest surprise of all. Timothy reached in and grabbed something wrapped in a tattered red cloth. The red cloth smelt of some kind of sweetness and had white printed patterns and a strange emblem of some description. A picture of a dagger with a lightning bolt in a strange triangular shape going around it. Inside was something heavy and metallic. Timothy unraveled it and held it up. A Pre-Fall handgun. My eyes watered. I couldn't believe it.

Timothy's treasures he had safely tucked away were exactly what he reckoned. There were loads of other items contained in the footlocker, but the gun was most precious. How he'd got it and then kept it out of Takers' hands was incredible to say the least. But at the same time, was useless without ammo, and there wasn't any. He had a lone bullet in the footlocker wrapped up in some old paper. The bullet resembled something that could've been fired from a cannon, not from a handgun.

"Pre-Fall fefty-cal," he said smiling again. "Ef only we had something to fire et."

He started packing things away back in the footlocker, but I was reluctant to give up the handgun. It felt balanced and weighty in my hands. It was like a precision instrument meant for performing the task of death. Timothy put his hand out and waited for me to hand it back. I paused. "What'll you take for it?" I asked him as I held it up to the light. That's when I saw it. An inscription on the handle. 'Donald P Bosco.'

"Not for sale," Timothy said plain and simple. Then he stuck his hand out for it like some little spoilt brat.

"Everything's for sale," I told him. "Don't give me the shits. There's something I can trade."

He stood up and wrenched the handgun from me. Then wrapped it back up, repeating his words not for sale. It was at this time I started to wonder about Timothy. He'd come across as meek and mild. The sort of bloke who could be easily played. Now he seemed harder. Almost seasoned. Or was he just stalling for the best possible asking price. So, I stood there and watched him for a while. He wasn't in a hurry to pack the gun away. Yeah, he's a player alright. He was on a mission for a sale. I could see it. But what was his asking?

The moment I went to the bug-out-sleigh and started fumbling through my items, Timothy stopped doing what he was doing. The game had begun, and his body language showed it. I consider myself as seasoned as the next when it comes to dealing. I read all the signs, and I wasn't about to let the prospect of owning a gun get away. The problem was I reckoned Timothy had enough crackle, and a few more shards was unlikely to sway him. I had to come up with something he'd want. More than that, something he'd need. So, I reluctantly took out something he'd most likely desire. I knew he wasn't good at fixing stuff. If he had any nous, those diesel generators wouldn't be such a problem. So, I was happy to give up my torque wrench and crowbar, thinking it'd be a good trade. He plainly said without expression, "Need to try harder." Bastard. He's playing the hard game. So, I quickly added a small paper sachet of Pre-Fall tomato seeds. I'd tried to grow them. It seems I didn't have what it took to get them going. From what Timothy said about where he came, he'd make good use of them.

Timothy smiled brightly when I handed them over. He knew the value of seeds. I paid good crackle to get them and now my investment was going to pay off. But the bastard still wanted more. "How about your eagle?" he asked. My heart sank. That was something I wasn't about to let go. The dealing suddenly hit the side of a stone wall and left me feeling as though everything was lost.

He must've noticed my hesitation. "Tell you what," he put in. "I'll kip et here with my treasures, and et'll be safe. You'll never have to worry about et. Et'll stay away from the Takers."

"The bones have to stay with it," I said after much thought. "It's important they stay together."

"Why?"

"Just is." I shrugged. I was even going to tell him about Charlotte but stopped myself, thinking the information wasn't relevant and the less he knew, the better. In my mind, I already decided to come and get it back after I fix his damn generator. How would the idiot know?

As soon I had that thought, Timothy responded. "Don't even think of coming back to get it, Michael. Only I know how to retrieve it without setting off the trap. If you attempt to get it later, everything will be destroyed." He then pointed down to a metallic box that was slightly U-shaped and set back in the depression just behind the footlocker. I'd only ever seen one before. Claymore. I knew they spit out death quick as a click of the tongue. The C4 *explosion was bad enough. The ball bearings had the ability of ripping anything in half. It looked ready to slice and dice just sitting there, but Timothy had it attached to something only he knew about. I think I just lost my beloved figurine forever. Or returning his gun into his hands was the only other option. He won. I lost. Plain and simple.*

Chapter Eleven

Small Things

Entry 726.

After finally getting to the end of the mineshaft and emerging into a gully exactly as Timothy described, it took more than a few moments for my eyes to adjust to the daylight. Ahead of us, rocky hills jut upward on either side. Sandstone boulders sit there as if they'd been delicately placed into position by some giant being. The place is alive with the sounds of insects and creatures I'd never heard before. An abundance of protein and any man can live here forever. If there is water here it'd give me reason enough to stay. I'd be able to survive easily.

As I sit here writing, Timothy is nursing some horrible sores on his feet. It wasn't until after I saw him limping along while wrestling with the bug-out-sleigh, that I asked him when was the last time he took off his boots? He looked at me with bug eyes and said he didn't know, only to add it was a long time. Shit. The bloody idiot.

"Didn't you notice how I took my boots off every time we stopped?"

"Yeah," Timothy said. "Your fit stenk. Thet's bad enough. I couldn't do both of us at the same time."

Jesus H Christ!

Next thing, a bird call. Some kind of bird I didn't recognise from a position high above the bank to our left. Timothy sprung up and began to prance around. Takers! I had the gun and began to wish hard I had the ammo for it. It may as well had been something to throw if it came down to it. Useless.

Timothy answered the bird call with an exact sound he had made by pushing his fingers to his lips and blowing. He smiled and for the first time I saw how yellowed his teeth were. A few heads bobbed up from behind a couple of rocks about forty strides up the embankment. "Over here," Timothy yelled out. I pounced on Timothy to silence his excitement once and for all, but it was too late.

"Relax Michael, they're my clan."

After the heads-up top became bodies, they began to shimmy down the embankment toward us, Timothy met them halfway and greeted them by touching his nose to theirs. I found this way of saying hello to be quite odd. I kept myself way back until I knew everything was okay.

Timothy introduced one of them as his sister, Cherith, which was hard to pronounce at first until I got used to it. She appeared younger than Timothy and her complexion was surprisingly fresh. She had the same facial tattoos as Timothy that curled around her left cheek and eye. The other was a brother and ran by the name of Seth who also had virtually the same facial tattoos only a little more expressive in the design. I commented on the tattoos and Seth answered, "Where we're from, we all have 'em, bro."

Turns out, when we depart this place, we'll all get the chance to carry Timothy. His feet are truly stuffed. The bloody idiot.

Entry 727.

We trudged the gully about ten thousand strides east. Carrying Timothy was already the task we never wanted. If I wasn't dragging, dragging, dragging, I'd have him on my back while Seth took over the bug-out-sleigh, Cherith erasing drag tracks from behind. Then we'd all change our positions again after another thousand strides or so. It was hard work. Added to that, Cherith is one tough girl, no doubt about it. When it was her turn to take Timothy on her back, she did it like a man. Flabbergasted, I was.

I'd never consider the trudging in full daylight. The heat is a killer. I drank twice as much retched fluid compared to at night. But Seth assures there'd be no threat this far east from the Takers. He seems to think if there're contacts, they'd be easy enough to deal with. So far none. Can't help thinking that's just more arse than class. I also can't help but wonder if Seth ever had the pleasure of Takers company. He's too complacent for my liking. I wonder if there's something about Seth under the surface. Something that carries with his complacency. Guess I'll find out soon enough.

I had my boots off for a time while we stopped to rest, and judging by the condition of my feet, I hoped our destination wouldn't be too far away. The sores between my toes, even though not half as bad as Timothy's, were already in the established stages of trench-foot. Timothy's trench-foot is full blown. He'll have a battle keeping his feet attached to his legs, I reckon. With no hope of an antibiotic, I fear he'll turn gangrene. All because the fucker was too damn lazy to take off his boots. Then what? We chop his feet off to save his life. The more I think about it, the more I wonder about his number of days. Then, I think about something else entirely different.

Without Timothy alive, there's next to no chance of retrieving my figurine. I must keep him alive. No question. After we get to Newman, after I fix the generator, I must go shopping out in the waste. My shopping list will be short. Antibiotic, antibiotic and antibiotics. Oh, and it'd be nice for at least one bloody bullet for my future handgun.

I'm now somewhat reluctantly Timothy's bodyguard. That is, until I get my figurine back. After that, I don't care much. I'm sure Timothy's clan will continue without too much trouble. Guess what? I'll be somewhere else. Where that'll be is anyone's guess.

Enough said. I'm out of paper. Time to get going. The Sun is about to dip below. Time to trek through the night.

Chapter Twelve

A Journey Begins

The weight of the last tattered and possibly blood-stained sheet of paper felt much heavier than it truly was. I'd read a lot of books over the years. I was well accustomed to the anticlimax one feels at the end of a good read, but this was something else. In my mind, my internal voice kept telling me, 'This can't be the end of it. There must be more.' If that was the case, where was it? And what would it take to get hold of it?

After having read what was written by Michael, who was an obviously educated individual, I found myself torn in half by the new questions the journal raised. The urgency to head south and rescue Chloe hadn't wavered. But I found myself also wanting to know the whereabouts of these so-called Lost Ones and also, to learn the fate of what happened to Michael and Timothy. I realized I'd never know without having access to more of Michael's writings. If it existed, was it possible to launch into an investigation and find out where the rest of it was? Or perhaps there may be the risk of starting something I'd regret. Either way, how could I ignore the adventure? And where would that adventure lead?

"Richard. Pray tell what you're thinking," Captain Bass said. "If it's the same as what I have in my head, I'm afraid we're both in a spot of bother, are we not?"

"In my head, I'm thinking there're too many questions and not enough answers. When that happens, I get the itches. One—What's the significance with the relics' relationship to each other? And why must they stay together? Two—Who is Charlotte? And why did she refer to the journal's author as 'Michael the Protector?' Three-There was a gun in dead man's chest. Where is it now? Four-Who are The Lost Ones? And why are they lost? Shall I go on?"

"Err . . . No. Stop there before you do yourself a brain hemorrhage."

I went on. "It'd be nice to know who the bones belong to. I'd like to think we could do the decent thing and return them to the right family. And! Once we retrieve the figurine, we should find out its history and where it came from."

"Young man! You're beginning to drown in the details. Let's finish one thing at a time."

"Need a whiteboard," I responded. "Everything needs organizing in a way we don't leave anything out."

"Richard . . ."

"We'll need portable recording devices . . ."

"Richard!"

"We'll need more men . . ."

"RICHARD"

"What?"

"Just stop, will you? We're not living in the times before The Fall. We shall never have the resources to go at this as though we've been given some government grant. My boy, everything we do must have a near invisible footprint. Trust me on this. Let us take some time and think what needs doing first."

"Chloe is first."

"And it shall be done."

Finally, firm confirmation from the captain. We were at last about to set sail for Antarctica. I should've been high on the happiness. I should've run from the great cabin, up the stairs to the ship's rail and shouted out her name. I should've shouted 'Chloe, I'm coming for you.' But I didn't. It seemed no matter how hard I tried, I couldn't get my head away from the journal. And, as soon as I realized it, I felt shame tear me into two pieces. How I hated it. But how could I help it?

The journal mentioned 'Ambers,' and in my mind, the word 'Ambers' rang true in some strange way. A memory from somewhere. Distant, going way back to when I was a kid. But it was a foggy memory. I tried hard to recover it. It wouldn't come.

"So, pray tell. Who do you think is the dead man?" the captain interrupted my thoughts.

"Dead man is either Michael or Timothy. It's a slim chance it could be anybody else."

"My deduction also, dear boy. Do you think it is possible that we shall ever find out for certain?"

"That depends."

The shame of it all. I almost felt a sense of disgrace that something else had crept into my life and was threatening to take me away from the one person I loved so dearly. But somehow, I managed to bite it all back. Somehow, I knew it in my heart that my future was about to change so drastically.

I got up from my chair and without any consideration at all, I walked past Captain Bass as though he wasn't there. I could almost feel his eyes upon me as I was about to help myself to another glass of rum from the decanter. My internal dialogue sounded off. This wasn't me. How could I be so ignorant and empty of manners? I spun and immediately apologized to the captain. "Crap, I'm so sorry. May I?"

"But of course. There's plenty."

Just then, something rocketed through my brain, sending off tiny shockwaves as a sudden realization leapt into my conscience mind. *But of course, There's plenty . . .* It occurred to me that I was having the luxury of drinking rum when there shouldn't have been any. From what I learned, only the Takers would have such a luxury. And the captain said it himself. There was plenty. An incredible sinking feeling swept over me. Maybe I'd gone from a situation that was bad enough, into a situation that was truly fucked-up. From this moment on, I decided that a good measure of caution must be taken.

"And how, may I ask, do we manage such a task?" the captain broke into my thoughts.

"I'm sorry, Captain. Where were we?"

"The dead man. The figurine. How do we retrieve them? We do not have the equipment, my boy. Only in Perthland will we ever find such items. That has a twofold disadvantage. One cannot expect to procure such items without drawing attention to oneself. And drawing attention to oneself means The Takers will know. Should that happen, our attempt at diving for the eagle has come to naught and the eagle figurine will inevitably fall into the wrong hands."

And there it was. A warning bell. I must play this with care.

I quickly changed the subject. "This rum. Where did it come from?"

I saw the captain's eyes narrow. He paused long enough to think about what he was about to say. The fact that he paused was another warning. Then his hardened expression melted away and he began to laugh. "You think . . . Oh, my dear boy. How could you think . . . I'm dumbfounded . . . I don't know what to say."

"That doesn't answer my question."

"Richard. Calm down, will you? This can be explained as easily as having a piss off the end of the bowsprit."

I said nothing. I assumed my expression said all the words necessary. The captain immediately stepped across the floor to a very heavy looking sea chest. Lifting up the lid, he beckoned me closer. Inside the sea chest was what I thought was some kind of solidified oil. After thinking about it, I realized I was looking at the material Michael wrote about in his journal. Crackle. And the sea chest was full of it.

"Crackle," the captain said, confirming all of my thoughts. "My boy, there is enough here to purchase most anything from the colonies for many years to come."

"And where did you get that!" I said. I wasn't totally convinced. Our captain would need to explain a whole lot more before he could take away my suspicions. But I also realized if I was in the presence of The Takers, I'd perhaps be dead by now. Jason and Eli as well. However, if I *was* in the company of The

Takers, what could I do about it? Fight my way out? To where? I was more trapped on *Victory* than I ever was on *Steinbeck*.

Captain Bass took a big chunk of crackle out of the sea chest and gave it to me. I felt the cold weight in my hand. I saw my own reflection in the surface and then I thought about how it was made. All those lives. All those billions of people. All gone. Wiped out when the bombs fell. Crackle has the blood of billions of souls compressed into it. Billions of birthdays. Billions of Independence Days. Billions of Thanksgivings. Billions of first walks, first talks, first dances, first kisses, all gone. I realized it and the first thing I wanted to do was smash it into a million fragments. But instead I fell to my knees. I felt something ripping up through my body I'd never felt before. What was it? Was it the pain and suffering of all those people? Was I somehow transmuting their anguish? Billions upon billions of citizens of Earth? I suddenly felt as though every tear ever shed was now falling from my eyes.

* * *

I felt a hand land gently on my shoulder and I realized Captain Bass and his *Victory* could not have been part of any Taker stronghold or fleet. I kept telling myself, it just wasn't possible. We'd be dead. But what he said next cemented our partnership and our cooperation in this coming venture for the eagle and the Lost Ones.

"You've read about it yourself in dead man's journal. You've read about the scroungers."

I nodded.

"That's much the same as what we do on *Victory*. But instead, we do it on the high seas. The more Takers ships we raid and sink, the more goods we're able to transport back to the colonies. The everyday folk can therefore survive a little longer. We help them. As much as we can. But it doesn't hurt to give *Victory's* crew some luxuries for their labors. That's our rum. It came from The Takers. And our business to the colonies still stands, Richard. So we must make haste and do whatever needs doing so we might find ourselves in Perthland again. The people there depend upon us."

With my mind settled, I began to think what our next steps must be. "In that case, Henry, we must be on our way. Tonight. Without any further delay." I was thinking about Chloe, but I was also thinking about what lay beneath the surface of the seas and how we could retrieve it. Then an idea came.

"*Steinbeck* has a two-man submersible there for the taking," I said. "There'll be no need to purchase diving equipment at Perthland." But something I didn't think about made me halt. How many years had it been since the submersible was ever used? Or was it ever used at all? One thing I knew about electronics. If not constantly maintained, electronics will fail. Plain. Simple. I wasn't, however, about to tell that to our captain. After we make sail, it could turn out to be an issue resulting in turning around the ship.

"Richard, my boy. If we move, we lose our location to where the eagle figurine was last seen."

"We don't have to be exactly accurate. Mark our current location on the ship's charts and when we return, the submersible will take us to where we need to be. Now. Let's get going."

* * *

I didn't realize how difficult it was navigating below decks at night until I tried it. Having had a few rums made things more difficult. Being injured with a broken shoulder and a bruised knee cap that was made worse with the ship's rolling, just made everything virtually impossible. But I did eventually make it to my allotted space between two cannons. Arriving there, both Eli and Jason were tucked in their hammocks fast asleep.

I did my best getting into my hammock as stealthily as possible. The potato soup and damper, as the captain called it, that was delivered to the great cabin, rolled around in my belly as I heaved myself up and in. I was silent, all the way up until my body went one way and my shoulder went the other. F-U-C-K!

"Ditch! Where've you been, Ditch?"

Oh crap! "Captain's great cabin. Jase, I have to tell you something."

Over the next couple of hours, I put Jason and Eli well into the picture. I'd told them everything I'd learned and read about. As I explained it, Jason never interrupted me. The fact Jason didn't interrupt said everything about his interest. And the fact Eli was also wordless meant he must've fallen asleep. Or did he? But both also reacted negatively the same as each other when I told them about the idea with the submersible. Both launched into hearty laughter as though I'd finally lost my mind.

"Ditch. It'll never work. And if it does work, how're we ever going to get it from *Steinbeck* knowing what's instore when we get there?"

"What do you think is going to happen?" I asked.

There was silence for a couple of moments. It didn't appear anybody knew for sure.

"We're on an armed vessel," I said. "When was the last time you saw guns of any type on *Steinbeck?* We've also got small arms. All they've got are batons and tear gas. Yeah, I get it. Our firearms are over three hundred years old. But they still pack a punch. And in my mind, I say bullets will always win over fists."

* * *

We discussed all our options and came up with a solid workable plan, passing in most of the night. Just before dawn, a plan was nutted out and it was time to get some much-needed sleep. I had no idea how close we were to Antarctica, or how many hours must pass before we finally drop anchor. The only clue to tell me was the growing length of each day. Already, the sense of time I was well accustomed to was gone. Living in a world which had a twenty-four-hour cycle of night and day had thrown my stable body clock out the window. After sun-up, our objectives will be heard in the captain's quarters where we'll receive a yay or nay from Captain Bass and his officers.

Once I found myself comfortable in my hammock, I closed my eyes and went over everything in my head. After arriving back at the Ross Ice Shelf, it would be important for Jason, Eli and myself to remain on board *Victory.* We'd left *Steinbeck* as prisoners, sentenced to death. If we were seen, it was mutually assumed between us that we'd be again taken captive. So instead, a party of men chosen by Captain Bass would disembark *Victory* and make contact with Skipper, making him aware that *Victory* had arrived on a rescue mission to relocate all souls to Australee.

Skipper would then be invited aboard *Victory* to inspect the ship's capacity to transport human cargo. He would also be encouraged to draft a lottery for the first transport. It would all be discussed at a formal dinner at the Captain's table in his great cabin.

The plan would ramp up with the capture and imprisonment of Skipper while partaking in evening mess. He'd be held prisoner on *Victory* for a ransom. That ransom would be the sum total of a lone two-man submersible delivered directly to the *HMS Victory* within twenty-four hours. That was the plan. How much simpler could it be? There was only one thing that worried me. What if Skipper no longer had the popularity vote? Certainly, he was on the top of the hate lists that a majority of *Steinbeck's* inhabitants carried around inside their minds. Perhaps a ransom wouldn't work for that reason. Nobody could give a shit about him. Then what?

A plan B must be put in place. For some reason, I lightly shuddered thinking what that might entail. Whatever the outcome, however, it was discussed that it will be with the good intention of everyone on board *Victory,* that as many souls as possible are transported, with the intention of the armed vessel to return as many times as required to evacuate the rest.

Chapter Thirteen

A Higher Purpose

I opened my eyes. I'd been transported to a place among crowds of people. High up on a stage, I sat overlooking them all. So many people were jumping and cheering in time to the beat. The beat I played. I played the beat loud. I played it hard.

Kickdrum, snare. Kickdrum, snare. Kickdrum, snare, kick-kick. Snare.

Rimshots. All rimshots. I played in my style. None of that syncopated bullshit. None of the traditionally mastered art of parradiddle-parra-diddle. None of the technically perfect rolls and beats that are divided sixty-four times into the four beats to a bar time signature. No. I was raw. I was powerful. And-they-loved-it.

Kickdrum, snare. Kickdrum, snare. Kickdrum, snare, kick-kick. Snare.

To my left through the curtain, someone arrived on stage. A woman I thought looked familiar. But there was no face. Only her back toward me. Could it be that I knew her? The crowd went crazy! But I played on. The same beat. The same heavy beat. Rimshots, baby. Rimshots. Four tom-toms on a rack in front of me. I didn't touch them. I was the last of the groove heavy hitters. I laid down the groove.

Kickdrum, snare. Kickdrum snare. Kickdrum snare, kick-kick. Snare.

From my right, another entered on stage. Someone I didn't recognize. A bald-headed guy with a bad limp shimmied over to the Marshall stack and grabbed his axe, whipped it up, and plugged in the cord. The Marshall stack responded with an earsplitting squelch. The crowd went wild! But I played on.

Kickdrum, snare. Kickdrum snare. Kickdrum snare, kick-kick. Snare.

On my left, someone I didn't recognize arrived on stage. A female with long black flowing hair. The hourglass body of a Hollywood movie star. Skin tight leathers shiny and black as her long locks that went all the way down to her ass. She strutted over to the Marshall stack and picked up her axe. She plugged it in. Another ear-splitting squelch but I played on.

Kickdrum, snare. Kickdrum snare. Kickdrum snare, kick-kick. Snare.

The crowd went nuts.

In the light, I managed to see the back of the bald guy's head. A tattoo. An eagle. A white eagle with a sword. Then he started grinding on his axe. The earsplitting sound through my fold back speaker was immense. All of a sudden, I could no longer hear my own beat. The sound guy! Tell him to turn up my kit! Before I screw-up! Before it's too late.

Kickdrum, snare. Kickdrum snare. Kickdrum snare, kick-kick. Snare.

The crowd went wild. Women started to take off their shirts. Some riding their boyfriend's shoulders while they showed their tits to the world. Screaming and jumping. Jumping and shouting while the band played. While I lay down my heavy, heavy, groove.

Then.

The front man stopped.

The chick in black stopped.

The woman I thought I might know stopped.

The crowd no longer shouted and screamed.

There's just me and the beat.

Kickdrum, snare. Kickdrum snare. Kickdrum snare, kick-kick. Snare.

The bald guy with the eagle tattoo and what I thought must be a fake leg turned and looked at me. "Ladies and gentlemen, a big round of applause for our drummer who will be travelling north into danger. Who knows if he will survive? He might die, ladies and gentlemen. He might die."

The crowd again went nuts. But this time, I knew it was all for me.

The rock chick dressed in black put her hand on her belly and began to laugh. She stepped up to the mic. "Ladies and gentlemen. I'm Teresa. This is Nathan and we're The Angels of Mercy!" Her strange accent. I thought she must be Arabic.

The crowd went completely out of their minds.

Then Teresa turned to look at me. She whispered so quietly, placing her hand over her mic at the same time. Somehow I heard her above the crowd. Somehow, I heard her above everything. "Richard, go north. Those Lost. Find them. Find them, Richard. Follow the path and the Moon won't fall. Follow the path and the Moon won't fall. Follow the path and the Moon won't fall."

The woman with her back toward me I thought I knew collapsed on the stage.

I woke up sweating. Panting. Dizzied. I was almost about to scream out.

I didn't know how or why but a hard realization came. Something in the pit of my stomach told me Chloe had died. I leapt out of my bunk with such energy I left my calico sling behind. I raced for the steps and flew up and out into the daylight. I ran for the ship's rail, already feeling ready to purge anything that might exist down in the depths of my guts. When I got there, the violent rush up my throat was immense. I tasted the acid bile as it pushed up my throat and out.

"NOOO!"

I shouted and two voices bounced back from the icebergs that littered the place.

"CHLOE! NOOO!"

I slid down from the rail and hit the deck, feeling heavy with my head about to explode in pain. I sat on the ship's deck with my head in my hands. My hands on my knees. Curled up almost like an embryo. Somehow, I didn't know how it was possible. I didn't know how it could *ever* be possible. I had to be sure. I moved my arm around. A little at first. Then I made big circles. My shoulder and my knee were completely healed.

* * *

Morning mess consisted of a damper with cheese from a goat and a large mug of black liquid that was called coffee. The coffee was hard to get used to at the beginning but as I consumed more of it, I found myself becoming addicted to it. I also found that coffee was a great remedy for a sore head. An old sailor sitting opposite at the table, eyed me with a grin, " 'Ung over, are we? That coffee will sort ya out. Trust me. The more of it inside ya, the better. So, drink that coffee. Drink it all up."

I didn't know what he meant about a 'ung over,' as he put it. That being what it was, I put my trust in the old sailor and drank several cups before leaving the table. He was right. The pain in my head left, even though my heart rate picked up in speed to a level equal to what might be the case had I been running. I felt a little sweaty and light headed. But there was no pain. Coffee. What a wonder.

We organized to meet in the captain's quarters shortly after mess. Jason, Eli and myself, along with first officer, William Fletcher, Surgeon Cristian Hamell and Master at Arms Thomas Brice sat around an oval table that shone and reflected the early morning light. I couldn't help but run my hands over it. It felt cold. It smelt like a hundred years. It looked as though it was made from a rich, dark, mahogany, the same kind of wood that was used as the trimming in Skipper's quarters. It made me think that perhaps it was a tradition to use mahogany in such ways. It was easy to think of trivial things. I found myself thinking of the inconsequential if only to take my mind away from the ugliness I felt in my heart. It appeared to work. I hung my head and searched for other unimportant things that I could focus on. But before I could, Captain Bass finally appeared at the doorway.

Captain Bass eyed me curiously as he sat himself down at the table. "No sling, Richard? Are you sure?"

"It seems I'm now all healed up. How about that?"

Captain Bass's eyes went immediately to Christian Hamell and then to Eli. They had no words. Eli managed a shrug. Christian Hamell shook his head a little as though he was as befuddled as ever.

"You've been drinking far too much coffee, Richard. It blocks the pain receptors, but you may well still be as injured. Mind you be careful. You could do more harm to yourself than you can imagine."

I smiled a little to myself as I reflected on the dream. In my mind, I told myself it was nothing more than that. A bad dream. That's it. Nothing more. Chloe is all right. There is nothing to worry about. I kept saying it, over and over. If I kept saying it enough, I'd start to believe it. And that was the reason why I told nobody about what I'd seen.

The plan we'd nutted out was put before the Captain. It was a big ask to assume he'd agree to use his men while Jason, Eli and myself lay low. But he did see sense in what we had planned. By the time our meeting was concluded, everyone knew what they needed to do. Jason called it our plan A. By calling it that, it implied there must be a plan B. There wasn't a plan B. Simply because I supposed nothing else could've worked.

Before leaving the table, there was only one concern left in my mind. It was the fact we weren't going anywhere in a hurry. With the absence of the prevailing winds, we'd found ourselves becalmed, as the captain had put it. The winds could pick up again in an hour, or they might not pick up for days. There was no choice but to wait it out. Or was there?

"Can I ask a question?"

I saw that the captain was ready to leave. He sat himself back down and eyed me. "But of course. What is it?"

"What would it take to move the ship under oars?"

"We only have the two longboats, Richard. If we tethered *Victory*, we'd still need a lot more man power and many more oars. I'm afraid we're stranded until such time as there's a change in the weather conditions."

* * *

I heard them up there. Seabirds. Gulls, and maybe the elusive albatross. I rubbed my eyes awake as the light of a new day dazzled my senses. Vapor shot away from my every breath. It was a clue I couldn't ignore. I bounced out of my hammock without a sound, taking extra care not to wake Jason. I shimmied around a cannon and poked my head out of a porthole to be sure we'd made land. We were home. Finally.

Chloe.

I hope you're alright.

Out on the glass-like water that sparkled with the early morning sun, the familiar craggy peaks of icebergs littered the sea in sporadic gangs. *There*, was the ice shelf. *There*, was the *Steinbeck*. But billows of black smoke rose in a funnel, reaching high then sharply trailing off at ninety degrees. I felt the contents in my stomach begin to curdle and separate. The hard realization. Nothing was all right.

"Jason."

Jason woke up as his usual grumpy self.

"Jase. Something's wrong," I said.

After Jason and Eli saw the black smoke emanating from *Steinbeck*, I realized our plan A was trashed. There was no plan B. It was with urgency, however, that a landing party must be put to shore. To find out what had happened. To find Chloe.

Eli put his head further outside the porthole and looked up. I noticed his skin paled. Pulling his head back in he looked as shocked as ever. "We're still at close-reef."

Jason and I exchanged our glances of bewilderment. "How did we get here, Ditch? There's no wind. And the sails are still tied up."

Chapter Fourteen

Sunken City

Even though the quarter deck was crowded with men, and the deck was abuzz with activity, I felt heavily forlorn standing at the starboard rail, looking out across the choppy waters. Behind me, the prevailing winds had returned, and it filled every sail. *Victory* pitched and rolled, cutting noisily through the waves. All hands got on with what needed doing; pulling at ropes, scaling the rigging, tying this, untying that, pulling and pushing as though they were truly born into the craft of sailing such a huge vessel.

And me?

I was alone as ever.

If there were a hundred men around me, I was sure it would still feel as though I was standing, looking out, feeling isolated and cut off from everything.

Thinking it over, what had happened on *Steinbeck* was completely unexpected. And I kept thinking back to that damned dream. The Angels of Mercy, they'd called themselves. If this was mercy, it was a bad joke and there was no humor about it at any angle. But still the memory of the dream lingered in my mind, and it felt as real as taking a piss off the bowsprit, as our captain had put it.

Everyone on *Steinbeck* was dead. There was no denying how it happened. The rampage came early. Among the dead were my wife and unborn child. We stepped over body after body in the search for Chloe. Bodies which had been savagely bashed to almost beyond any possible means of recognition. I'd never seen such carnage. I fear the image of those poor souls will stay with me forever.

Jason and Eli started their search for Chloe from the flight deck. William Fletcher, Captain Bass and I decided it would be better to start below decks. I found Chloe where I thought she'd most likely be. She was with my mother in her stateroom which had been set alight. Both had died in the fire. They were burned so badly it was impossible to hold them in my arms one last time. As I knelt down beside my wife, I noticed she'd used something to scratch the letter 'R' in the metal floor. My first initial. She was thinking of me when she died. How it hurt me to see it.

We managed to take their bodies from *Steinbeck*, up the hill past Emert's Turn to the cemetery. I said goodbye to Chloe and my mother with all the strength I had left. But no matter how much I tried, I couldn't swallow down the feeling of anger at myself for their abandonment. I hated myself terribly for doing that to them.

But even so, above everything that had happened, we managed to procure what we needed. What *they* needed. The two-man submersible.

Every time I see the submersible sitting on *Victory's* poop deck in such contrast between what was old, and what was very-very old, the cost of getting it there chills me. I was no longer happy about it. How could I be? I'd lost so much. And it cost so much. It no longer mattered about what it was going to be used for. The eagle figurine could stay where it was. The dead man's journal; I swore the next time I saw it, I'd put a match to it. And the lost ones could damned-well stay lost.

I stood at the starboard rail, the toe of my boot just slightly hanging over the edge. What would it take? To take one step too far? One step and I could go to sleep. My tired mind. I was so tired of thinking. Sleep would be nice. And I thought wherever I go from here, perhaps I'd find Chloe again. There'd be little effort just to step over the rail and step off the edge. A little effort and much relief.

As I swung my leg up and over the rail, I grabbed a rope and held myself there for a moment. What was I waiting for? Let go of the rope, I told myself. Just let go. I loosened my grip slightly. Looking down in the water was a huge creature I knew I'd seen before. The same all white orca who'd pushed the slab of ice north. The same all white orca who'd sunk the Takers' ship. And it was rumored this orca was one of several who saved *Victory* from being becalmed. I loosened my grip fully, and I fell.

I didn't know how it was at all possible. The need for oxygen while under the water never mattered. I grabbed onto an orca dorsal fin and rode.

The great white orca pulled me down, all the way down. I felt my ears want to burst. I felt as though a hundred men were sitting on my chest. But still, we went down. I looked on. The water darkened as we dove and out of the darkness, the hulks of what were once shops that I'd only ever seen in pictures appeared out of the murk. It was as though a thick fog had rolled in and had covered everything. Then out of the gloominess emerged broken buildings with shattered windows. Roads that had been smashed to pieces. Cars and trucks lay on their sides and on their roofs with their doors left flung open to somebody who'd never show up.

The orca took me further.

We passed a couple of street side signs. One said, 'Battery Point' and I knew it in my heart this was once the Hobart in Tasmania that I'd read so much about. We followed a sign that said, 'Elizabeth Street'. The orca took me into the city center, and out the other side to a bridge that arose from the bottom of the sea like a dead giant. The sign on approach said, 'Tasman Bridge.' We followed the bridge to the other side through suburbs of housing estates were normal folk must've once lived.

Skeletons lay everywhere.

Human bones were stacked in the middle of roads, in suburban yards, in open doorways, in cars that were piled with suitcases. Suitcases that were still tied down.

Skeletons of the young and the old. Babies in prams. All of which seemed frozen in time. It was as though these souls were attempting to take shelter or were trying to escape. Then I knew what I was seeing. I was witnessing the last minutes on Earth as The Great Seep washed through. People everywhere tried desperately to get away. But to where? Nobody had any chance at all. There were signs of panic and madness everywhere I looked.

The orca took me to a clearing, and in the middle of the clearing was one single skeleton dressed in the same clothes I'd seen on that day we'd nearly perished on the ice. I knew we had arrived at where the submersible was supposed to take us. I knew we'd found the dead man.

As we got there, the orca slowed to a stop. I almost instinctively put my hand out and plunged it into his pocket. My fingers curled around something. It was no eagle figurine. I pulled away a big wad of what I knew were papers. The wad of papers looked exactly the same as what I'd already read, and I knew it was more of dead man's journal. In my mind, I decided I must now find the eagle. I darted around the dead man's clothes. I worked them over, zealously. I searched every pocket more than once, more than twice but there was no eagle.

* * *

I broke the surface and took oxygen like I'd never needed it more. The water was choppy, *Victory* was at close-reef, and I knew they'd responded to a 'man overboard.' How was I going to tell the captain what had happened? A hundred thoughts in a split second drilled through my mind. But in my hand, I grasped the wad of papers. It was living proof of where I'd been.

With the water seething around me, I grabbed the rope which someone had flung down. When I finally got to the top, I was greeted unceremoniously with a ferocious punch to the jaw. I found myself flat on my back and my brother standing over me. I knew if I got up again, he'd have another go. So, I got to my feet. And down I went again. I got to my feet and this time someone was hanging onto Jason. My brother's face was red. Fury, I knew, raged inside him. I couldn't blame him. I wanted to exit, taking the easy option. If it was me, I'd have done the same thing. He could've beat on me as much as he wanted, it didn't matter. When this all unravels, it'll be worth it.

* * *

It took almost a week to painstakingly dry out each single page. Jason, Eli and myself met daily in the captain's great cabin where each page had its own place to dry. I had to hold myself back from the urge of reading as I went. Had I attempted to read a page while it was still wet, I ran the risk of putting my damn finger through it. So I lay out each page separately and put them back together only when they again became stable.

The day came when the journal was put back together. I couldn't help but feel a certain eagerness building inside me. Jason and Eli tried to hide their excitement as best they could but failed. Even Captain Bass appeared impatient to get going. I guess we all knew that we'd finally find out more of what happened to Michael and Timothy, perhaps even find out what had happened to the figurine and uncover clues that may lead to its whereabouts. The question remained, however, whether there was enough to lead us to it? And if so, what would it take to recover it.

Chapter Fifteen

Charlotte

I met Captain Bass in the great cabin to continue my reading commitment, but this time I had an audience. Eli and Jason stopped whatever they were supposed to be doing and joined us. It felt very odd. It felt almost as though I was a teacher and these eager faces staring up at me belonged to my pupils. As I picked up the papers and held them, I made sure one final time they were all bone dry. Happy with that, I started at the top of the first page being aware that my brother and the doctor, as well as our captain, appeared to be almost salivating. They eyed me excitedly as though I was holding up a big cut of prime meat. I also found myself wanting to get going if only for the reprieve I'd get from my other much darker thoughts. I wanted to escape all the hurt and upset and this was an opportunity. I was so glad the relief was only seconds away.

Dropping my eyes on the first sheet that was as badly dog-eared and tattered as the first part of the journal, I was pleased the writing continued at entry 728. If it didn't, that meant there was a hole in time which might've led to the possibility of missing vital clues.

Entry 728.

Newman is everything Timothy described. The entire place from what I can tell is walled up and it resembles some kind of fort. The walls are as high as thirty hands in some places and it's made of odd scraps of wood and other materials that they've collected. Rusted tin sheet, pieces of gyprock, wire, steel, slabs of concrete and even great chunks of asphalt. From the outside, it looks like a junk pile. And everything's lashed into place with ropes, hooks, nails, and screws. But it's strong. Seth assures me, it'll stand up to any Takers raid.

"What about the trucks, Timothy told me about? If the north-erners have them like he says, that means the Takers have them as well. They can smash through the barriers."

"The Takers don't have thim. Only carts drawn by their droppers."

"Droppers?"

"People thet work for thim. They call thim droppers because when they drop dead, they get eaten."

"Slaves?"

"Sort of. They give thim labour but they're more for food. And the Ambers from up north haven't bin down here in a while. Even if the Takers attack us with ranged weapons they'd get nowhere. We've got contingencies in place for an evint like that. You're safe, Michael. There's no nid to worry."

Tracking the edges of the sentry walls as Seth calls them, we came to an opening and heads popped up from behind a pile of rusted forty four galon drums. After greeting the sentry guards and making ourselves known, I stepped down a flight of rickety steel stairs and into a darkened musty smelling tunnel. It was my turn to carry Timothy. I put him on my back for the 101st time and I was so sick of it, I felt glad that it wasn't for much longer. It doesn't matter what anybody tells me. I still reckon Timothy won't last long without medication. It's up to me now. I'll have to get them and sort him out. If he dies, I'll lose my eagle. That's just not happening.

Climbing the steps at the other end of the tunnel and emerging again into the sunlight, I looked out over rows and rows of green.

Green!

I've never seen it before. There's crops just like Timothy described as far as I could see. The crops swayed in the breeze and rippled like liquid. Seth told me it's corn but they also grow wheat, barley, and rye. There's vegetables, the same as those I tried so hard to nurture and get going but failed. Tomatoes. Pumpkin. Celery. Even horse radish. What a surprise.

As I adjusted my eyes trying to believe what I was seeing, Cherith grabbed Timothy off my back and took him away. Timothy said nothing, the bastard. Not even a thanks. He just disappeared into the distance, not a word said.

Seth grabbed my attention just as I was about to shout out 'thanks for nothing.' He pointed to the far east side of the compound to a hill that rose up from the flatlands. "See that?" he said. "That's our fertiliser pile. Horse shet, cow shet, donkey shet, chook shet, pig shet, but no people shet. We're not like the Takers. We don't put people shet on our crops. Thengs grow because we prep the land and we have water. After harvest, we turn and rotate the paddocks. We don't plant the same seed in the same paddock twice."

That was when the first warning sounded off in my head. I should've listened to my gut instinct. Timothy told me these people only have meat in deep freeze. That's why they needed their generator fixed. So then, where did they get all that manure? Their animals are supposedly dead. My mind went, 'Turn the fuck around and run, you wanker.' I couldn't. I was too far from the sentry tunnel. I had no idea what kind of weapons these people might have. They might have guns and ammo. They might even have bolts and crossbows. They might have anything. If I made a run for it, I was sure they'd either tackle me, or shoot me as I ran.

As soon as I thought about it, the second warning ricocheted around in my brain. Nobody has firearms but the Takers. What made Seth think they could stand up to them? The only thing that can answer a gun fight is more guns. A horrible thought came to mind. Maybe I'm now in more shit than I know.

Entry 729

I thought it'd be better to play out what needs playing out, and make a break for it when I got close enough to the tunnel. An old memory told me, 'If you hold your hand out long enough, you'll catch bird shit.' The trick is not to hold your hand out. Keep everything to yourself. And this is what I'm doing right now. I swallowed all my suspicions. I said nothing to nobody.

After they'd taken my stuff away; my belongings and precious gun with a single 50 cal bullet, they'd given me a place to sleep in one of the farm sheds. Something in my head told me I might not see those things again, and I worked hard trying to force my mind to think positive thoughts. But Timothy is a bloody liar. The place stinks of cows. And it doesn't take much intelligence to work out they've fed them only yesterday. It made me wonder about the generator. Do they even have one?

Entry 730

This guy called Murk turned up and said he was to take me to my work station. Work station? What? Was I some kind of slave now? That being what it was, Murk wasn't a guy you'd mess with. The guy is beefier than a Brahmin. And probably twice as angry. I said to Murk, "There's a diesel generator that needs fixing. That's why I'm here."

He laughed and said, "Yeah, that's what Temothy tells all of thim. He even wears the right kind of diesel perfume when he goes out looking for droppers."

Droppers! Shit!

As soon as he said it, Murk tightly gripped my upper arm. I thought my blood was going to squeeze out of my eyes. Pretty soon after that, there were more of us so-called droppers. I saw them hunkered down, swinging sickles, chained together in long lines. None of them were smiling. None of them even talked about anything. The next thing I knew; I was added to the chain and doing the same damn thing.

Swinging a sickle is a pain in the arse. Under the beating sun, it's twice as bad.

I tried to make small talk with one of the other droppers. He was reluctant to say anything. He kept on swinging that sickle, at the same time acting as though he was deaf and dumb. I felt Murk's big curled up fist between my shoulder blades and I got the message to shut the hell up.

Entry 731

A new day of swinging a damn sickle awaits me. At least it's a way of getting out of this stinking barn. I wasn't alone this time. Last night, several of us were dropped off like pieces of litter in this stinking cow shed. Before the sun went down, they threw some plastic plates under the big wooden door. They'd made us a heap of what the chain masters call clag. They also pushed a container of brown bore water toward us before shutting and locking up for the night.

With the heavy chains off my limbs, I grabbed my plate of clag and found a place to eat away from everyone else. I hoed into it with my fingers, thinking at the same time what I must've looked like from the outside. Here we all were tucking into something that was made from crushed wheat and water. To be honest, I'm pretty sure this clag could be used like glue to stick things together. But eating it was better than nothing. I ate all my clag and washed it down with that wretched brown bore water.

After I'd finished my plate, I pushed some dirty hay into a heap and thought it was well enough off the ground to get a good night's sleep. Before I knew it, one of the other droppers was scoping my plate for possible left overs. I only left the tiniest amount. I was gonna save it for breakfast. But when he got close enough, I thought maybe I could finally talk to somebody.

"What's your name. I'm Michael."

This guy looked at me a little startled as though nobody had ever attempted to talk to him before. Then he pointed to his mouth.

"What's wrong with your mouth?" I asked him.

He opened up and showed me. These guys don't have a tongue. He showed me in sign language what happens to new droppers. They cut their tongues out! The takers like their food supply nice and quiet.

Fuck!

Now what?

I got up and tested every possible escape route I could find. The place is solid. The ground is much too hard and compacted to dig a tunnel with my bare hands. The only way out is through that big door.

I grabbed the handles and gave it a big shake. "Let me out of here!"

I did it again but the droppers behind me seemed to be amused, making a laughing sound that wasn't quite a laugh. It was very spooky.

"Let me OUT!"

I screamed it a few times to nobody. The sun started to go down and night time came.

Entry 732

They came in just after sun up. Murk burst through the big heavy barnyard door with another behind him, wearing doctor's garb that was so grimy and dirty; it was hard to tell it was supposed to be white. Without any hesitation, they went straight for me. Murk grabbed me. I tried to fight him off. I had no strength. The other guy held out his huge rusty knife. I knew what was coming. I was going to lose the ability to speak.

Murk grabbed my hair and forced my head back. "Get on your knees, dropper!"

I fought him. I fought him hard. Murk's big hands tried to force my mouth open. My head spun. My brain went, 'fight him, fight him, fight him.' I clenched my teeth has hard as I could. But I was fading. I relaxed a little. My mouth opened slightly. Murk's fat fingers entered my mouth. I felt his flesh. I felt his bone. I bit down hard, and I instantly tasted that coppery taste. His bone went 'crack.' I bit down and spat away Murk's big fingers. He reeled back, screaming like a little girl.

The hit I got across the face was aided by an implement. My skin peeled back and opened up. The wetness oozing out was hard to mistake for anything else other than my blood. It ran down my face and neck, and by the time it reached my shoulder it had already gotten cold. There was nothing further I could do. They can take out my damn tongue. They'll never stop me writing.

That guy with the dirty whites got down and did what he came for. I knew Murk would help out even though he was down a good hand. I felt fingers dart and rummage around inside my mouth. Then the blast of pain shot down my throat and into my stomach.

Entry 733

I thought I'd be dead by now. Three weeks fighting an infection and only today am I able to write something. Eating nothing but clag and drinking stinking water somehow kept me going. Today, I join my gang and work the fields. I wonder if this is going to be for the last time. I feel like I've been cheated. Why can't I just die?

Entry 734

I've lost the sense of time. I have no idea how long I've been here. Maybe a lifetime and a bit more. More new droppers arrived. More tongues were cut out. More dead droppers were laid on the backs of carts and pulled away by the Takers walking food supply.

Entry 735
I thought I saw someone familiar. Was I dreaming?

At sentry wall mending detail, I happened to get my eyes on a scrounger who'd turned up to sell wares. I cast my mind back and I remembered who this scrounger was. It was Charlotte, of all people. The young scrounger with a face like an angel. The scrounger who sold me the eagle figurine and bones. I would've shouted something. Anything to grab her attention. But now, I can't say anything to anybody that they would understand. Now, words don't mean anything. She probably wouldn't have recognised me anyway. I've lost so much weight and my hair's fallen out. I've lost most of my teeth. I don't need them to eat clag, so I can't complain. Maybe tomorrow at sentry wall mending detail, Charlotte might be there again. This time I'll let her know I'm around.

Entry 736

A funeral was held for Timothy. He'd died from infections to both legs, I heard them saying. His feet were so bad they had no choice but to amputate. I should be happy he's gone but I'm not. One— I don't know how I'm ever going to get my things back. Two— I've resigned to the fact that I'm never going to get out of here. I'll die soon and I'll end up on a Takers' dinner plate.

Entry 737

A party of Takers arrived for their weekly collection of dead droppers. There was something different this time. They didn't bother to enter the sentry tunnel as they usually do. And from what I could tell, they all seemed to be on edge about something.

But that was before something DID happen.

From my workstation outside the Newman compound, I heard a low earthy rumble and it seemed to be coming from a distance to the north. It was a mechanical noise and something I'd never heard before. Dust clouds were kicked up high in the desert sky. After it got close enough, something in my head told me they were the trucks from the north I'd heard so much about. And they'd picked a bad time to arrive at Newman.

The Takers scattered toward the sentry tunnel, instantly taking cover behind several forty-four gallon drums, and concrete barriers. Almost involuntarily, I turned to seek refuge behind ancient roadside debris. I pulled at my chain and it wouldn't budge.

As a member of a gang of seven droppers, it was useless. It was as though my gang knew it was an opportunity to gain their own freedom; to die where they stood. The idiots were reluctant to go anywhere that might be safe. I stood there, agog, out in the open, knowing shit was about to go down.

Several Newman dwellers raced with arms raised towards the incoming fleet of Ambers. It was an attempt to warn them off, but far too late. By the time the Newman dwellers got away by forty strides, the Takers opened fire and cut them down as they ran.

A Taker popped up from behind cover, holding a missile launcher. The tracer of a missile screeched across the sky, then struck an inbound fuel tanker. The tanker exploded, tipped over on its side and erupted in a cloud of black smoke. Several Newman folks screamed at the Takers to stop the madness. Then a Taker, without any nuisance, drew his pistol and shot a guy who complained.

The rest of the Ambers' fleet rushed to a stop and were immediately peppered with small arms fire. The Ambers' vehicles turned long, slow, U-turns and headed off in the direction they came. More Newman residents emerged from out of the sentry tunnel, two of whom, almost point blank, were shot in the head.

From out of nowhere, that familiar face I'd recognised as Charlotte entered the affray. I didn't know where she came from and it didn't matter. Lightning fast, as though non-human, she retrieved her long recurved blade from her bejewelled cross-draw sheath. Instantly, as if she wasn't affected by the forces of gravity, she moved swiftly between them, mowing down Takers one by one until they all had been relieved of limbs and heads.

I rubbed my eyes, not believing what I'd seen, but as I looked skyward I caught sight of an enormous eagle. The eagle joined more of their kind to become seven; one of which was entirely, and completely the colour of white.

I lifted my eyes from the journal amid the sounds of an almost childlike objection. Clearly, both Jason and Eli could've stayed and listened all night, but I was fast losing my ability to read aloud. My voice was getting croaky and my words were becoming more like mumbles. Apart from that, I had to stem the barrage of new questions that were beginning to emerge.

"What is it, Richard?" Captain Bass asked. "You're looking more befuddled than you were during our last reading."

I was forced to hold my breath and think about what I was going to say next. Yes, I was still enthusiastic as ever to find the crystal eagle but I was also weary. "I hate it when you think there might be an answer, more questions arise. It means there's more work involved and more trudging to do."

"Oh?" Captain Bass got up from his chair and headed for his decanter. "This is unlike you, if you don't mind me saying. I've only known you for a short time and already I see you as an adventurer. Now, it feels as though you're ready to give up."

"It's not that. It's not that at all."

"So pray tell what you mean?"

"It's to do with Charlotte," I said. "She seemed to have this power. This ability. But even so, she appeared to avoid the cruelty of how the droppers were treated. Why did she let them live like that when it's clear she could've helped them? But also this. Michael saw several eagles, one of which was all white."

"Your point?"

I took a breath. I knew this wasn't going to be easy. "The orcas. Seven of them," I said. "Just the same as the seven eagles . . ."

"One of which was all white," Eli said straight away.

"There's a correlation, do you think?" Captain Bass asked in a tone as though he was genuinely mystified.

"There's a correlation, all right. And this also has something to do with the relics, and the reason for them to stay together. We must find the crystal eagle, Captain Bass. Whatever the cost. Whatever the human endeavor. And in my mind, the more I read of this journal, the more it feels like we're on a race with time."

"There's more in the journal," Eli put in. "Maybe Charlotte *did* help the droppers. We won't know for sure until we have the whole story."

Eli was right. Of course it could've been exactly as he said. That question, however, would go unanswered for tonight. We all needed sleep. We all needed our wits about us. We were on the edge of discovering something that was fated to reveal itself. To all of us. Maybe a destiny. I felt it to the core of my body. I wondered if Eli and Jason felt the same. I wondered if Captain Bass felt it as well. What he said next confirmed my feelings.

"You're albino just as much as the orca and the eagle," Captain Bass said, just as I thought it was good time to head off to my allotted hammock. And as he said it, something went through my mind at the speed of light that I didn't at first want to acknowledge; but perhaps subconsciously I already did. Maybe I knew it from the time the orca took me down in the ocean. It was as though we were both somehow joined.

"You haven't read the *Holy Bible*," Captain Bass continued. "So you wouldn't be aware of the *Old Testament* and the seven archangels either. Perhaps some further reading is on the table."

I didn't know what to make of it. But there was a part of me that just couldn't let it go. Curiosity sparked up and I was no longer tired. I was alert and alive, finding myself leaning in toward Captain Bass as he went on explaining.

"There're seven of them. The messengers - and hands of God. Michael the Protector . . ." *There it was. Michael the Protector as Charlotte had called him.* ". . . Gabriel the Messenger, Raphael the Healer, Jophiel the Creator, Uriel the Guardian of Beasts, Azrael, the Angel of Death, and Chamuel the Keeper of the Light. Their job? The fight for the righteous and the battle against evil on earth."

After Captain Bass had said it, he simply turned and headed for a refill of rum. "There was one other," he went on. "The fallen angel. Lucifer was cast out of the kingdom of God. Cast out because Lucifer wanted to be God unto himself. So he was given a choice. Accept God as his creator or he can be God elsewhere. So for Lucifer, he chose the latter. He is God of Evil, or the Prince of Darkness as most are aware.

"So, young Mister Gabriel. You're albino, and your name suggests you're more connected than you might think. Same with you, young Jason. To be honest, all three of you are. Eli here shares the name Raphael. A healer no less! Coincidence? I say not! The more I think about it, after what's been put before all of us, there's a mission revealing itself that is turning out to be vastly more important that we can imagine."

Shit!

My head thumped as the realization came. It all made sense. It all made perfect sense. On *Steinbeck*, we all shared the names of these seven archangels. We didn't know it. We weren't aware of it. And perhaps someone sharing the name of Lucifer decided it was better to do away with and erase any literature or reference to *The Holy Bible* or to *The Old Testament*. It might have been a completely different story living there had we all known the significance. And now, only three *Steinbeck* dwellers survive. Fate or Destiny? I felt it was turning out that way. Now, with every fiber of my being. Sleep would have to wait. I grabbed the journal.

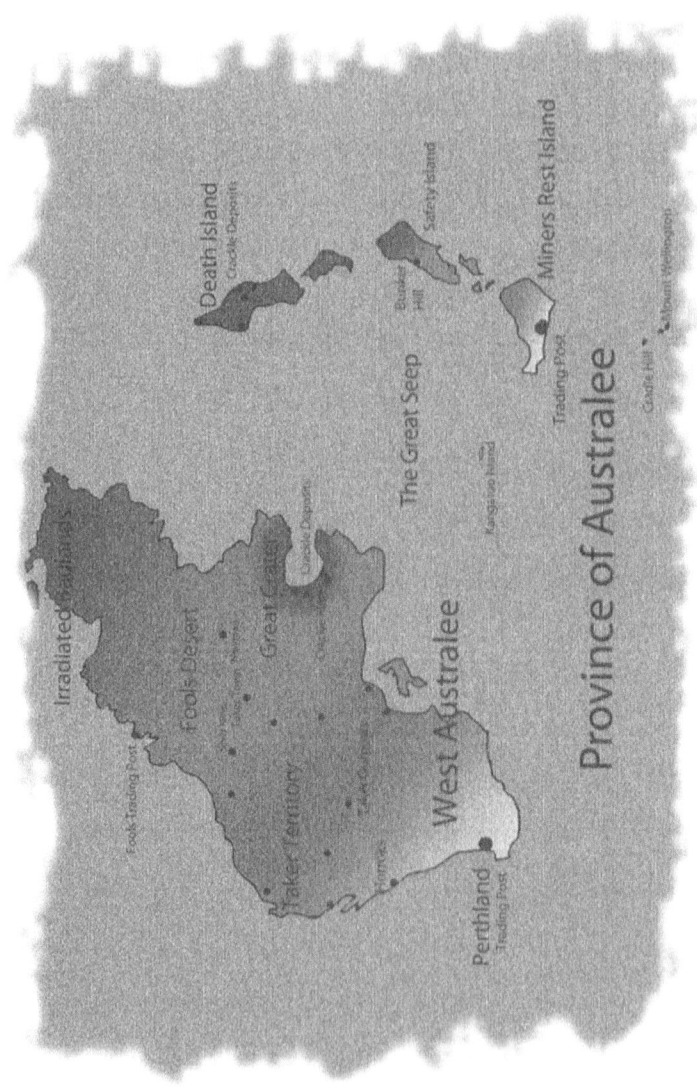

Chapter Sixteen

They Can Go and Eat Themselves

Entry 738

On the outside of the compound, us droppers were detailed to clean up the mess. Picking up body parts wasn't what I had on my wish list for the day. But instead of burying or burning the Takers' remains, Seth chose to have everything placed in containers and stored in deep freeze. The thing was, I couldn't have cared less even if we were going to grind those body parts into a powder and use them as blood and bone fertilizer. But then I realized Seth planned to put the body parts in with the next export of dead droppers, so the Takers can literally go and eat themselves. A bit of poetic justice if that was the case. The sad thing was, I'd never know what the outcome would be.

As I bent over the huge trough that held the Taker grossness, one my chain members tapped me on the back. He pushed his finger up to his lips in a sign of 'shush.' It was a little odd knowing we couldn't form or mouth verbal words even if we needed to, but that was beside the case. It was his way of warning me to be quiet because our gang master had his back turned and he was just a little beyond the range of quiet noises.

My chain member held out his hand, and in it, was a key. It was the key that can set all of us droppers free.

I signed to him, "Where in the heck did you get that?"

He signed back, "I picked Murk's pocket."

"Shit!" I signed. "He'll know soon enough. We're all gonna die."

My dropper friend just shook his head slightly and smiled. His hands were already unchained. Without any further delay, he pushed the key into my hand and he took off. I thought I was a fast runner. This guy ran like the wind. It was then I realized why he took off in a big hurry. Murk gave chase. Murk didn't have a weapon. They don't give out weapons to gang masters, simply because there's not enough to go around. So, on foot, our sixth dropper was gone, and with big Murk chasing him down.

I saw the opportunity. I didn't waste my time. The key in my hand found my lock and I was free. The other droppers? Who gave a shit? I gave them the key. I was outta there!

I ran as hard as I could go, back toward the west. But it wasn't long before my malnutrition caught up with me and running at full force slowed to an uneven non-rhythmical lollop. But I was by this time far enough away that I wasn't able to be seen by the other Newmaners, or the other gangs of droppers who were always on work detail outside the compound.

Now was the time to get back into survival mode. It was still full sunlight. And one of the things I never do is walk the waste-land while I can see things at any distance. The general rule of surviving the flat-lands is, if I can see them, they can see me. I needed to get to cover and hole up until night. Then I could start thinking about how I'll get my stuff out of the footlocker without being blown to pieces.

Entry 739

I'm at the gully before the entrance to the silver mine. I'm a little nervous. If the worst happens, these will be my last words.

That was the end of reading all the journal. But we all agreed that Michael's life didn't end in the tunnel after he retrieved his belongings. If he was blown to pieces, as he put it in his writing, his skeletal remains wouldn't have ended up floating on the ocean. So, the question was, what happened, and where do *we* go from here?

"We shall make haste and sail for Perthland," Captain Bass said with one finger pointing into the air. "From there, we shall see about getting your backsides to this place they call Newman. I think, if you're ever going to find the relic, you should start there."

"You're not coming with us?" Eli put in.

"I have a ship. But you shall have my support when we dock in Fremantle."

I was a little disappointed that Captain Bass wouldn't join us on the journey, but I agreed we needed to start at Perthland if we were to ever stand a chance. We also needed a map and see for ourselves where Newman really is. "Do we have a map of the area?"

"Absolutely." Captain Bass stepped behind his desk and opened a drawer that I could see contained large rolls of sea charts. He retrieved an old looking map and printed underneath several islands were the words, 'The Province of Australee.' There was no resemblance at all to the maps of Australia that I'd seen in *Steinbeck's* Library. For the first time, I saw what had happened to the continent of Australia after The Great Seep had killed so many millions. It was a sobering sight. The thought of all those lives lost almost made me ill. I had to stem my anger and put it away. Now wasn't the time to transmute the pain of millions of people.

Captain Bass unrolled the map across his desk and placed a candle holder on one edge to hold it down. Eli stepped closer and placed his hand down to hold the map open. Already my mind wondered how we could ever get there.

I discovered Newman was virtually in the center of the land mass called West Australee. And right in the middle of an area known as Fool's Desert. The map also showed several Takers' outposts. To get there from Perthland, we'd have to traverse Fool's Desert while avoiding Taker contacts but that wasn't all. Newman was also in close proximity to Great Crater. An area which the map showed as being highly radioactive. "The coast to the east of Newman is far too radioactive," I said. "And there're too many Takers' outposts to the west. To the north we have the Irradiated Badlands. And Fool's Desert just south of that. Newman looks truly boxed in."

"That leaves Perthland as our *only* option," Jason said as he studied the map closer.

"I agree but how do we get to Newman from the south?" I asked after a moment of looking things over.

"There is one option," Captain Bass responded. "There's a caravan that departs Perthland and travels the old Trans Access Track to the north. Perhaps it might be a good idea to . . . err . . . tag along, as it were."

* * *

The Port of Perthland came into view as the sun's rays pierced the horizon to the east. For my eyes, it was a beautiful thing. I'd made it. Land. And not only that, my chance to make a new start finally started to feel real. As soon as I had that thought, Chloe's sweet face appeared in my mind. A few seconds ago, I was happy and looking forward to the adventure. Now, all I felt was hurt and guilt all over again.

"Looks like we made it, Ditch."

"Yeah. Looks like we made it," I said to my brother as he stepped up behind me.

Jason eyed me and it was as though he knew what my mind was thinking. "Rick. It just turned out that way. You're gonna have to get over it. You've gotta get your head clear for what's coming up."

My brother was right. But the hurt still lived in my heart for Chloe and my mother. Part of being human is hurting. And part of being human is learning to live with it until time takes the hurt away.

"Time, little brother. Time is the healer." Jason said it exactly as I was thinking it. I looked at him and gave him a smile. "Don't ask me why. But something tells me more hurt is coming. More hurt for me to get over, huh?"

After thinking about it, Jason replied, "I'm not going any-where, Ditch. I'll bury you. Not you, me. Got it?"

Not saying anymore on the subject, I thought of Chloe and I promised myself that whatever the future holds, she'd always be in my heart. I would always remember her. I'll always be thankful for the memories we have of being together.

* * *

As *Victory* docked in Fremantle after being hauled into place by what appeared to be a timely old diesel tug, the first thing I no-ticed was the noise. I wasn't accustomed to so many people shouting over the top of each other. Then I realized what all the shouting was about. There was a market at the end of the docks. People were making their living from selling wares as soon as goods were delivered. Goods that came in on ships.

It wasn't too long before a crowd of Perthlanders arrived at *Victory's* dockside. Then I remembered the discussion I had with our captain about the commodities she brings to the colonies. They were items that had been taken from the Takers. As I looked out among the dozens of messily dressed individuals with cheer-ful faces, it was as though they were all there waiting for the ship to unload. It turned out I was right. In the next moment, a sudden burst of activity toward the rear of *Victory's* quarter deck told me the unloading had already begun.

Captain Bass appeared behind me and placed his hand on my shoulder. "This is what we live for, young lad. This is what makes it all worthwhile. Seeing their happy faces and knowing they can get along a little longer with the items we bring them. And I don't mind saying that most of these things were stolen from them in the first instance. It brings a whole new meaning to the word 'justice,' wouldn't you agree?"

I *did* agree. It was heartwarming to see. "Robin Hood."

"What was that, Richard?"

"That's who you are to them. You're Robin Hood. You take from the Takers and give to the colonies."

"Well perhaps you might be correct. But let's not dilly-dally any longer. We have a caravan to find and you three have a whole lot of distance to cover. But first, you'll need cooler clothing. It's hotter out there than you can ever imagine. Oh, and another thing. I feel it's vitally important for the bones to stay on *Victory.* They'll be safe behind our cannon. When you find the eagle figurine, make your way back to Perthland and wait for me."

I agreed. Jason and Eli agreed. It seemed like a logical thing to do. But at the same time, I was surprised that Captain Bass wanted to go out of his way to help us. I pictured Jason and Eli with me as we learned all about our new environment. But this captain was not only willing to go ashore and show us where things were in Perthland, but he'd already decided to negotiate with the caravan driver on our behalf.

* * *

Captain Bass issued us with calico purses full of the stuff they called crackle. Judging by the weight, I guessed there was enough to purchase anything we needed. I was almost about to object to the amount Captain Bass had given us, oddly thinking it was too much. I offered my purse back, which he politely refused, then Captain Bass pointed with a finger back to *Victory's* poop deck. "Your two-man submersible. Consider it sold. And I'm afraid you'll need every shard you have for this journey. I'm not doing you any favors. I gave you fair price for what I've purchased. Let's leave it at that, shall we?"

"You're a good man, Henry Bass. A good and decent man."

"And that, my dear boy, is why I cannot leave my ship. Let it be said, though, I am mildly jealous of you for the journey you're about to embark upon. Perhaps I've been at sea a little too long. But business is business. This is what I've chosen to do."

"And they all depend on your expeditions."

"That they do, young Mister Gabriel. That, they do."

Heading down the worn looking timber decking of the docklands, a mixture of odors attacked my senses. The smell of fresh cuts of meat from a butcher's stand, mixed with the strong stench of a fishmonger's stall. The dye used for coloring clothing and leather; the heavy smell of cheeses in a stall where goats were kept in timber and wire enclosures. The cackling noises of poultry and geese and boxes and boxes of eggs on display. And above all the smells and animal noises, were the loud voices of the stall holders, hollering out their special prices for the day.

"Get ya fresh chook here! Lop the head yaself and save! Only four shards!"

"Damper! Get ya damper while it's hot. One shard for damper. Two shards for three!"

It was then I noticed someone staring straight at me through the crowds of rushing people. A woman dressed in earthy colored cottons with flowing black hair all the way to her waist. And her complexion; so milky white and perfect. Her eyes, black as a cold winters night. It was in that moment, impossible as it was, I was sure I'd met her before, but where? Then I remembered the dream. She was Teresa. But that was even more impossible.

I left Eli, Jason and Captain Bass at the poultry stand and rushed through the crowd to catch up with her. "Teresa! Wait!" But she was gone as I reached the place I'd seen her. I slowly scanned a full three-sixty. "Damn it!" She wasn't anywhere to be seen. For the sake of one last time, I scanned again. This time slower. "Where are you?" Just as I thought I was hallucinating and about to give up, Teresa appeared again, standing just outside what I thought was a hut with fine looking glass-blown art pieces on display in the windows. She walked through the door to the inside. At last I knew where she went. "Wait! Teresa! Wait!"

PART TWO

THE LONG WALK

Chapter Seventeen

The Vanishing

I punched through the door. "Teresa!" As my eyes adjusted to the glinting of glass trinkets everywhere, I found myself alone standing in the middle of the floor, surrounded by shelves upon shelves of intricately-blown glass creations. I wondered if there was a back door. Teresa could've found an exit to the outside. There was no back door I could find. Teresa had vanished into nothingness. And yet, in a far corner, a lanky old man with a crooked arm, wearing jeweler's headgear sat eyes down in a cubicle oblivious to anything. On his cluttered desk were art pieces in various stages of completion. He looked up and eyed me curiously. His long grey beard was tied into several plaits with little bows at each end and jiggled as he spoke. "Can I help you, mate?"

"Teresa. There was a woman . . ."

The man took his headgear off and eyed me, this time appearing to be genuinely surprised. "You've got the wrong place. Try the house of ill repute on Cliff Street. If you're after the company of a woman, there's plenty to choose from."

"No," I said. "I was outside. I saw her come through the door. This door."

"You're mistaken. I've been here all morning and no customers yet. But be my guest. Have a browse. There may be something here that you might like. These hands make everything here. Take two, and I'll give you a special deal."

I was in no mood for shopping, but how could I resist such beautiful work. On the shelves were sculptures of unicorns, penguins, bulls, and horses. Dioramas of domestic pets they called dogs and cats. Creatures of the sea including sharks and dolphins. Even birds of prey like the condor and the eagle. But when I saw the eagle sitting there on the shelf, something inside me immediately snapped to attention. I went to the shelf. I picked it up. The glass eagle with its wings spread out was beautifully created; awe-inspiring.

"It's an exact copy of the real one that's made from rock crystal called *The Angel of Bunjil*," the old man said as I held up the eagle to the light. "It's as exact as I could get it, I suppose. That there, is one of the first sculptures I've made, going back nearly forty years ago. I'm sorry. It's not for sale."

"If this is a copy, the real one must be truly magnificent. Can I see it?"

"Unfortunately, I don't have it. That's why I'd never forgive myself if I sold my sculpture. It's the only record of my recollection. One day my memory will fail me. If I still have this sculpture, I hope I won't be so challenged. There's a story with her. A story written in a journal."

"Journal?" I couldn't believe what I was hearing. "Are you sure?"

"Of course, I'm sure," the old man said. "But it's not complete. There're pages missing. For almost half of my life, I often wondered if I'd ever one day have the chance of seeing the entire journal from start to finish."

The old man paused, then eyed me more intensely than before. He took a step back, put his hand to his chin and for some reason seemed to hold his breath. I saw a slight smile curl on his lips. He put his eyes down and let out a huge sigh that could never be misread. It was a sigh of relief. "It's the journal of the one they called 'Michael the Protector'," he continued. "And after all these years, something deep inside me is telling me you have the missing pages of that same journal. I'm not mistaken, am I?"

I didn't know what I must've looked like to him. I tried to hold my composure and not seem so excited, even though inside I was going completely nuts. If he had the last part of the same journal that I'd spent the previous weeks poring over . . .

"Are you okay? You look like you've seen a ghost."

"I'm albino. I always look like I've seen a ghost. The real crystal eagle. *The Angel of Bunjil.* If you know where it is, please tell me how I can find it. I need it. We all need it."

In that split second, Jason and Eli along with Captain Bass burst into the shop; beads of perspiration glistened on their faces. "Mother of penguins!" Jason spat. "You're like a little kid. You gonna tell me where you're going next time? Disappearing around here isn't an option, Ditch!"

Jason grabbed my arm, but I pulled away. I told him to look around the place. Then I showed him the glass eagle. In that moment, everything changed. I told Jason, Eli and Captain Bass everything the shop owner had told me. They were no longer in such a hurry to get away to the caravan.

Captain Bass approached the shop owner, appearing to do his best not to seem so utterly eager even though I knew he was feeling as excited as I was. He held his hand out to the old man. "I'm Captain Henry Bass of His Majesty's Ship of the Line, *Victory.*"

"Marty," the old man said and shook the captain's hand. "Marty McBride."

I was getting anxious. I felt like asking Marty, 'Where's the eagle, where's journal, and can I have them?' But I knew that wasn't going to do any good. In the next split second, Captain Bass asked Marty, "Where's this journal and may we please have it?"

Oh no. I held my breath. Now we were going to be refused.

"You don't have to ask," Marty said. "I was going to offer you the journal anyway. But please do me the honor of letting me see it one last time in its complete form; how it should've been before everything went bad. After all these years, this day has finally arrived. Now, it's best to let it go."

Before I was able to add anything further, Eli butted in. "Have you seen the crystal eagle? We need information. It's of utmost importance that we find it?"

"So, everyone keeps saying," Marty McBride said as he got up from his chair and placed both his palms on his desk. From his body language, it appeared from the outside at least; he was in regret. "But before we go down this road, there is something I must say to clear my conscience. I've had to bear this weight for forty years. This seems like a good time to let it all go.

"I was a Taker. I'm not proud of it. I was one of those pieces of shit. Some might say I grew a conscience when I was out raiding. I suddenly realized the life wasn't for me. I stopped going out on raids. I stopped taking things just for the sake of taking them. Every time I ate something, I became sick. So, they locked me up. I became a prisoner; a dropper. But I escaped. I absconded. I made my own life down here in Perthland. But, always looking over my shoulder and sleeping with an eye open does things to a man. My health has paid a heavy price for it. I'm now on the Takers' blood list. If they capture me, I'll die by the way of the blood eagle. I'm not afraid of death. I've stared death in the eyes more than a few times. But, the blood eagle; it's not the way I'd like to leave this life. That's why I make these little pieces of art. So, your question was, have I seen it? Yes, I have. Not only that, I know where it is right now. That being what it is, I'm guessing you've also recovered the Sacred Bones?"

Captain Bass pointed toward the docks. "We have the Sacred Bones and they're safe on *Victory*."

"Well then," Marty said. "Let's make things happen."

* * *

With the new twist to the entire situation, Captain Bass thought it was a good idea for all of us to regroup back on-board *Victory*. I couldn't help but be amused as I saw Marty's facial expressions. After he'd stepped across the gangway and onto *Victory's* quarter deck, it was rather like seeing a child light up for the first time after receiving a birthday present.

Being taken by surprise so suddenly caused Marty to almost drop an intricately decorated wooden box which he'd brought with him. I guessed what was in it. The glass eagle he'd made. He juggled the box in both hands before he caught it again. A near miss but it was heartwarming to see Marty's eyes full of joy. His happiness was quite contagious, and it almost made me get a little misty.

I was happy also in most part because, in my grip, was the rest of Michael's story. With the entire journal safe in our hands, I knew it would give us the extra clarity we needed to search for the crystal eagle called, *The Angel of Bunjil.* And as a bonus, we also had an actual first-hand account in the mind of this person we took onboard. What more could we ask for? With his forth-coming information, we could put firm plans into place to find it, and I knew it in my heart that it was just a matter of time until the complete mystery unraveled. In the back of my mind, however, I also knew that all of us were being guided in some way, one step at a time by something I couldn't quite comprehend. I shivered slightly thinking about it. How can a person in a dream become real and then, disappear? But to answer that question, I'd need also to answer the question of the orcas. And then there was eve-rything that was in Michael's writings. My brain pounded with the blood from each heartbeat. Maybe there'd be the day when everything made sense. I had to let it go for now.

* * *

By 1900 hours, my job of showing Marty around the ship was complete. And by 1930 hours, we'd all found ourselves at the captain's table for evening meal. I was seated at the table with Eli to my left, Jason to my right. Captain Bass was seated at his usual position at the head of the table. On his right was First Officer William Fletcher, then Surgeon Cristian Hamel. Lastly, taking up the guest of honor end of the table, master craftsman extraordinaire, Marty McBride.

Tonight's affair was a silver service at the Captain's pleasure, to which everyone at the table was impeccably dressed for the occasion. Ship's officers wore their decorative navy blues which were pressed with precision and were meticulously made lint free. For some reason, our captain had also issued Eli and myself with naval officer's uniforms; rank of ensign. For Jason, he'd climbed back into the red, royal marines uniform he'd donned during the tussle with the Takers ship, *Excelsior.*

With *Victory* being freshly resupplied, I wondered what might be served up instead of the normal damper or dumplings, goat's cheese, oranges or lemons. I wasn't, however, prepared for a meal that consisted of lamb and mashed potato with gravy. The potato and gravy weren't unfamiliar. I'd never had the lamb before. It was the very best meal I'd ever had the pleasure of enjoying. After finishing such a satisfying meal, I started to wonder if our captain was putting on a show for the benefit of our newcomer. I thought perhaps Captain Bass was softening Marty up. Then I thought I was seeing something that was out of context to everything else that was in front of me. Was our captain gay? As soon as I had the thought, I thrust it to the back of my mind. Surely not. But then, why not? What difference would it have made? And it certainly was no business of mine. The captain had every right to his happiness. It didn't matter at all where he found it. But my suspicions of Captain Bass putting on a show to soften our guest a little was confirmed after we'd all retreated to his great cabin.

* * *

In my mind, I still remembered vividly how Michael had written about the time he and Timothy opened his box of treasures. Of one of the many items was a box of Cuban cigars. As I thought about it, here in front of me was a captain enjoying a cigar with his guests, complete with a crystal glass of rum. What I saw with my own eyes was a Jules Verne novel. Everyone was small talking to each other. But nothing substantial about our quest was forthcoming. I decided to change all that.

"So don't keep us in any more suspense. Please let me read some of the pages in Michael's journal," I said rather loudly over everyone. It was a subject that played heavily on my mind even through the act of enjoying such a gorgeous dinner. I decided I wasn't about to retire to my hammock without knowing more about Michael. Now that I'd almost rudely silenced everyone in the room, I was about to hear it for the first time.

Marty looked down at his empty glass and twiddled the stem back and forth in his fingers. He then handed the glass up for a refill which Captain Bass willingly obliged him. He took a breath before sitting down in the same chair that I'd sat in while reading to Captain Bass. He picked up the pages that were in a ragged pile to his left. As he handed me the pages, his voice lowered. "You'd better prepare yourselves for this."

Chapter Eighteen

Prophecy

Marty McBride made himself comfortable in his chair, hitching an ankle up to his knee and taking up his glass of rum. After drawing an audible breath, he began to speak with words that seemed heavier than only moments ago. "As you'll find after reading the final pages of Michael's journal, the prophecy of the *Angel of Bunjil* and the Sacred Bones will only come to pass after the relics are reunited and returned to their rightful keepers. That being what it is, I'm compelled, now, to tell you the *complete* story."

Here it was — the moment of truth. Now was the time we'd find out about all the intricate details we'd missed. I was looking forward to settling my mind, and I could go to my hammock have a decent night's sleep.

"Rosemary Keene, a survivor of The Fall, wrote her memoir called *The Book of Hearts*," Marty explained. "Before the bombs, Rosemary was a nurse who'd worked at a secret location in the

Northern Territory of Australia as it was known back then. She was part of an elite group of individuals who'd been given an exit strategy away from the coming destruction."

"What elite group of individuals?" Jason asked.

"Ambers. These people were genetically created to resist the effects of radiation and so, therefore, they'd become a master race on Earth. Keene also goes on to write about a group of Ambers who failed to exfiltrate from danger, and are now known as The Lost Ones.

"On that final day, Keene chose not to use her ticket to safety. She tells of her incredible story of survival, and not only that, how she endured the after-effects, the radiation fallout, and most amazingly, how she endured the wash-over, also known as The Great Seep. But in Rosemary Keene's account, she describes the death of Nathan Masters and today, her story; *The Book of Hearts* has become a legend.

"One set of relics you have with you on this ship are known as The Sacred Bones. They belong to Nathan Masters. Some years before the Fall Wars, Nathan Masters operated as a special forces soldier who was given the task of rearing an orphaned ten-year-old girl named Angel—a girl who possessed special abilities."

"What special abilities," Eli asked.

"Angel had the power to heal, and also, she possessed a height-ened sense of perception, more so than what's deemed the typical level human of awareness. After the bombs fell, Nathan Masters contracted radiation sickness and died from the effects."

"If Angel was a healer, why didn't she heal him?" I asked. "If she had these abilities as you say, it seems logical that she'd do just that."

Marty immediately held up his hand and carried on. "In *The Book of Hearts*, Rosemary Keene explains how Angel *wanted* to heal Nathan. The legend also describes Angel's pain. She was torn between being healer and friend. She knew Nathan wanted to die. As hard as the decision was - she let Nathan go in peace. It meant Nathan could finally be reunited in death with his long-lost love, Teresa."

"Teresa?" Captain Bass asked. "The same Teresa as in young Mister Gabriel's dream, no less?"

Marty looked directly at me. His inquiring eyes drilled into my bones. "Did she have long black hair and black pupils, so black; you could see your reflection in them from across the room?"

I nodded. "What happened to Teresa? In my dream, she was a young woman. That means she was young when she died."

"Nathan Masters killed her. He shot her in the head, point blank."

I immediately recoiled in my chair. I couldn't imagine any reason why Nathan would do such a thing if he and Teresa were in love. But just as I had those wonderings, Marty enlightened me a little.

"Nathan didn't have a choice in the matter. He was made to do it. Nathan Masters was held captive by a group of thugs who called themselves the Guardianship of Milestone. And today, these thugs are the Takers. They're the direct descendants of the original arseholes.

"According to Rosemary Keene's account, the crystal eagle figurine known today as *The Angel of Bunjil* was given to Angel as a birthday present from her partner, Jenny. But unbeknown to Angel, Jenny wasn't just human. Jenny was something else completely extraordinary. Jenny was also Charlotte, an eagle who Angel had befriended as a child. And Charlotte was . . . and still is, the Angel of Death, Azrael."

"Angel carried the crystal figurine with her right up until the time Nathan Masters passed away. When he died, Angel placed the figurine on Nathan's body, and she made a vow that she'd return and give him the burial he deserved."

"Where did she go?" I asked. "Where did all of them go?"

"Unfortunately, there's no record of where they exfiltrated to in Rosemary Keene's memoir. But she wrote about the prophecy of their return that will come to pass once the Sacred Bones and the *Angel of Bunjil* are reunited and returned to The Lost Ones."

"And that's the reason the Takers seek to destroy the relics," Jason said. "No relics, no prophecy."

Marty McBride nodded vigorously. "When the Ambers return, there'll be one mighty showdown between good and evil on Earth."

As the evening went on, I became a little cautious about our guest. It seemed every time we wanted to know more about the possible location of the *Angel of Bunjil*, Marty stepped further and further away from giving us the direct information that we needed. It was a little odd for Marty to be so aloof knowing he'd seen the crystal figurine with his own eyes. Even if it was long ago, the information would've given us a starting point. But Marty held back on giving us anything. Why?

By 2317 hours, I'd had enough, so I asked Marty directly. Loudly. Over everyone in the room. "Marty, do you know where the *Angel of Bunjil* is or don't you? It's not a trick question, it's a straight yes or no answer."

Everyone in Captain Bass' great cabin held their tongues. Only sounds of cracking and creaking emanated from oak timbers as the ship moved on the waters. I knew I'd said the same as what everyone was thinking. Maybe I was a little rude. It was late and my weary eyes needed to be shut down.

Marty appeared to hold his breath, looking a little annoyed while he placed his empty glass on the mahogany side table. "I could answer you in a way you'd like to hear it right now. Or, I could let Michael give you your answer through his writing. Which would you have?"

Marty was right. Not only did he put me back in my place, it made sense to wait until the entire story was made known. Now I had a choice. Go grab some sleep or stay up for the night with some light reading. Of course, I chose to stay up.

Chapter Nineteen

Marty

Entry 740

I'm glad I'm able to write. It's been a while. Getting hold of paper and then finding something to write with seems harder now than it used to be. I have to do it out of sight. I have to do it when they think I'm doing other things. Other things they get me to do. At least they have me work outside and I'm no longer trapped in that room. It's a room where nightmares live. It's a room that contains the most horrifying things my eyes have seen. My biggest wish is for the ability to un-see. But in that room down below the ground, they're there. The not quite dying; not quite living. The ones who've been selected for their meat. The ones who've had parts taken from them, but they still live. They say nothing but make noises. They make noises and cry. They cry in their pain and their anguish. They're fresh food for the Takers. The Takers feed them. They take parts of them away, and they slowly die.

Entry 741

I think about it all the time. Why did I enter the silver mine after I heard their voices? I could've stopped. I could've stepped back and thought about something else. Maybe there was another way in. I didn't explore it. How could I have done things differently? But no. I waltzed straight into the obvious. I blasted down the tunnel, running noisily toward their voices. But I had to. I had no choice. They were going to take my things. I had to save them. And then, the explosion.

I thrust my hands up to my ears. The shockwave almost knocked me over. I could see it. The footlocker was on the ground. It hadn't been damaged. But bodies lay there. It was too late for them. I ran toward it and I was so glad that everything wasn't destroyed. The next thing I thought of was to get away before more came. And more did come.

I ran as hard as I could with my footlocker in my arms. I ran to the west entrance, past the great stack of rubbish where I'd once eaten to my fill. I could see it. There in the distance. The light at the end of the tunnel. I nearly got there. Nearly.

"Stop! Or you're dead!" The voice reached my ears. Then the unmistakable ca-clink of a weapon being cocked. I stopped where I was.

"Put it on the ground!"

I did exactly that. I put the footlocker down at my feet, and I raised my hands.

"What's your name and where ya from!"

I couldn't say anything. How could I? But I managed to make a mumble.

"What's the matter with you! Can't ya talk!"

I shook my head. I wondered if he could see my reaction in the darkness of the tunnel. I shook my head again even harder.

"Well, looky-look. We've got a runaway dropper. Which camp ya from, dropper!"

I mouthed something. Whatever the heck it was.

"Oh. Can't speak huh? That's right. I forgot! Your tongue was on someone's dinner plate. Ha-ha-ha."

What a smartarse. My anger started to burn. But just as I was able to get physically violent, a sharp thud from between my shoulder blades sent me over onto my hands and knees. From there, I can't remember anything.

Entry 742

Once, I ran from seven chain members. Now I'm chained to twelve. They keep us working in the day. They keep us working pulling things. Pushing things. Picking up things and carrying things to places. It's mundane and meaningless. A purpose of our labors must be somewhere, but I can't see it. They don't eat greens, so they don't grow them. They don't grow them so there's no sickle to swing. So, they get us to pick up things and put them down. Pick them up again and put them down again. All day. Every day. Day in. Day out.

At night they throw us in a hole — no ladder to climb down. If we break a leg, we'll get sent to that room of unspeakable horrors. It's too high to climb. It's too hard to dig. So, we wait in the hole until the sun comes up again.

In the darkness while in the hole, I felt someone next to me. I felt his hands touch my hands. I immediately pulled my hands away. He grabbed them again and pulled them toward him. I didn't know what he was wanting, but if he was wanting what I was thinking, what would it have hurt? and who would know about it? Maybe it wouldn't be that bad. Maybe I just had to let myself go. Maybe it would save me from insanity. But as he took my hands again, it wasn't that at all. It was a way to learn a new language. By the touch of a hand, we worked out how to communicate. Before the week was out, we were having conversations.

Entry 743

My new friend on the chain said his name is Marty McBride. Each night after they throw us in the hole, we talk about anything at all. Using our hands, we can tell each other stories. We can take ourselves away to somewhere in our imagination and share our experiences. We can cheer each other up if we're sad. We can silently laugh together at things that are funny. We can even be mad at each other if we say something wrong. But Marty told me something tonight that took me by surprise. Marty told me he kmows a way to escape.

Entry 744

The bastards must have sensed something. They put Marty and me at the opposite ends of the chain. Now, I don't get to talk to him when we rest for clag. I'm so pissed off right now; I can't write.

Entry 745

In the hole, Marty grabbed my hands, and we started to talk about our plans. We'd have to time it right. But I said to Marty, I can't go if I don't have my eagle. And I can't go if I don't have my Sacred Bones.

"What are they?" he asked by twisting and touching my hands.

I told him the entire story up to the minute. By the time I was finished, my hands felt like I'd dragged them through sand.

Marty agreed. My things were much too important to leave behind. So now our escape would have to include their recovery. The question was, how?

Entry 746

Picking up things. Putting things down. Does it ever end? But just before clag time, the same things happen every day. They get us to pick up concrete blocks and place them into a pile. The chain master always takes his seat and puts tobacco into his pipe. He always puts his shotgun within reach to his left. He always wears the keys on a big ring on his right hip. He always opens a can of bully beef or beans and starts to eat it in front of us. He always smiles before each mouthful. He always finishes each can and folds the lid over to the outside of the tin. He always puts the can on a piece of concrete to his right. It was the same set of actions every, single, day, without fail. So, Marty and I built our plans around this sequence of events.

Entry 747

Marty and I ran from that place after we got ourselves free. We're now out of sight in an old creek bed far west of the silver mine. And I'm so glad we've been able to get my things. The Takers had taken stuff out of the footlocker. But they'd left the eagle and bones. Why? I don't know and I don't care. Not only that, we now have a shotgun and ammo. I don't know if it was just plain old luck, but it bloody-well seemed that way. The shot gun took a bit of getting used to but as soon as I pressed the trigger a couple of times, I worked out what that shotgun could do.

The bad news. Some of the Takers are dead and if they find us, we'll get executed by the blood eagle. A nasty way to die.

We'll take off again after sundown and we should reach my home before dawn.

Entry 748

Home again but it's not good. They raided my house. They took everything. There's nothing left here but a hulk of a place. My most precious backup food supplies and water are gone. All my tools. All my furniture. All my belongings. If it was too heavy to carry, they'd smashed it to pieces. There's debris all over the place. Fuck I'm angry. But Marty says we can start a new life at a place he knows about. It's another twenty nights stride west of here. He says it's on the coast and there're people living together in a community. I've never lived with other people before. And I've never lived in a community. Maybe they won't like me. Maybe I won't like them. But it sounds much better than staying here in this dump. To think it used to be my home. Bastards!

I'll gather what I can gather, and we'll start west after sundown.

Entry 749

Marty makes everything look so easy. There're bugs when we need them. If we find small animal bones, there'll be stuff left on them. Sometimes there'll be live echidnas wandering and it's just a matter of getting past their sharp spines, and then they're food. Once there were five in a row. Five! We ate like Takers that night. But water. Yeah, pissing again. Gees. I didn't have to do that when we were chowing on clag three times a day. How those bad things can get forgotten so quickly.

Marty says three more nights and we should be there!

Entry 750

It was so sad to see Marty's hopes drop so suddenly. After we came over the top of the hill that overlooked the community of Kalbarri, it wasn't long before we both realised it had been taken over by FUCKING-BLOODY-TAKERS!

Entry 751

We made camp on the hill for the night. I had so many pieces of paper in my pockets, I decided to lighten the load and leave a big wad of my journal in the footlocker. Marty and I spoke for a while with our hands. I was surprised that he wanted just to give in and go down there knowing he'd be placed on another freaking chain, or worse, die by blood eagle. But the thing was, it meant we didn't have to drink our own urine. And to be totally honest, I was getting so sick and tired of carrying the bloody footlocker even though it was a lot lighter than it used to be. So, Marty's idea of just getting it over was slightly attractive in that respect. But we also had the shotgun, and I thought, how about if we go down there and kill as many of them before they kill us?

Marty didn't grab my hands to reply. He just walked over, picked up the shotgun and tossed it as far as he could get it. Then he sat down next to me and for the first time in my life I saw a grown man sulk. I used to do that when I was . . . five?

He grabbed my hands and said, "Can I have a look at your eagle figurine?"

Without a reply, I opened the footlocker and gave it to him. He studied it for a while, then asked if he could keep it in his shirt pocket. For good luck, so he asked.

"Sure. No problem. Be my guest," I replied.

Marty then squeezed it into the top breast pocket of his checked western shirt. It looked a little odd. It looked like he had a breast. I grabbed his hand and said, "What happened to your other boob?" He laughed and I was glad I was able to cheer him up. Then he looked at me all serious. "Let's go," he said with his hands.

"Where?"

He pointed down the hill, then grabbed my hands, "let's take down as many of the bastards as we can." Then he started beating on his chest. He must've remembered what was in his pocket. He grabbed it out, smiled, and gave the eagle back to me. This time Marty picked up my footlocker and started down the hill. I placed the eagle in my pocket and grabbed the shotgun on the way past thinking at the same time, 'I'm gonna be dead soon, but it'll be fun getting there.'

Marty and I were a bit more than halfway down the hill when someone noticed our approach. There was yelling and carryings on in the distance but worse than that; there were voices behind us. Two Takers were on the chase towards us coming at us down the hill. I stopped and crouched behind some post-fall debris and I waited until they were in shotgun range. Spinning around, I signalled to Marty, "Run Marty, Run!" Which he did. He picked up the pace, footlocker and all. But he was running right into the arms of the Takers who were down there already waiting for him.

If I could've screamed something I would've. I would've screamed for him to run to the coast. "No Marty. Run to the coast and find a boat. Don't die. Save yourself." But it didn't matter how much I wanted to yell out to him, I couldn't. I wasn't capable. But Marty kept going.

I turned my attention back to the Takers who were almost on top of me. I popped up from behind cover and blew the bastards away! The wind blew their cloud of blood all over me. Some, I got in my mouth and I spat the filth away.

Spinning back toward Marty, he was almost out of sight, but it was as though he'd heard my thoughts. Marty had veered off to *the right and headed for the coast. He'd find a boat and he'd wait for me if I lived. If I knew my friend Marty, that's what he'd do.*

I cracked my shotgun and loaded more shells. Now, I was in no mood for the bullshit. I headed downhill toward the Taker stronghold. I touched my eagle figurine in my pocket for good luck, wondering at the same time how many Takers I could take out before I died.

Just as I was about to take the fight to the Takers, I felt an enormous amount of air pressure all over me. The downforce almost pinned me into place. I looked up, saw it, and I knew I wasn't alone in this fight. The huge eagle landed on the ground in front of me, it was no longer an eagle. My breath left me as I saw the young and fresh face of Charlotte.

"Michael. Go south," Charlotte said. "Go south, now."

"But Marty . . ."

"Your friend no longer lives. You must go south from here and take The Angel of Bunjil."

"The Sacred Bones, I must have them too."

"The Sacred Bones will find you again. Go. Do not look back. You may hear it, but you shall not bear witness as I slay with my sword."

I turned away from Charlotte and faced south, amidst the sounds of booms and explosions to my rear and I suddenly realised I was again able to speak words verbally using my own voice.

Chapter Twenty

Confession

I saw it in his eyes, the pain he must've felt back then. After I'd read the final words in the journal, I knew why he'd chosen to hold off on telling us anything. How Michael must've loved Marty. Marty McBride was dead and had died a long time ago. Now, it was obvious who this humble glass-blower was. It was also clear about the dead man we'd found floating in the water. But just as shocking as the truth was, it was also a relief not only to me but, to Michael who was seated in front of us with red-rimmed eyes, appearing to hold back a wave sadness.

"Michael the Protector," I said.

"For over forty years, yes."

"You could've told us back at your shop," Jason said.

"I agree. But others have asked for the whereabouts of *The Angel of Bunjil* after they visited my shop. I didn't know who they were. I invented a cover story, and it stuck with me all these years. For all I knew, those who've asked for it were Takers. Even though we're safe from raids in Perthland, I remained cautious.

Takers have infiltrators in both genders. We've caught several of them over the years. I was doing my job at protecting."

Captain Bass walked over to Michael and kneeled before him. "I'm honored and privileged, sir, to make your acquaintance."

As Captain Bass said it, Michael burst into tears.

* * *

I tried hard to imagine it, but I could never appreciate what forty years of carrying pain and suffering could do to a man. Michael shed those many years of sadness in less than an hour. After he'd finished, he sighed and politely asked for another glass of the captain's fine rum. "Of course, there's the question of *The Angel of Bunjil* and where to find it," he said with words that felt a little happier."

I still had the pangs of sorrow for Michael inside me. Even though Michael was about to let us finally know where to find *The Angel of Bunjil*, the sadness of his story still played heavily on my mind. I wasn't as eager as I once was to find the crystal eagle. It was almost as though I didn't care anymore. My mind stepped back to all the loss we've had to endure over this journey. My mother. Chloe. How I missed Chloe. Our unborn child I'd never meet. I remembered how I felt as I stood at the rail and looked out over the water. My motivation to end everything was strong, and I remembered how I was just a moment away from peace. I could've been with Chloe again. Perhaps I could've even been with our baby.

Michael broke through my thoughts by holding up the wooden box he'd brought with him. The glass eagle was most likely an offering of gratitude to our captain which I knew he'd love and give pride of place in his great cabin. I realized it was a very generous gesture of friendship. I remembered Michael telling me it wasn't for sale. Now he was giving our captain something that was most precious. I was misty-eyed before. Now, I was tearing up and trying desperately not to become a blubbering mess.

Michael opened the box and smiled. "I haven't seen this in so many years," he said at the same time as drawing the eagle out. But it was no glass eagle.

My legs wobbled a little. Eli let out a gasp. Jason said, Shit! Captain Bass dropped his glass of rum, and it smashed on the timber floor. Michael had *The Angel of Bunjil* with him all this time. And it was as beautiful as everything we'd learned. The eagle posed with its wings spread out; a gold inclusion ran diagonally through it from the base to a flared wing tip. We were all stunned into silence.

* * *

Not able to sleep, I left my hammock, and I navigated my way up the steps to the quarter deck to get some air. The smell of coal wafted in on the soft breeze which carried a briskness that caused the skin on my forearms to prickle. Ordinarily, I wouldn't have noticed the cold. I thought I might be finally acclimatizing to the new environment.

The view from *Victory* across Perthland at night was beautiful with the light of candles and lanterns dancing through windows and on poles. I wondered what it must've looked like before The

Fall when electricity was everywhere. Maybe one day in the future, the people of Perthland might have electricity again, and it'd become as second nature as just breathing. Maybe one day, humans would learn to treat technology with respect and not hurt the planet. Ultimately, that was the reason humans had got the entire world into the mess it is now. But as soon as I had that thought, I realized I'd not had the experience of a world before The Fall, and I could only imagine what it was like. Reading about things, however, was not as real as living it. I'd have to settle for what my imagination could provide.

Eli stepped up behind me which caused me to startle. He apologized then said, "You can't sleep either, huh?"

"Me? No. I have so many things in my head right now; I don't know if I'll ever have the pleasure of sleeping again. I keep thinking of the next phase, and I don't know why we haven't thoroughly thought of it before. How, exactly, are we ever going to contact the Ambers in the north?"

"Our minds were on other things."

"That's right, Eli. But now, we're left with the dilemma."

"You're talking about the radiation?"

I nodded. "It's scary. Every time I think I might have a solution, the fact that there's radiation up there that can fry anything living blows my ideas away."

Eli paused for a while and said nothing. He stepped up to the rail and looked out. "It's peaceful out there, isn't it?"

I agreed. "Those people in their beds tonight don't have to worry about when the next Takers raid might come. That's the only reason why its peaceful, Eli. The entire populous of Australee should be able to sleep in peace. But it's not that way. Not yet anyway. What will Australee be like after the prophecy comes to pass, I wonder? Will it be for the good and for the better? Or will the Takers find a way back and all this that we're going through now will be for nothing."

"We don't have the power to see into the future," Eli said. "All we've got to work with is the here and now. We'll find a way to contact the Ambers. The answer is out there somewhere. After we've done our duty, what happens after that, we have no control over. So, you're giving yourself extra to worry about when there's no need."

Eli was right as usual. And I kept forgetting about the divine help we've received that I was only starting to fully understand. Perhaps we'll get more guidance from the archangels as time goes on. But I also thought that I must be careful and not take for granted anything from that moment on.

* * *

After breaking fast on damper and eggs from a chicken, we all met in the captain's great cabin and I knew in my heart that by the time we left there, there'd be a firm action plan put into place and I'd no longer have to endure the nights spent tossing around in my hammock. Not only was it not doing my health any good, but it also meant I'd stop getting kicked by Jason who was always nearby.

As I stepped through the great cabin door, Captain Bass was already in deep discussions with Michael, and I saw them both bent over the map of The Province of Australee. Eli was with them, standing arms folded with a hand to his chin looking on as intent as ever. But as I looked around, I couldn't see Jason.

Captain Bass stepped from behind his desk and met me in the middle of the floor, looking as cheerful as a cherub. "Come. Come, dear boy. I think you may enjoy hearing what we've discovered."

"Where's Jason?"

"I've sent him on an errand with William Fletcher. He'll be back shortly, I assure you. Come."

I approached the map, and I saw that plot lines had already been marked out. It appeared that there was much discussed already without my presence. I was a little disappointed but knowing time was of the essence, I let it go.

Behind the captain's table, Michael's footlocker was left open, and inside it, I could see the crystal eagle and the Sacred Bones were placed together. Finally, the relics were reunited, and I reflected a little on what was known as the legend according to Rosemary Keene's account in *The Book of Hearts*. *The Angel of Bunjil* rested once again with the body of Nathan Masters. Captain Bass noticed my eyes on the footlocker. He smiled warmly as though he too was relieved that we were able to bring the reunion of the relics to a conclusion. But somewhere in the back of my mind, I knew we'd won a battle and the war was yet to be decided.

Just as I had the thought, the door opened, and Jason stepped through holding a gadget which I already knew about. A yellow box with a handle that made clicking, squelching noises. A Geiger Counter. It was nice to have, but it still didn't fix the problem. "What? Are we to draw straws to see who goes north?"

"We've already decided," Eli said. "It's going to be me."

"What? You can't. You're our doctor!"

"Haven't you noticed, Richard? I was the only one who ever got close enough to the McMurdo ruins without getting sick. What does that tell you? And, I have the same skin and hair as an Amber. Coincidence? I don't think so. All the Raphaels on *Steinbeck* could've done the same thing. I think we shared the same gene as those of the Lost Ones."

"Wishful thinking," I said. "Can't you see that? You're getting swept away with the adventure. It's making you see things that aren't there."

"Ditch!"

"You have no proof that you can survive the radioactivity and you won't have proof until it's too late."

"DITCH"

"I won't let this happen . . . I won't . . ."

I felt Captain Bass' hand land on my shoulder. "Richard, we've decided. We're ready to go and go we must. We weigh anchor at the hour of ten. We shall sail north as far as we can go until the Geiger Counter tells us it's no longer safe, and then, Eli takes it from there. It's settled."

Chapter Twenty-One

Death from Above

Victory's **sails bellowed out and strained** with the gusty winds that whipped up from the south. Monstrous seas crashed over her decks—sailors dashed and scurried through wash after wash with their obvious seasoned ability. None of them tripped or slipped or stumbled or fell. It was as though they ran around with sandpaper stuck to the soles of their shoes. But in times like these, they wore no shoes at all. In prep for the southerly gales, they roughed the bottoms of their feet with corn husk.

Hours after the winds had died; after emptying the contents of my stomach over the starboard rail about seven hundred times, the raging seas settled into a subtle swell, allowing everyone one on board to get some much-needed respite from *Victory's* severe pitching and rolling. As I stood there, looking out, there was no longer any sign of land. I was alarmed and thought the wind had taken us far away from where we were supposed to be. Captain Bass joined me at the rail and with only a few words; he took away my concerns and swapped them with something else to worry over. "Don't worry your head, young Richard. If we can't see the land from here, it means the Takers can't see us. We must be out of sight because if they know where we are, they can use their artillery guns to sink us."

"Artillery?"

"Howitzers, Richard. They have them in positions along the west coast of West Australee. You thought the north was fraught with danger from radiation. That might be the case. But getting there is equally as perilous. We must all have our wits about us." Captain Bass slapped me hard on my back and stepped away. But after he'd left my side; a low drilling sound flew overhead. As the object hit the water off the larboard bow, it exploded sending up sheets water high into the sky. I looked up as shrapnel tore through the sails. Pieces of timber rained down from the masts and yardarms. Then another shell flew; drilling overhead with the same awful sound.

Captain Bass spun and immediately commanded his crew. "All hands! All hands! Battle stations! Mister Fletcher! Beat to quarters!"

"Aye, aye Captain," William Fletcher said, then spun and shouted to the crew, "We shall beat to quarters!"

Within the minute, a lone drummer began beating on his snare drum, and the quarter-deck came alive with activity.

Captain Bass took up his position near the helm. "Evasive maneuvers! Mister Brice. Evasive maneuvers, god-damn it! Mister Finch! Run up all batteries if you please!"

Victory lurched violently sideways as another massive explosion erupted out of the water sending a monster wave shooting straight up. "All hands brace!" The leeward side of the wave hit *Victory* with an incredible crunch, sending skillful sailors off their feet. Some fell from yardarms and crashed into the deck with an audible snap from their limbs.

Another shell came in drilling across the sky. I involuntarily got down and thrust my hands to my ears. The incoming shell struck *Victory* amidships, exploding like a hammer from the gods, splintering timbers and sending men through the air; their blood instantly turned the spray of salty water a ghastly shade of violet.

"Mister Brice! Get that helm hard over! Hard over! Do you understand me, Mister Brice!"

"Trying, Captain."

It all went racing through my mind. We were so far from shore we couldn't see it. But they saw us. How?

I raced over to the captain's side and shouted over the noise of explosions and rushing, shouting men. "They're using radar to track us. It could be x-band marine radar. It doesn't matter if we can't see the shoreline, Captain Bass. They can see us on their scanners."

"It doesn't make any sense, Richard. How is this possible?"

"They used the same radar tracking system on the *Steinbeck*. We must move further out to sea. We have to get *Victory* out of range."

Immediately, Captain Bass commanded his coxswain. "Mister Brice! West by southwest if you please!"

"Aye, aye!"

Another shell found *Victory* and exploded on impact, sending massive solid oak boards skyward as though they were mere matchsticks. In that instant, I knew it was the end for the once proud flagship of the British Royal Navy.

The Footlocker!

It went screaming through my mind. I need to get there. Right now.

Without any explanation to the captain, I turned on my heel and bolted for the stairs. Just as I got there, a shell dropped from the sky and struck the quarter-deck, top dead center. Instantly, the detonation caused the ship to dome upward and explode with debris sent screaming up, licking the sky with deadly shrapnel. I flew down the stairs to the great cabin, hoping like crazy it was intact when I got there.

To my rear, I heard men shouting the words I never wanted to hear. "Abandon ship! A-BAN-DON-SHIP!"

Another almighty explosion ripped through the ship, and I heard the cracking of masts as they collapsed onto the decks; men I knew had become trapped under the huge timbers and were badly injured or dead. Those still alive screamed out their anguish.

"Abandon SHIP! The ship is sinking! Abandon ship!"

"Away with the longboats! Away with the fucking longboats!"

In the great cabin, I opened the footlocker. I grabbed some of the Sacred Bones. I grabbed *The Angel of Bunjil,* and I thrust them deep into my shirt. As I looked through the great cabin window from the rear of the ship, the stern; once high up from the sea was now almost at sea level. The ship began to keel over. I had but moments to get to a longboat. I ran like I'd never run before.

On the quarter-deck, Captain Bass strutted back and forth. He helped his sailors get to the safety of the longboats, as yet another explosion violently rocked the ship. This time, a gaping hole opened before me, and I could see down through *Victory's* decks to the water's surface below.

"Richard! Get in the longboat!"

"You're coming too, Captain Bass. None of that, 'captain goes down with ship' bullshit."

"Richard. Just go, will you?"

"You first! Then me!"

"Just go!" Captain Bass shoved me over the edge. I fell half in the water and half in the longboat. I saw Jason's face, and I was glad he was okay. I saw Eli's shocked face behind him. Another shell drilled overhead, and this time, it missed and fell into the water a good distance away. After the shell exploded, a wave pushed up and almost caused *Victory* to stand true again. It as though it was meant to be *Victory's* last wave. *Victory* slunk back down into the water lower than she was before. Voices of men behind me screamed. "She's goin' down!"

I looked over to where *Victory* lay on her side. On the rail, I saw Captain Bass holding on and dangling in the air. His facial expression was void of any emotion as the hulk of *Victory* gurgled her last breath and slowly sunk under the surface, taking Captain Bass with her.

There was no way I could believe what had just happened. "NOOO!"

I ripped off my shirt. The things I had stashed in there fell onto the longboat floor. I got myself to the edge about to leap into the sea. Jason grabbed me and hauled me back. "Leave it, Ditch! He's gone. Captain Bass has gone!"

* * *

We'd been floating on the sea for what seemed like hours. The shelling had ceased. The ocean had calmed. And an air of sadness had descended upon us. No-one spoke. I wondered how long the shell shock might last. But in the back of my mind, I knew we were all still ducks in a duck shoot, as Captain Bass had once put it. We needed to get as far out to sea as possible. I was aware of the ability of x-band radar. It not only picked up seagoing vessels, but the x-band system also picked up much smaller objects. I wondered how much time we had before the shelling started again. With a bit of luck, perhaps we were already in the area of radar where it exceeded the range of the Takers' howitzers. It was the only sliver of hope we had left.

Around me, the men who were lucky to survive the onslaught sat calmly as one volunteer began a roll call. After the roll call, we discovered we'd lost more than half the crew. To make matters worse, we had no oars. Crew hastily put the longboats into the sea. Out of the panic and the madness, the oars somehow never made it into the hands of the men. We were bedraggled and beaten, crammed into two longboats that were roped together, floating aimlessly in an ocean, floating wherever the current took us. I was certain the question in everyone's mind was, how long could we last?

Out of the corner of my eye, I saw something under water. I leaned over the edge of the longboat and looked down into the depths below to confirm my suspicions. I wondered for a second, could it be one of the orcas? I couldn't help but think they'd turned up much too late. I was almost angry, and I felt betrayed. But after looking harder into the water, I realized it couldn't have been an orca. Orcas aren't yellow where this object appeared the same shade of yellow that I'd seen before. Suddenly, I was lighter. And when the object broke the surface, everyone rose from their seats in the longboats and cheered.

The yellow two-man submersible that once belonged on *Steinbeck* appeared from below the surface. After the hatch opened, a smiling Captain Henry Bass protruded. "You there, young lad. Pass me that rope, if you please."

I got myself to the edge of the longboat and happily shouted to Captain Bass. "I thought the submersible would never work!"

"Turns out, young Richard, all that was wrong were flat bat-teries. We charged them with the wind turbine on Victory's poop deck. Do you remember me telling you we installed it for emer-gencies? Hmm?"

With the longboats tethered together, and our captain towing them in a steady northeasterly direction, it was with no doubt in my mind our mission would have to proceed over-land. We'd have to take a long walk.

* * *

We reached the west coast of West Australee without incident. As we approached land, I could see in everyone's eyes how nervous they were feeling. If I was on the outside of my body and looking in, I was sure my eyes would've reflected the same concerns. But disembarking the longboat and hitting the sandy shore, I looked around, and there seemed to be nobody anywhere.

"Where do you think we are?" I said as I found a higher posi-tion to see into the distance.

"We appear to have luck greatly on our side," Captain Bass responded. "Judging by the elements of land that I've come to know, I'd say we're in the vicinity north of Drummond Cove and somewhere south of a place called Horrocks. If that's the case, it's a short distance north to the Horrocks trading post. With a bit of luck, we should be able to pick up supplies before we take our journey inland."

"The Takers run the Horrocks trading post," Michael put in.

"Yes, I'm aware of that, Michael. You must stay out of sight and far away from the area. Nonetheless, they'll trade with per-sons such as I even though at exorbitant prices. The bad news is, one never knows if the Takers will take those items away when you're no more than two hundred yards up the street. We'll need to take extra precautions. Perhaps I'll go it alone at first while the rest of you stay back. We shall then see what happens."

The long walk was confirmed but expected. I readied my mind for the journey. Already, the sun's heat bit deep into my skin; I've never felt so hot. I wondered how long it would be before my skin turned into a raging inferno. Being albino, both Jason and I were completely at the sun's mercy, more so than the others. Maybe if we're lucky, this place called Horrocks might have suitable long sleeved clothing that may give us the protection we needed. But just as I thought it, I realized it was impossible. We had no crackle. No crackle meant no supplies.

"Captain Bass. You forget we have nothing to purchase supplies. We're not able to get supplies if . . ."

Captain Bass cut in as though preempting the end of my sentence. "We have crackle, dear boy. It's in the form of something else at this moment. I'm quite sure the submersible will get us what we need. What use is it now?"

I wasn't totally happy, but I knew it was our only option. Trading the submersible with the Takers just felt odd. It felt wrong. It was almost as weird as doing trade with them in the first place. But what choice did we have? From what I'd read in Michael's journal, we were about to traverse a most unforgiving land. Without the right preparation, we'd all die. Plain and simple.

Captain Bass was finally able to do a more accurate headcount, and with the loss of so many men, he named the beach 'Mandown Beach' in their honor. We all worked together to gather and piled up sandstone rocks to form a pyramid which stood eighteen hands high. First Officer William Fletcher said a few final words as we all stood somberly with our heads bowed.

Chapter Twenty-Two

The Angel and the Mad-Man

We made camp on Mandown Beach. Captain Bass and William Fletcher left in the submersible and headed north to the Takers trading post known as Horrocks. Our instructions were to stay camped until our captain and his first officer made their way back. They would either have the supplies with them, and we could immediately begin the trek to the east, or we'd be invited to the trading post and take up trade as we saw fit.

As the hours dragged on, I began to wonder if resorting to making contact with our enemy was a good idea at all. These people were responsible for the deaths of at least thirty members of our crew. And here we were, walking up to them in the hope they'll trade. It was almost an insult. My anger raged inside me all over again. As I played in the sand, doodling with a stick, the reasons we were all there in the first place seemed to be distant in my mind. I was beginning to lose hope, and I felt trapped.

More hours had passed, and the sun sat low on the horizon to the west. A cool breeze whipped up and was cold enough to cause me to shiver. I looked over to Michael who'd fashioned a carry bag out of a piece of his calico shirt. In the bag; along with the *Angel of Bunjil*, he carried the only Sacred Bone we had left which we both thought was a femur. I smiled a little and thought that Michael will always be the protector until this journey concludes. I was almost jealous, only because I was no longer on the roster for their care.

The sailors of other ranks got together and collected enough sticks for a fire. Soon after, a bonfire raged roughly three hundred yards away from where I sat doodling. Everyone including Eli and Jason crowded around the fire and began to sing what they called ditties. Everything felt so relaxed and peaceful. But as the sun sank fully under the horizon and stars began to appear, I began to wonder about the amount of time Captain Bass and William Fletcher were taking.

"Michael!" I shouted and waved him over.

Michael made his way up the beach sat heavily down beside me. He handed me the bag containing the *Angel of Bunjil* and Sacred Bone. I took it from him, and I placed the bag down at my side and put my hand on it. I reflected a little and looked back at what had taken place in my life to bring me to this point. All the people I've loved, and then they were torn away. But as I sat there and reminisced, I noticed Eli was no longer around the bonfire. Jason, however, joined in with the sailors as they sung their sometimes-strange ditties.

"Eli was there with them," I said. "But he's not there anymore."

"Oh that," Michael snickered under his breath. "Eli went to see a man about a dog."

"What?"

"He's answering nature's call. He said he had to go, most urgent. I told him, 'why're you telling me?' He said, he had to tell somebody in case somebody needed to know where he was. Then I told him the slang term for it. He was mystified. Just like you."

"That's a good one. I'll have to remember it. Go and see a man about a dog doesn't sound anything like taking a dump. How did they come up with that?"

Then in the distance, from somewhere south of where we were, three flashes lit up the twilight sky.

"What was that? Did you see it?"

"See what?" Michael said.

As soon as Michael answered me, three dull thuds, one after the other rang out. In my heart, I knew what they were. The burst of lights were muzzle flashes. The low rumbling thuds came from the barrels of howitzers. But around the campfire; over their singing, Jason and the others would've never seen the flashes or heard the burst of fire. I looked up, and I saw shell tracers streaking across the sky towards us. Michael looked up at the same time. "Shit!"

Shit!

"Jason!" I screamed out.

But he and the sailors kept on with their singing, oblivious to anything.

"JASON! RUN!" I screamed out louder than before.

I got up. Just as I commanded my legs to run toward the fire, Michael grabbed my shirt tail and pulled me back "No, Rick. It's too late!"

I stood there willing for it not to happen. Jason noticed I was staring straight at him. He waved at me; then innocently beckoned me over. I couldn't help but watch the tracer as it drilled in across the sky then, instantly, the shells exploded on impact. Jason and all who were around the fire were gone.

"JASON!"

"Rick. Quickly. We have to get to cover."

Michael grabbed my arm and forced me to run in the direction away from where the bonfire was reduced to a huge gaping crater in the middle of the beach. As we ran, Eli popped up from behind a dune and beckoned us over to him. There was no more artillery — only the eerie silence with the thick smell of exploded ord-nance hanging on the cool seaside air.

* * *

At sunrise, there was still no sign of Captain Bass and William Fletcher. But I'd had enough. My anger for the Takers now burned inside me. Retribution pumped around my body, and I was sure I could do the damage of a thousand men. I got myself out of that hole where we'd found cover. I clenched my fists and rose to the highest point on top of the dune. If I were a wolf, I'd have certainly howled loud enough to be heard across oceans. But I was no wolf. I was a mad-man. I was enraged, and my anger gave me the power to kill any Taker I put my eyes on. My blood was steam. My biceps were pistons. My fists were hammers. Show me a Taker. Steer me toward him. Let me slowly take his body apart. Let me rip the head from his shoulder.

"Richard. Give me your burden. Do not harbor such anger."

As soon as I heard the voice, it was as though it was speaking inside me. I spun around, then spun some more. There was no one I could see. "Who are you! Why did you let them kill my brother!"

"I am you, and you are me. We are one. You and I are one, Richard Gabriel."

"Why-did-you-let-them-kill-my-brother!"

"There can only be one true heart. Give me your burden. Give it to me now."

I fell to my knees and felt sickness rip up from the pit of my stomach. I threw up something black and ugly looking like crude oil over the sand. I felt a hand on my back as I threw up more. But after it was done, my hate had left me. I was no longer furious. It was as though everything I ever hated in my life no longer mattered. A new peace had descended. I was lighter. I was stronger. I felt like I could walk any desert unchallenged.

"Richard. Is everything okay?" Eli met me at the top of the dune. "You were sick? You'd better let me examine you. Black bile usually means internal injuries."

"I'm fine, Eli. But Captain Bass and William Fletcher have been captured. We need to rescue them."

* * *

Even though he'd been away from the area for nearly forty years, Michael knew the area better than Eli and myself. We stayed close to the water and tracked the beach north. By close to mid-day when the sun had already turned my white skin a fiery shade of red, Michael assured us that the Takers trading post was just around the next bend. The question I had in my head was, what in the heck were we supposed to do? We had no weapons. We had nothing but fists. They had guns. They even had artillery. My internal dialogue told me it was going to get ugly and we'd come off worse than any Taker. But Michael still seemed confident we'd find a way.

As we came around the edge of a dune, I saw two Takers, one male, and one female, swimming naked in the ocean. On the sand were their belongings. I was convinced from where I was standing; I could see a rifle was among the items that lay in the sun on towels.

Before I could say anything, Eli picked up his feet and ran. He bolted toward the Takers belongings, and when he got there, he grabbed up the Takers' rifle. I saw him as he cocked what I thought was an M4 assault rifle. Eli ran toward the Takers who were swimming in the waves and opened fire. Within a moment, the wash from waves brought two dead bodies onto the shore. Both Michael and I exchanged our shocked glances. Who I saw wasn't Eli. I didn't know who that guy was.

"Why the fuck did you do that, Eli? We could've had something to trade. The two Takers for Captain Bass and William Fletcher. But now that's not possible."

"They had towels, Richard. Towels! When was the last time *you* had a damn towel? Huh?"

What was going on? Two people were dead over the fact they had towels. Was this beach turning us into mad-men? Nonetheless, they were the enemy. And these assholes took Jason. I immediately thought back to the archangel Gabriel and my anger was no more. And now, we not only had their weapon, but at least one of us could use their outfit.

After gathering up the Takers clothing, we worked out that the woman's outfit was out of the question, but we could use the leather for other purposes. It'd be a complete waste to leave them on the beach. It was agreed that Michael had the privilege of wearing the Takers' leather and canvas outfit. It seemed to fit him perfectly even though I argued my point one last time.

"I still think I should be the one to infiltrate and find out where they have Captain Bass."

"No," Eli said. "Richard, you may not be white anymore. But you're the same shade of red as a Red Delicious apple. You'd stick out. And we don't go around 'sticking out' when we're infiltrating. I can't do it either. I look too much like an Amber. It must be Michael."

"So, stay here and wait until I get back," Michael added.

* * *

"I know where they're being held," Michael said as he suddenly returned to where we were hiding. "But it's not good. They're on the Takers blood list. If we don't get to them in time, they'll die by blood eagle. It's to do with something about Captain Bass and a wind turbine generator. They think he stole it from them."

"Shit!" Eli said. "So, what do we do next?"

"We go and break them out, of course. But getting there. It's a long way east of here. Twenty nights stride."

I thought about it for a while. "The same place you talk about in your journal?"

Michael nodded slowly. It was as though, suddenly, his memories returned. I saw it in his eyes; he disengaged from reality. He returned to his torment and haunting. I grabbed him by both shoulders and shook. I shook hard. He looked at me with eyes that said nothing at all. I shook again. "Michael!"

After a moment, Michael returned from where he'd gone. His pupils were again full of life. "I'll go back the trading post and get some water and supplies. I don't expect you guys to do the same things I've had to do in the past. The desert isn't a nice place, and without the right preparations, people can die. Easy as that."

One Flew into Fool's Desert

Michael led the way into the grey and dusty desert, armed with an M4 assault rifle firmly placed at his hip. I strode behind him, humping two gallons of water in opaque plastic bottles on a long stick across my shoulders. Eli was in the rear, swiping footprints into nothingness with a hunk of old fence paling and a scrap of rag.

As we walked, my thoughts returned to Captain Bass and his first officer. Then something horrible occurred to me. There was no doubt in my mind they'd both be turned into mutes, in the same way they'd once done to Michael. But I couldn't imagine how bad it was for Captain Bass. What good is a captain who couldn't command his men? Just thinking about it made me feel so sad. And he wasn't even aware that his men were gone.

I thought the stars at night in Antarctica were beautiful. I'd realized that all my life, I'd taken for granted the months of an uninterrupted jeweled night sky. In the desert, I couldn't take my eyes away from the band of the Milky Way, nebulae, and clusters of stars that formed into galaxies. I wondered if there was other life out there. I wondered if they'd evolved into intelligent beings and evolved like humans. I wondered if they started to make mistakes and changed the course of their planet's environment. I wondered if they turned into power crazy, greedy, hurtful sons o' bitches who'd ended up nuking their world into oblivion. Maybe it was a course of passage that all intelligent life must traverse. Maybe intelligent life needs to virtually annihilate itself before the ones who're left realize how wrong they were. And I wondered if it was the same everywhere. I looked up, and I wondered.

I realized that looking up, and walking along, was never a good idea. Michael had stopped in front of me, and I crashed into the back of him. Michael gestured with his hand for Eli and me to get down. We did, but I also wondered why he crouched down so suddenly. "What is it?" I asked.

"It's dinner for the next two nights. But only if we're lucky."

I peered into the distance, but clearly, Michael had better skills than me. Eli worked his vision and said he saw nothing.

Michael looked back over his shoulder and sighed. "I'll need to teach you night vision skills. Concentrate your field of vision a little left or a little right, and you'll see things with more clarity. It's to do with using your rod cells which are more tuned for seeing at night; as compared with your cone cells which are tuned for seeing during the day."

I didn't know what the heck he was talking about.

"Try it. See that tree trunk over there."

I nodded "Yeah, I see it."

"Now look slightly away from it."

He was right. "Holy crap!"

"Magic," Michael said. "But you need at least twenty minutes of total darkness before it develops. If you get white light into your eyes, you're stuffed. You'll need another twenty minutes before it comes back. I'm surprised you blokes didn't know about it considering the part of the world from where you came. Six months in a year of darkness; you'd have to be using your rods."

"We had electric lights," Eli added. "We stayed on board *Steinbeck* during winter. But even so, by the time the sun came up again, I was treating many of our people for severe cabin fever and melancholy."

I patted Michael on the back. "I think I see it now. A kangaroo?"

"You wish. There're no kangaroos anymore. Just these . . . things, that look like them. They're carnivores. Man-eaters. We call them 'Rad Roos.' Kangaroos have mutated over the decades since The Fall. If you see one of these beasts during the day, run. Run as fast as you can. It's the only hope you have left. If they get you, they'll rip your guts open with their nine-inch claws. If you can't find a tree high enough in time, you're dead. The thing is, you'll never see one by itself. They're pack animals. Kill one of them; you'd better hope you can kill more. They'll all turn on you. They'll seek you out and hunt you down. But there's a technique to hunt them. You get them to all turn on themselves."

"How?"

"I found out that they don't like being hit in the head. They think one of the pack has picked a fight. So then, they'll fight each other until one gets killed. You must get close enough so you can throw a rock. If you miss, you'd better have a tree close by so you can get to safety. Even then, they'll wait for you to come down. Or they'll hide and make you think they're gone."

"Mother of penguins! Is it worth it?" Eli asked.

"Well, if you want my opinion, dying of starvation is worse. At least if you get done by a Rad Roo, it's guaranteed to be quick."

"We have our rifle," I said. "We have a better chance if we shot one."

"No. Our ammo is valuable. We don't waste it on Rad Roos. And we're not taking one down either. The fact they're here means they're on a hunt. There's prey in the area. It can be anything from dingoes to echidnas. That's good for us. We'll leave the Rad Roos alone."

We waited in the shadows of the shrubbery for the mob of Rad Roos to move on. It meant we could get up and continue our journey, or hunt the creatures the Rad Roos were interested in. But they seemed to be quite contented staying where they were. We were stuck. No way forward. No way back. "How much ammo?" I asked Michael.

Michael quietly took the magazine out and held it in his hand. "By the weight, I think about nine rounds. Give or take. And no, we're not shooting them. We wait. Patiently."

I sighed and turned to check on Eli, but he was gone. I spun and tapped Michael on the back. "Eli's gone!"

"What! The bloody idiot! Didn't I just say . . ."

Just as Michael had said it, I saw out of my night vision someone protrude from the bushes fifty yards in front of where we were. Eli had a huge rock in his hand. He launched it, and it struck a Rad Roo square in the back of the head. The Rad Roo shook its head and then looked around at the rest of its mob for the aggressor. The spat was on. Two huge Rad Roo males squared off and danced around as though they were world heavyweight boxers. Then one got up on its tail and kicked out with its huge claws. His opponent did the same, but this time connected. The injured Rad Roo let out a terrible scream that sounded like a mother in the final stages of labor. The beating went on.

Eli made it back to where we were. I spun around and saw his face in the pale moonlight. "That wasn't so bad," he said. "We'll have fresh food after these big roos do what they need to do. Then we'll go and clean up."

But just over his shoulder, I saw a set of huge canines glinting and glistening.

"RRUN!"

I'd never ran so fast or so hard. My heart pumped like the rattle of a snare drum. As I ran, I looked for a suitable tree. I saw one and thought I could make it. Behind me, I heard the padded hopping of a Rad Roo closing in. I reached up with my hands to grab a branch. My foot snagged something in the ground, and I went down skidding on my face as the Rad Roo bounced over my head.

Getting myself up on my hands, I saw the roo do a turn in the dirt before it stopped momentarily and sized me up. The tree was my chance, and the big branch was just above my head. I had to get there. I had to jump up at least twenty hands high. My life depended on it. As soon as I got up, the Rad Roo was coming at me like a furious bull. I jumped. I couldn't quite make it. The tips of my fingers only just missed the life-giving tree. I fell again, realizing there was nothing else I could do. I was too late. I put my hands over my eyes.

A burst of gunfire rang out and hit the Rad Roo which skidded to a stop right at my feet.

"Get in that tree!" Michael shouted from somewhere. "There's more. Get up in there!"

Then more gunfire rang out as I again jumped and this time; I grabbed hold of a branch. I climbed up and out of danger.

* * *

Remembering what Michael had told us about the Rad Roos, I stayed up in the tree until full sunlight, and with the sunshine, I could see the carnage of dead Rad Roo carcasses that littered the area. I counted them — seven dead Rad Roos. Michael was already skinning one of them with a crackle blade he'd scored from dead Takers. I couldn't see where Eli was, and I hoped he was okay.

Getting out of the tree, I approached Michael, and I could already see how unhappy he was. I said a few words which went ignored. It wasn't until after I asked Michael if he knew where Eli had gone until he said anything at all.

"I don't really care, Rick. I'm so fucking pissed off right now, I don't know what to tell you."

Then Eli, as though hearing his name, emerged from the bushes. Michael charged at him, crackle blade held over his head. I got in the middle of them. "Hey! Calm down! This is *not* how we're gonna get our brothers out of imprisonment. Calm down!"

It took a bit of effort, but I got there in the end. I managed to avert a disaster between Michael and Eli. But what I saw next broke my heart — the water bottles I'd been carrying lay on the ground in the distance. The Rad Roos must've used their claws to puncture them and then they'd helped themselves to the most precious items we had.

"Yeah," Michael said. "We've got meat. We've got skins. We've even got sinew for making things. But what a price! No water. One bullet left. It's back to drinking piss. You blokes will now know what it's like to do those things. I've tried hard not to do them again. There's no choice now. Eli, you bloody idiot. Why didn't you just let me handle it?"

"Easy," I said. "Let's not do this again."

"You know what?" Michael went on. "After this is over, I'm going back to my own place. The place where I grew up. At least I know how to survive. Not like you two. You're fucking hopeless."

"I'm sorry," Eli offered. "I thought . . ."

"You thought! What did you think, Eli? Did you think it would be easy? Wake up sunshine; nothing is easy out here. Everywhere you go, there's something or somebody who wants to kill you. Let me give you a little lesson in life in Fool's Desert. Every time you eat something, be thankful because there may not be anymore. Every time you drink something, be thankful because you're not drinking your own piss. But now we have no water, and only ONE bullet left, it'll be a miracle that we'll even make it to the Takers' garrison. So wise up. Listen to what I say. Do what I get you to do. And we might just get there. Is that all right with you!"

Michael turned his back and immediately got on with skinning the Rad Roo carcass. As Eli stood there after being firmly put in his place, I started stripping the meat from the bones of the Rad Roo, wondering at the same time, how it would taste after we cooked it.

I couldn't help wondering about Eli. First the Takers on the beach, then this. He was becoming unstable and hard to trust. For now, I thought I'd keep those feelings to myself.

Chapter Twenty-Four

Fletcher

We arrived at the Takers' encampment under cover of night, much to Michael's contentment. It also meant we could rest up before sunrise in roughly two hours. It'd give us the time to sort things out in our minds and to figure out what to do next. Along the journey, I hoped we'd use the time to work out a tangible plan, but that wasn't the case. The last nine nights of trekking was empty of anything verbal apart from what needed to be said to get by. After we finally arrived, I was so weary, all I wanted to do was lie down and go to sleep. I was sure Eli felt the same. Over the last sixty miles, we strode with Eli complaining bitterly about his hunger. Oddly, he didn't complain as much when we needed to drink our urine just to survive.

Michael was right. He'd once written in his journal that trekking across Fool's Desert for twenty-three nights does things to a man. It wasn't until after I'd taken my shirt off to let it air dry from my perspiration, I noticed how much weight had come off my bones. I realized I was much too weak even to consider

mounting a rescue using what Michael had called, 'extreme violence.' I already knew deep inside my mind that the rescue would
never work if we all got physical and went in there all gung-ho.
Not only did we have just one round of ammo left; time was
against us, and in our state of health, going in there looking for a
frenzy of bloodletting was asking for trouble. I also began to realize that the visit from Archangel Gabriel had somehow gifted
me with a way of seeing things differently. Although I didn't
know exactly what it was, I knew I was on the verge of learning
something extraordinary.

As we sat in the shadow of the Takers' stronghold that was
positioned up high on a hill, Michael pointed to the base of the
hill, and he assured us the opening to the silver mine might still
be there. Even though the entrance was covered in desert weeds
and shrubbery, the telltale indent near the entrance could still be
seen.

We hunkered down in a ditch and got ourselves away from any
possibility of getting busted. Ditches; I hated them. I hoped it was
the last time that I smelt the desert and the dust right up to my
face. But this time, Michael didn't attempt to get any rest. While
Eli snored heavily in the background, I heard Michael saying
things under his breath. I thought he saw things; maybe he hallu-
cinated due to the effects of dehydration. After I asked him what
he was talking about, Michael shut up and looked at me with the
same eyes my brother had given me all that time ago. There was
hopelessness sitting there behind Michael's eyes, even though he
tried to hide it by looking down and away. It was the exact same
reaction that immediately took me back to the time with Jason

while sitting on the edge of *Steinbeck's* flight deck as we discussed options for escaping the blackout.

Michael looked up at me and said, "This is it, Rick. This is how we go out. The mongrel bastards win every time."

After Michael said those words, something inside me suddenly erupted and came alive. I couldn't have disagreed more. I locked eye contact with him. "When we go in there to liberate Captain Bass and William Fletcher, it's not going to be the outcome any of us are expecting. Their liberation isn't going to be by extreme violence as you keep saying. I don't know why I know this. I just know it. I want you to get your head back in the game, Michael. We have a job to do, and we need you. We must succeed. And we will succeed. All we have to do is turn up at the Takers' gate and knock. What happens after that has already been fated, and we have no control over it."

"Well, look at you," Michael said, smiling a little. "What happened? Are you giving me pep talks now? This wasn't you a few days ago. But you know what? You're right. Whatever happens, is whatever happens."

* * *

"Are you sure you want to do it this way?" Eli asked me, then rubbed his eyes as though he didn't believe what he was hearing.

"I'm sure. Just trust me with this one. Everything will work out. But before we go, we'll stash everything here. The relics, the rifle; everything."

After I dug a hole in the sand and buried our belongings with the relics, I placed a sandstone rock that was in the shape of a heart on top of it, so it'd be easy to find. I looked at Michael and nodded. He returned my nod with a nervous looking smile.

We had no need for the silver mine. It may as well have not even been there. Instead, all three of us walked with conviction up the track to reach the Takers' garrison main gate. My heart was pumping, and I swore it was in my mouth, but I kept going. We all kept going in an arrowhead formation; me leading, Michael to my right, Eli to my left. We walked up the hill and stopped in front of a huge steel gate which had coils of rusty razor wire running the length of the top, and continued along the garrison's old bluestone walls, disappearing away into the distance.

I walked up to the gate, and I was almost overwhelmed with the stench of death that emerged from the garrison. With one hand, I covered my nose and mouth. With the other, I smacked the gate with the heel of my hand, which resulted in a deep clang and an echo, and I knew that someone in there would've heard it. The gate squealed noisily open by roughly four hands. The surprised stare of a musclebound freak of a Taker gazed straight at me. "What the fuck do you blokes want. Fuck off, before I put a bullet through you."

"I'm Gabriel," I said. "This is Michael and Raphael."

"So what? I said fuck off before I put a bullet through your heads. You've got three seconds. ONE."

I sucked back a huge gulp of air. "It's in your best interest to release the two men who you're holding. Henry Bass and William Fletcher."

"TWO. And don't make me fucking laugh. Fuck off. Last chance."

"Release them right now. I demand it. *Your* last chance."

"Right!"

The rusty steel gate slid fully open with an ear-piercing squeal.

"Do what I do," I said over my shoulder to Eli and Michael. "And whatever happens, don't move. Just hold still."

I got on my knees and put my hands on my head. Eli and Michael did the same.

"I hope you're right," Michael whispered.

They sprung from behind the rusty steel gate and came at us. The big guy who'd told us to fuck off came at me and landed a hard punch to the side of my head. I heard a loud crack. It wasn't what I was expecting. The big guy reeled back screaming in agony, holding and shaking his hand.

"Mutha-Fukka!" he yelled at the same time as he examined his broken hand and busted fingers.

In an instant, another massive Taker came for me. He wound up a huge baseball bat which I saw was modified with nails to do more damage. He lifted it high above my head and he brought it down with mammoth force. The baseball bat snapped and broke into a thousand splinters. The big Taker looked at the remnants of the bat he was holding in his hand and tossed it over his shoulder; then he retrieved his pistol from his holster. After cocking the weapon, he came at me and held the barrel point blank to my face.

"You can use that weapon," I said. "But what if that bullet doesn't come out? What if your gun explodes in your hand? But let's not discuss it. Go ahead and pull that trigger. It's the only way we'll find out."

Fear; I had none of it. But I saw it on his face, the big Taker thought about pulling the trigger. I had no idea if he'd kill me and it didn't matter. From my peripheral vision, I could see eagles circling on the wind. There were seven of them that I could make out. So, without any trepidation, I knew what was about to occur.

In the next moment, the two big Takers spun and left us where we were. They disappeared behind the gate and then slammed it closed.

I heard Eli mutter the words, 'mother of penguins,' under his breath.

"What now?" Michael asked.

I looked up and caught sight of the seven eagles which were circling, speeding up into tighter circles, as though they were making themselves ready. "Well for one, let's all get up off our knees," I answered Michael. "No reason we should ever do that again. So now, we'll wait, and we'll see what happens next."

* * *

We waited for long enough to think we were forgotten, as the seven eagles above us flew tighter and tighter circles. During the time we were there, it was easy to hear screams of pain and suffering coming from somewhere on the other side of the gate. It was incredibly difficult to stand there and do nothing to help them. As soon as I felt the anger rise, I remembered Gabriel's words and I looked up again. Six eagles now flew in a circle where the albino hovered in the center. If someone told me the white eagle was looking directly at me, I would've believed it. And as soon as I saw it hovering, the anger I once felt was gone.

The gate squealed opened by four hands, and they'd pushed someone through the aperture. William Fletcher fell on the ground as though he was only semiconscious. But it wasn't William Fletcher. It was a man who'd had pieces taken from him with unspeakable ruthlessness.

I read the words in Michael's journal about that room of appalling horrors. After I saw with my own eyes what these people did to fellow humans, the true revulsion touched me in a way that cut deep into my soul. It'd be easy to give up like the scrounger who took a shard of crackle to his own throat. It'd be easy to turn away, find a patch of ground, raise some crops, survive and not think about anything anymore. But this? *This* must stop, and *we* must make it happen. I looked up again, and all the eagles had stopped circling. They were all hovering, line abreast as though they waited for me to command them.

I took a breath and instructed my legs to walk towards William Fletcher who seemed lifeless on the ground. As I walked, the gate squealed open again and, in my mind, I thought Captain Bass was next to step through. I held my breath and waited, knowing well he'd be as injured, if not more, than William Fletcher. But instead of Captain Bass, a young woman with bright red hair and freckled complexion was thrust outward, and the gate behind her squealed closed.

The three of us rushed urgently to the gate. I looked down upon William Fletcher's face. His eyes were taken out. And judging by the lack of sounds and the amount of blood coming out of him, they'd also taken his tongue. The stumps of both arms were wrapped in blood-soaked rags, and they didn't even bother with his missing foot.

While Eli was busy with William Fletcher and making him as comfortable as he could, I caught sight of Michael's expression. He looked as though he was ready to blow up. As soon as he turned away, I knew he was on a mission to destroy whatever he could destroy. But I grabbed him in time. I pointed skyward. "Their day is here, Michael." It seemed to settle him down. It seemed to take away his anger and pain.

After a moment, the woman with red hair introduced herself as Abigail. She said the Takers had no use for her anymore and seeing as William Fletcher wasn't able to talk, it was her job to let us know the whereabouts of Henry Bass.

"He's at Newman," she told us. "They said his body was too old and his meat would be tough. They've put him on a caravan and sent him east."

Just as I realized it, Michael confirmed it with his next words. He went on to explain that Newman was the place they'd kept him on a chain before he made his escape. But I needed no reminding. I also realized that Michael knew where Newman was and how long it would take to get there. I looked back down to William Fletcher. It was impossible for someone so injured to travel such distances. He'd never make the journey. I thought about it in my mind. I knew Eli was thinking the same, and I was sure Michael was with us. There was no need for words. I could see it in their eyes.

We retrieved our belongings from where we'd buried them, and I used our last round of ammunition to take William Fletcher's pain away.

After we'd buried William Fletcher in the same place we'd once buried our things, we shouldered our belongings, and I looked up for the last time. The seven eagles still hovered line abreast, and I realized they were waiting until the four of us were finished in the area. Michael approached me and said, "It's important that you don't look back, Rick."

"What'll happen if I do?"

"Just don't, is all. Trust me."

As we began our long walk toward the east, the sounds of complete chaos and destruction erupted behind me and was hard to ignore. It seemed even harder not to look over my shoulder. I nearly did. But Michael stopped me. We walked away from the sounds of explosions, and bursts of fire. The screams of terror and anguish. It was a sound I'll always remember.

Suddenly I thought about Abigail. It felt like slow motion as I spun and desperately shaded my eyes. "Abigail! No!" It was too late. Abigail gave in to the temptation and turned around. I caught sight of her facial expression as she became frozen in time. In an instant, she was no longer living. I reached out and touched her with the tip of my finger. Abigail had become a statue made of something harder than ash and something softer than rock. I took a breath and put my head down. I faced east and walked on.

Chapter Twenty-Six

Nothing Is What It Appears

I caught myself thinking that if Michael had made it the first time across Fool's Desert, it must've been more ass than class. But Michael surprised me by his knowledge of the area and by the demonstration of his survival skills. The desert bloodwood gave us food, but by also using the sap, we were able to heal the sores and blisters that were always a side effect of constant walking. We used the sap also as a repellant from marauding Rad Roos. The Rad Roos hated bloodwood trees and stayed away from them. By using the sap, we sent out a message to all Rad Roos in the desert that we were nothing more than walking bloodwood trees.

Michael also knew where there was water in the far east of Fool's Desert. In the middle of grey dusty nothing for miles everywhere, Michael took us directly to an oasis of water which gave us life and energy when we needed it the most. As I fell into the earthy smelling cool water, I smacked my face a few times to make sure I was fully conscious and not dreaming.

While we were at the water hole, we began to discuss our options for when we arrived at Newman. My memory of Michael's journal told me it was a place filled with danger. The Newman people appeared to only look after their own. I saw them in my mind as a tribe, and everyone on the outside of their compound was considered a threat. Maybe they were even worse than the Takers. As I thought it over, it appeared The Fall had reduced any surviving human inhabitants down to the rules of tribal warfare. But Michael assured us that if we played the part of scroungers selling wares, we'd not find ourselves dropped on a chain or offered up as food to the Takers.

"What do we sell?" I asked Michael. "We've got nothing but these Rad Roo skins."

"That's why I insisted on skinning them," Michael said. "They're worth good crackle out here, and they're always in demand. The demand is high only because people get killed if they specifically go out hunting Rad Roos."

"And you think this will get us inside the compound?"

"It won't work. Scroungers sell other things. They'll see right through us," Eli put in.

Michael put up his hand. "It'll work out. Let me do the talking."

I thought about it for a while, but it still didn't sit well with me. Then I realized Michael's motivation. "You're going for unfinished business, aren't you? After all these years, you think Murk is still there?"

"He could be."

"Could be? You risk jeopardizing our mission because you want payback?"

"He's got my gun, and I want it back."

"That was forty years ago, Michael. Things have changed. Forget about the unfinished business. We're there for Captain Bass. We negotiate for his release. Maybe we can use the Rad Roo skins as payment seeing they're in demand. We get Captain Bass out. We continue north to make contact with the Ambers. End of discussion."

After I'd said it, I saw it in Michael's body language that he was never going to leave it at that. But there was something else that played on my mind. After we leave Newman, then what? Do we all trek north into the Irradiated Badlands? Do we all die from radiation sickness?

"There's no need to leave Newman," Michael said at the same time I was thinking about it. "The Ambers deliver diesel to Newman, remember?"

We stayed at the water hole for longer than we planned. It wasn't a good idea. It gave us a false sense of security. It also meant we'd have to stride the final stretch in daylight. But Michael made waterskins out of Rad Roo hide and sinew. Finally, we were able to carry water on our long walk.

* * *

By the time we were within reach of Newman, our water was long gone. Along the way, we tried to save as much water as we could, but it was hopeless. The waterskins Michael made leaked worse than *Steinbeck's* lifeboats, and everything was lost. With not having water for what seemed days, nothing could've described us more accurately than walking skeletons arriving on death's door.

From out of the flatlands, in the middle of the day, the mirage of Newman's compound walls came into view. I struggled to pick up my feet and place them. My shoulders drooped, and my arms failed to swing. Eli was somewhere behind me. I heard his footfalls slide then drop into the desert dust. I watched Michael in front of me. I kept willing him forward, hoping he wouldn't fall. If he went down, I wasn't sure there was a way I could help him.

Slowly, and painfully, we trudged on.

I heard Eli as he hit the dirt hard. I spun, and I saw him spread-eagled with an arm raised.

I got myself back there and kneeled at his side. "Eli. Are you okay?"

After I'd said it, it seemed like a dumb thing to ask. But Eli responded with one word only. The same word I had in my mind for the past twenty-thousand strides. "Th-Thirsty."

"Michael," I yelled. "Michael, stop."

It was as though Michael didn't hear me or he didn't have the energy to fight his forward momentum. He kept up his steps going forward.

"Michael!"

As soon as I said it, I saw him stop. I thought he might turn around. He didn't. His body slowly fell forward, and he face-planted the earth.

"SHIT!"

Somehow, I got up off the ground. I didn't want to leave Michael and Eli. I had no choice. Before heading for Newman, I covered Eli and Michael with a Rad Roo skins, hoping that would make a difference. Hoping it would help keep the sun from burning them.

The mirage blurred in the distance. I squinted my eyes then relaxed them. I squinted them again and tried to breathe. Every breath I sucked back felt as though it weighed a ton. I willed every step forward and down, forward and down. I pushed my hips in front of my legs hoping like crazy that gravity would take over and move everything else. Gravity. The very second, I thought of it . . .

* * *

I felt hands patting my face. I heard a voice. A female voice. A muted voice. I tried to open my eyes. My eyelids ignored my efforts. I felt cooling water on my body. I felt cooling water all over me. I knew, somewhere in my core; I was dead.

The female voice said it again. The same words again. But it was like hearing her from a distance. She was speaking to me from the other side of the desert. But I knew her voice was sweet and lovely. I couldn't understand her words, but it was like hearing a song. I felt myself floating toward her. Her sweet and lovely voice. Chloe. Chloe's voice.

"Open your eyes," Chloe said. "Open your eyes, Ricky."

I tried to open them. But I wanted the opposite. I wanted to sleep; I was so tired. Sleep. How wonderful and beautiful is sleep? Dream on . . . Dream on . . .

"Open your eyes Ricky!"

I felt hands on my face — a sharp slap.

I opened my eyes.

The light was immense as it dazzled my senses. I saw a blurred outline of someone standing there. I saw a blurred shape and her hair, so dark. I closed my eyes.

"Richard. Wake up Richard . . . You must wake up."

More water over me. So lovely, the water.

I saw her again, that woman with long black hair and eyes so black they were the center of galaxies.

Then, I felt a sharp thud to the side of my face.

I opened my eyes wide, and I shook my head. I looked up to the woman standing there. She smiled down at me. I saw her take in a huge breath of air. A huge sigh. "Well you sure know how to worry someone, don't you? Welcome back."

"W-Where am I? What happened?"

The woman said nothing. She stepped to my side and lifted my head off the pillow to allow me to drink. I took a sip then wanted more. I wanted so much more.

"Hey. Easy there." The woman took the cup away. My body kept drinking from it. "I'm here to look after you. I'm Cherith. And you need your rest."

As soon as she told me her name, I knew where I was, and I realized how bad I was in it. I'd gone from something terrible, headlong into something truly screwed up. I tried to get up. Cherith pushed me back down. "Rest. You need to rest."

"Eli . . . Michael . . . Where are they?"

She said nothing.

I asked it again. "Eli and Michael. They were with me. Where are they?"

She again avoided my question but asked for my name.

"I'm Richard. Richard Gabriel."

Cherith stepped to my side and quickly changed my IV drip, all the while smiling her beaming white pins. She touched the top of my hand as she walked away.

"My things. My bag with my belongings," I said after her.

Cherith stopped and faced me. "We've locked your items away for safe keeping. When you're better, you may have them back." She smiled briefly before adding, "Seth will see you in a while. But rest for now."

After she'd gone, I instantly checked the drawer to my side. There was nothing in there. Something at the back of my mind told me they weren't going to give my precious items back to me in a hurry. I relaxed as much as I could. I relaxed, but at the same time, I wondered about Eli and Michael. Then blackness came.

* * *

Seth closed the door quietly behind him and eyed me intensely as he walked with light footsteps toward me. By the time he pulled out a chair and sat by my side, I knew it in my heart that Eli and Michael had died. I expected Seth to speak, but I also knew what he was thinking. It wasn't about the death of my friends. He sat there eyeing me as though he was wondering if I was strong enough to pull my own weight on a chain.

Seth leaned forward in his chair before he said anything. He put his hands together and rubbed them as though he was cold. "We did everything we could, I'm sorry. You friends were both deceased when we found them out there. But one of your friends wasn't a stranger. I met him a long time ago. Michael."

Things went through my mind — many things. I should've felt nothing but sadness. I didn't have the time. I needed my belongings back, and I needed to get the heck out of the place.

"Thank you, Seth. And thank you for everything. Now, If I could please have my things back, I'll get going, and I'll burden you no longer."

"Burden? Not at all. Please stay. Stay as long as you like. When you're strong enough and feel up to it, you may like to help out in the fields. In return, we'll give you lodging and meals. Meet our people. Join our community. Perhaps you might like to stay forever. Our home is your home."

"Thanks. But no thanks. I'll have my things back if you don't mind."

"What's the hurry?"

"What's the hurry? How about being locked on a chain and made to work like a slave. How about having my tongue cut out? That's two reasons. There's more."

Seth sat back and laughed. Sick bastard. Then he said something that shook every atom in my body.

"Yes, we've read Michael's journal. We've all read it. That man had an imagination that entertained everyone here. We had no books. But Michael gave to this community in ways nobody else could. He was an entertainer — a fiction writer. In his journal, he even gave the people of Newman their own unique accent. I asked him where he came up with the idea. Michael said he'd read a bunch of books about the Maoris in New Zealand and their history before The Fall. He got the idea from those books. Michael gave everyone Maori tattoos in his journal. Do you see any on me? Hmm?"

I studied Seth for a moment and thought about everything he'd said. "I need a moment."

"Sure. I'll leave you be. I can show you more of Michael's work if you like. He's written many books which are works of fiction based on fact. We keep them for entertainment. We've kept them for over forty years."

What was I supposed to do with this information? Was I supposed to believe it?

"What about Murk?" I asked.

Seth smiled and leaned forward in his chair. Over his shoulder, he called out Murk's name. In the next moment, the door opened, and a thinly built middle-aged guy wearing clinical whites stepped through.

"This is Murk," Seth said. "Murk, this is our new guest, Richard Gabriel."

Murk stepped over to me and offered his hand. I took it and shook. "You don't fit the description I've read about."

Murk smiled and said, "Pain in the arse, that fella. Sad that he's dead though."

"Michael was good at stretching the details and distorting the truth," Seth went on. "I asked Michael once. I said, Michael, why is it that you can never write how things really are? Do you know what he replied? He said, because the world is a stage. So, I'm glad we've got that off our chests. It's good that you're getting better, Richard. I'll be showing you around the compound soon enough."

Seth got up from his chair and turned to leave.

"Can I see them?" I asked. "Eli and Michael. Can I see where you've buried them?"

"Of course. Rest for now."

But there was something else that bothered me. Captain Henry Bass.

Chapter Twenty-Seven

Orientation

From the window, as I looked around the place, it was exactly as Michael described in his journal. But there were no gangs of slaves. There were no chain masters. There were no armed guards. There were no screams of terror. Everything Michael had led me to believe about this place couldn't have been further from reality. My eyes scanned the area, and I saw teams of workers in fields of green with their bare backs in the sun, glistening with sweat. It made every bit of difference to see them working because they wanted to work. Their body language showed it. They loved what they did. They enjoyed it. And there were no shackles or restraints of any kind.

After I climbed into my clothes and walked the small passageway to the outside, I stopped to take in the sweet air. It was gorgeous, smelling of fresh garden aromas that I'd never experienced before. The compound was huge and much bigger than the picture I had in my mind. To my left, I saw the fields of corn

Michael had written about, stretching to the far end of the compound. Beyond that, I could see the shapes of buildings and barns
and a mill that was driven by the winds; the same kind I'd learned
in books describing Holland. In front of me was a collection of
gardens consisting of various varieties of vegetables. At the far
end of the gardens, I heard the cackle of chickens and geese. Another large building behind the shack where they'd kept chickens
I assumed was for livestock.

On my right, I saw a collection of small buildings stretching to
the far end of the compound, and people walked and talked with
each other in what seemed a relaxed atmosphere. Some sat on
chairs and enjoying the sun. Others talked over fences while holding mugs and enjoying whatever they were drinking. I heard the
sounds of small engines and I saw something that took my breath
away. People were using small engine powered implements to cut
grass and shape it down. I was mesmerized by everything I'd
seen. But a strange white square structure stuck out of the ground
near the windmill. I wondered what that might be used for. I remembered Seth had asked me if I'd like to stay forever. I thought
it was a good possibility that it might be the case.

"Good morning, Richard. Feeling better?" Cherith said from
behind me. "Would you like some coffee?"

"Coffee?" The last time I'd had coffee was on the *Victory*. So
many things had happened over the journey. I'd traveled so far
and done so many things. Many people had died. My friends. My
family. Everyone I knew. Now I was getting coffee? "Yeah. Coffee. I think I'd like that a lot."

On the verandah, I sat down in a long wicker lounge which smelled a little old and musty, but for some reason, it felt like home. My eyes filled with tears as I looked around. I became overwhelmed with the happiness I saw everywhere. I looked from one corner of the compound to the next. Was I dreaming? Was this for real?

Cherith met me on the verandah with two mugs. "It's got milk in it. I thought you looked like a white coffee kind of guy," she said smiling, as she handed me a mug.

"Are you making fun of me because I'm albino?"

Cherith giggled and looked away.

"I've never had milk. I've had goats' cheese but not milk." I started to realize how limited my horizons actually were. I took a sip of my coffee, and I enjoyed the taste. It was strange. It didn't have the same kick as the coffee I had on *Victory*, but it was pleasant.

"So, Seth will be showing you around. You'll meet all our clan. You'll even meet an old sea captain who recently joined us. He takes the children after school and tells them about his seagoing adventures."

As soon as Cherith said it, I knew who she was talking about and what a relief he wasn't dead. "Henry Bass?"

Cherith eyed me curiously. "Oh. You must be the Richard he talks about."

"I hope he tells you all good things about me. But changing the subject, what is that big white square thing sticking out of the ground over there?"

"That's is our outdoor cinema. Tonight, we're watching *Big Country* with Gregory Peck and Jean Simmons. It's one of my favorite movies. But I can't go, unfortunately."

"Why can't you go? You're free to do whatever you want. Just go and see it."

"Well, it's because I don't have a date," Cherith said then blushed a little.

I was almost going to tell Cherith how happily married I was, and that dating wasn't an option. But as soon as I thought it, I realized for the first time that I'd never see Chloe again. I was no longer married. Suddenly, it was as though I now had the time to properly mourn the loss of my wife. But having found myself in such a wonderful place, I saw myself settling in this sanctuary called Newman. But something else appeared in the back of my mind. *The Angel of Bunjil* and the Sacred Bone. My mission. I must not let good things cloud my judgment. I had a job to do first. Then I could come back and join the Newman dwellers.

"Cherith."

"Yes?"

"I'd love to go and see a movie with you."

But before Cherith had the chance to add anything else, a familiar voice shouted my name from a distance away. "Richard! Could it be you, dear boy?"

I couldn't believe my ears. "Captain Bass!"

I launched myself from the verandah and ran to Captain Bass who limped and walked aided by a walking cane toward me. When I got there, he took my hand and shook it vigorously. "Oh, I'm so glad to see you, dear boy; I'm so glad indeed."

But after our greeting had concluded I caught Captain Bass eyeing over my shoulder as though he was expecting to see the others. How could I tell him there were none? His facial expression dropped from being happy to being concerned. "All of them?" he asked slowly.

I nodded. I had no words.

"The entire crew? All of my men?"

I nodded again.

"Jason . . . Eli and Michael?"

Tears backed up in my eyes. I could no longer hold them.

"Good heavens! I . . . I . . . am so sorry, dear Richard."

"As am I, Captain Bass. But the Takers encampment has been destroyed. They're no longer there. We've given William Fletcher a proper burial. They'd done too much damage to him."

Captain Bass lowered himself to the ground and sat. It was as though his legs just gave way from under him. I sat on the ground with him and waited for him to return from his thoughts. When he did return, it wasn't anything I expected.

"All of the Takers from the central garrison are gone, did you say?"

"There's nothing left of their encampment. They won't bother the Newman dwellers anymore. The people here can live freely without fear."

"But my dear boy, now that the Takers are gone, it's much worse than you realize. The people here had a ceasefire agreement. Now that the garrison has been destroyed, the agreement is no longer. Newman is now open slather for the taking. There's a war coming, Richard. Once other Takers' outposts learn about the destruction of the central garrison, they'll come in the numbers. We must now prepare the people. At once, before it's too late!"

* * *

I didn't mind watching an old black and white movie. And the sounds of crickets and frogs in the background didn't seem to take away from the atmosphere. There were roughly sixty people at the outdoor cinema seated on blankets and in foldaway chairs. We'd all brought little containers with garlic and lime with cloves to keep mosquitos away. I had no idea what mosquitos were until Cherith told me. But after I felt their sting and heard their drone, I believed every word Cherith had said.

I would've enjoyed the movie more than I did. I found my mind on the things Captain Bass was concerned about. I wondered how much time it would take for the word to get around each Takers' outpost. Then I tried to calculate the time it would take for them to react. It didn't matter how many times I'd tossed it around in my head; there were so many variables to consider; I ended up with completely different answers.

As Cherith and I sat on a blanket and the scent of everyone's homemade mosquito repellant was thick in the air, my thoughts returned to another place and another time which now seemed so far away. I wondered what Chloe had gone through. I wondered what my mother had gone though. Their final waking moments was sure to have been catastrophic for them; not just horrific. Here I was enjoying a movie, at the same time knowing what they had to endure. And I wasn't there to do anything about it. Suddenly I felt violently ill. I made my quick excuses and I returned to my quarters before my physical sickness became something ugly which I had no control over.

* * *

My orientation of the compound with Seth ended at my small but comfortable and functional farmhand quarters. Seth urged me to stay on for a second time as more hands were needed for the coming corn harvest. How could I deny him? Considering the welcome I've had so far, how could I not agree? But Seth didn't know about the destroyed Takers' central garrison. I wondered what his reaction might be after Captain Bass and I explain what had happened, and worse, what's likely to happen in the coming short future. It was agreed between Captain Bass and myself, that nothing should be said until such time as we both meet with Seth in his office to discuss what needs to be done next. As Seth smiled and walked away, leaving me at my door, I felt an urge to spill everything. It took everything bit of will to hold it back.

Chapter Twenty-Eight

Take That

Over the loudspeaker, everyone was woken by a song called *'Bright Side of the Road,'* I didn't know who it was by, and nobody seemed to know for sure. At first, it was a nice way to get out of bed. By day five, I wished someone would play something else. By day ten, the song no longer did anything for me. But even though, it was effective as an alarm clock for everyone who needed to get ready for work.

We continued with strengthening the fortifications around the Newman compound and all the while, I hoped with all my heart that the Takers wouldn't come while we were vulnerable.

Cherith met me at the south wall. As I worked with adding new material to the fortification, the wall was reaching new heights.

"Hey, come down from there," Cherith shouted as she looked up and cupped a hand over her brow.

After I'd got myself down from the ladder, Cherith handed me a tall glass of cool water, which I took and guzzled down. I didn't notice how incredibly thirsty I was until I started to drink. Cherith must've read my mind. I sat down in the shade and wiped the buildup of sweat and dirt from my forehead. Cherith sat beside me. But as she lowered herself down, I noticed from her body language that something was on her mind and was upsetting her.

"What is it?" I asked her as I playfully put my arm around her and tried to cheer her up.

Cherith wasn't one to mess around with her words. She came out and said exactly what was on her mind without any delay. "How do you think we'll go?"

I thought about it for a while. I was almost going to fluff things up, so it'd be easier to digest. But if I knew Cherith, she'd not settle for anything fluffed up. I told her, word for word, how I thought things would go. "We don't stand a chance, Cherith. We'll be overrun before the battle even gets started. And that's why we're putting so much time into getting the last resort bunker ready. I think shelter in the bunker is the only chance left for saving the families and the children."

"So, we climb down into a hole. We're good for how long? A week?"

"Two weeks."

"Okay. Two weeks, and then what? Will the Takers be gone by then?"

"That's the plan. When they're gone . . ."

"What, exactly." Cherith got up, stood back and folded her arms. "What should we do, Ricky? What? And what about you?"

I couldn't answer her although I wished I could. I wished hard I could see into the future and tell her no harm would come to her and the kids. I wished I could tell her I'd be okay and so would everyone else. But I knew by the end of the coming war, many of us would die, myself included. What other choice was there? We had to prepare the best way we knew how. I drew back to the words from someone who'd told me a long time ago; hope for the best but expect the worst.

* * *

Using huge horse-drawn carts that were made from old flatbed trucks with the cabins cut off, we collected ancient Post-Fall debris from Old Newman town center and used anything else we could find to make our compound stronger than it ever was. New to our compound were strategically positioned watchtowers which doubled as sniper nests if they were needed. With the new fortifications almost complete, I guesstimated that in two days of hard work, Newman's security would rival any Takers' outpost. The problem was, however, the lack of any significant firepower.

The weapons we had available ranged from a small number of antique bolt action rifles and only one of them was fitted with a scope — handguns and revolvers which were useless only because we had a limited reserve of ammunition. Everything else we had at our disposal were string weapons; bows, crossbows, and slingshots. But we had an ample supply of hand to hand fighting weapons. We had shields, knives, and swords made by our blacksmith from collected scraps of high carbon steel. We had bludgeons encrusted with razor-sharp shards of crackle. We even had garrotes made from the wire of an abandoned broken up piano we'd come across in Old Newman. As I went over it in my mind, if the Takers breach the wall, we'd give them a good showdown but, in the end, it was inevitable we'd be defeated. Every one of us would die.

In the center of the compound, the last resort bunker was complete. We supplied the bunker with enough water and food for the families to last for two weeks, which was exactly as I calculated. The entrance to the bunker was cleverly disguised under a row of outhouses, and it would take someone with intelligence to work out where to locate the entrance and how to breach it. I judged by what I already knew about Takers; the families would be safe until their supplies ran out.

On my list of things to get done were to help build an array of trebuchets. We'd need to position them at locations around the compound, in areas where we thought the Takers would begin their assault. Three huge trebuchets that were made out of reclaimed scrap stood ominously, thirty hands high, ready to do the damage. We needed more. The more, the better. Somewhere in the back of my mind, I had the image of 39-caliber howitzer shells raining down on us, and I tried not to think about it. The truth was, we were so unevenly matched, it would take nothing short of a miracle to stand up to the Takers and fight them until they were all dead.

I stood atop the central watchtower with my binoculars as guys outside the compound south wall placed markers where I needed them to go. I commanded the trebuchet operator on the ground in front of me, "Loose when ready."

The trebuchet swung its massive arm. A bag of flour was sent skyward, and I watched through my binoculars where it hit the ground. "Marker," I flag signaled the guys out there. Immediately, two guys ran and placed debris and rocks marking the location of the impact.

* * *

By the end of the day, the area outside the south wall of the compound had been target-marked, and the three trebuchets we had were set up with the correct trajectories. Just as I was finishing up and ready to climb down from the watchtower, I looked out to the north. I saw a group of eagles hugging the terrain, flying low and coming toward me.

"No. We're not ready," I said loudly to myself.

The white eagle led the formation as they approached, but there were more than the seven I'd seen before. Two had joined the seven to become nine. A black eagle, as black as a crow, and I knew, an American Bald Eagle, much larger than the rest, flew with them bringing up the rear. I cast my memory back to the dream that still lived vividly in my mind. Could it be these newcomers to the seven were the Angels of Mercy? They cried out with ear piercing eagle cries, passing over the top of me in arrowhead formation. As the eagles disappeared into the southern sky, my heart plummeted, and I knew the Takers were about to launch their attack. From the top of the central watchtower, I urgently grabbed a leather cord with my shaking hands and rang the bell. "Get the children!" I screamed. "Get the families and the children to the bunker. Now!"

By the time I reached the ground, men and women scurried madly with crying children in their arms as they raced for shelter. "Get the children to safety!" I kept screaming. Cherith ran up behind me. I spun and eyed her urgently. "What're you doing! Get to the bunker!"

"I wanted to give you something," Cherith said, at the same time wiping her tears away.

Cherith handed me something heavy wrapped in what I thought was a red bandana. After I unwrapped it, I held the pistol in my hand. A pistol with an inscription. *'Donald P Bosco.'*

Out of all the panic and madness around me, I was somehow surprised. "This is Michael's gun."

Cherith nodded. "It's fully loaded. I've been saving bullets as I've found them. I always knew Michael's gun was for a purpose. It's today, Rick. Make every bullet count." She pulled me into her arms and kissed me. Then I watched her as she spun and raced for the bunker.

Now, I turned and fixed my mind on what needed doing.

After I checked for rounds and cocked the weapon, I slipped the pistol behind the small of my back. I raced to my quarters and busted through the door. I picked up my rifle with the twenty-times scope and shouldered it. With time running out, I raced for the south watchtower.

Getting to the watchtower, three trebuchets were pushed to the boundary walls and were loaded with explosive bags of nails and anything else we could find that might do serious harm. I climbed the ladder and raised my binoculars. I waited. Archers made their way up ladders and took up position along the rim of the southern wall. They loaded their bows with explosive tipped arrows. The compound behind me grew silent as those who were about to fight held their position.

We all held still and silent.

Through my binoculars, I watched for signs of movement to the south.

Then.

They came.

The first line of Takers stopped just outside of Old Newman town center. I saw through the lenses of my binoculars they were roughly a thousand strong. Where are the eagles? I couldn't see them. But the Takers had all halted their advance. It wasn't long before I found out why.

A long series of low rolling booms rang out from somewhere in the far southern distance. As soon as I heard them, all the horrors I had in my head became a reality.

Howitzers!

"STAND-TO! STAND-TO!" I screamed. "TAKE COVER! INCOMING! TAKE COVER!"

I got myself to the ground as quickly as I could. Unshouldering my rifle, I bolted for the south wall. Howitzer shells screamed and drilled through the sky. An enormous explosion in front of me, knocked me off my feet as the south wall took a direct hit. Men were shredded, momentarily turning the sky a cloud of blood red. As bodies and parts of bodies landed around me, some were still alive and screamed out in pain. I ran to one man who was minus both his legs. I pushed my hands up to his stumps to stop the bleeding. "MEDIC! M-E-D-I-C!" I screamed at the same time another shell landed in the middle of the compound and exploded, sending the central watchtower toppling to the ground.

"M-E-D-I-C!" I screamed through the smoke and the blood.

Doc Drouin ran to my side. "I've got this. Go!"

Another shell drilled through the sky and exploded on impact with incredible force. I knew this time it was the east wall. Through the smoke a distance away, I saw the outline of Captain Bass, and I knew he had his detachment on the trebuchets ready to go.

Men were screaming from the west. I saw Takers already breaching the wall. Gunfire broke out. I raced to get there. As I ran, I retrieved my pistol. I raised my weapon and caught sight of Takers pulling themselves over the wall and down. I aimed and fired. Takers' heads snapped backward as their dead bodies fell to the ground. I continued to fire. More Takers fell.

From out of nowhere, nine eagles landed in front of me then instantly they transformed into human forms. One of the archangels faced me. "Get to the west watchtower. Do not look upon the face of the white archangel, Gabriel." Then she drew her sword and was gone. An angel with the tattoo of a white eagle and sword on the back of his head, spun and burned his eyes into me. He gave me a wink, reached and drew his recurved kukri, then disappeared into the smoke, thrusting his blade through invading Takers. I stood awestruck as the angels dispersed into the fray, slaying as they went. Running for the watchtower, I popped the heads of Takers who were in my way.

I climbed the west watchtower. And at the top, I saw what seemed several thousand Takers who were all sprinting across the desert, heading our way. Raising my rifle, I shot down Takers as they ran, sniping in quick secession until my ammo ran out. Dropping the rifle, I grabbed my sidearm and fired in rapid fire. Knowing my ammo was finite, I killed as many Takers as I could.

A tremor shook the platform at my feet. A deep rumble rose up through the watchtower, and into my body. Out in the south, dust rose up high into the air. As I turned to face the west, I raised my binoculars. I couldn't believe what I was seeing. A stampede of Rad Roos bore down on the thousands-strong Takers.

Just as I saw the Rad Roos from the west, from the north, the thunder of mechanical beasts cut through the noise of battle. The outlines of trucks raced across the desert pan. Trucks and tankers, and I knew . . . I knew they could be none other than the Ambers who we'd spent so many days and months in the hope of tracking down. The Lost Ones had arrived.

I faced west again to the sounds of men being ripped to pieces. Rad Roos, thousands of them, encircled Takers and closed in. One by one, Takers were ripped apart by the Rad Roos' nine-inch claws. The desert became a sea of blood with Takers' body parts abstractly strewn as far as I was able to see. But in their numbers, the Takers kept coming.

Trucks and tankers rushed vociferously to a stop. Ambers sprang from doors, shouldering weapons I'd only ever heard about. Then they lit the place up. The Ambers ripped into the Takers, letting them have it with their M134 miniguns. The multi-barreled guns spun at high speed and glowed red hot, spitting death and destruction wherever the Ambers pointed them. The Ambers walked slowly in lines abreast with their miniguns setting the place ablaze, cutting down Takers as they advanced. I watched on, and I saw Takers literally cut in half and then immediately shredded with the many hundreds of thousands of high-speed projectiles coming from the M134s

Rad Roos from the south and the west and the east. Ambers from the north. The Takers who were left alive and who were able to run dropped their weapons, turned, and bolted. The people of Newman roared their happiness. By the end, what was left over was a ghastly battlefield of the dead and the dying, in a sea of gore stretching to the horizon in each direction.

Chapter Twenty-Nine

Aftermath

I didn't know what I'd do if I had to listen to that song again. I made sure I was up early and far enough away from the loudspeakers. As the sun broke through the horizon to the east, I stood beside the gaping hole that was left in the compound wall. The break of day brought with it the true horror of war.

Ravens. Millions of them. They'd descended on the battlefield, and it was as though they were there to take the souls of the dead to some dark place. The battlefield was alive with the ravens' squawking and screeching, as they got busy with their pecking and prodding. For as far as it was possible to see, the ground before me seemed to be alive with shimmering waves of black upon red.

I hadn't come to the east of the compound to gloat about our victory over the Takers. A victory, yes. But somehow, I knew there'd be more. Our triumph was over a single battle; and not a war. Somewhere in my heart, I felt there'd be the day when the righteous descends upon evil in one final conflict. When that day would come was anybody's guess. They shall have their day of reckoning. They shall be made to pay for their crimes.

On the east side of the compound, I kneeled in front of Eli's grave. In a way, I was glad Eli never had to deal with the horrors of last night. I was equally glad for Jason whose grave had been placed without a body next to Eli's. But, if only I could visit Chloe's place of rest one last time. Perhaps one day I might have the opportunity to travel back to Antarctica, even if it's only to visit Chloe and my mother for one last time.

I put my hand down on Jason's resting place. Even though his body wasn't there, I knew his spirit would be wherever I chose it to be. "This is goodbye, brother. I'll see you on the other side, huh?"

I got up and turned away. With a sigh, in my mind at least, I began to continue the long walk.

* * *

We spent the next five full days collecting bodies and body parts, piling them into heaps and setting them on fire. I would've liked to have seen the entire battlefield cleaned, but with so many of the dead to deal with, it was virtually impossible. Apart from the immediate area of the compound, the Ravens were left with the task of cleaning what we were unable to handle. But, if we'd never had help from the Ambers, the task of cleaning up would've taken much longer than it did. I was thankful to them. We all were. It meant the people of Newman could get back to their lives and not have to worry about disease.

At the end of each day, tired and exhausted, I retreated to my quarters knowing the next day would come, and it would play out in much the same way. By day six, however, life began to return to normal with the Newman dwellers. As for me, I had a job to finish.

I met Seth during the morning of the seventh day. After Seth handed over my calico bag containing *The Angel of Bunjil* and the Sacred Bone, there was only one thing left to do. And that was to hand the relics over to the Ambers before they left and returned north. My job would be over. I would've finished what I started. But, after that, what? I couldn't help but feel empty with that thought running around my head. I'd thought about staying in Newman only superficially. Now, I had to make up my mind one way or another.

In the early afternoon, I'd met a tall and slender looking Amber who shared the same bright red hair, fair skin, and freckles as the rest of them. He introduced himself as George De Niro and took my hand, shaking it with a grip so firm, he momentarily cut off the blood supply from the rest of my body. George was in charge of the Ambers' convoy and said he makes the trip once a year from Amberton in the north to Newman and then back; and has been doing it for the past forty years. After I handed over the relics, George opened the bag, and it was like he'd been reunited with a long-lost friend. He put a hand to his face and took a step back. "This is wonderful!" he said happily. And the smile on his face was priceless enough for me to leave everything right there. But my quest was never going to end at that moment.

"I'm grateful and happy to see the relics. I'll hand them to our high priests after we return."

After he said it, I knew I wasn't going to be happy until I saw the very end of the journey with my own eyes. "If you must give the relics to your high priests, then I will be the one to do it. I've come so far, and I've been through so much. I'd like to be the one to take the relics to them."

George took a few moments to think about what I'd said. "If you come with us, you'll die."

I nodded. "I'm aware of that."

"You'll die in pain."

I nodded again. "I know what pain is."

"Come with me," George said.

I followed George to the west wall. Before we reached the entrance tunnel, he told me to wait. George stepped away and left me there but returned a few moments later with something yellow and plastic in his hands. "Put this on. It won't save you, but it'll slow down the onset of radiation sickness. You'll have time to hand the relics to the high priests."

"I'll die after that?"

George nodded slowly. "You've got balls. I gotta hand it to you. We'll all hope for your quick death. But we must go right now."

Cherith. I needed to at least tell her that . . . "I'll be a moment. I just need to . . ."

"We have to go now," George said urgently. "If you want to live long enough, we must leave. Our vehicles are all highly radioactive. You've already taken a big count. So, put on that rad suit and let's go."

* * *

The Amber's convoy of three troop trucks, three flatbeds, and two diesel tankers left Newman in the afternoon of the seventh day. I rode shotgun with George in a huge tanker as it bounced heavily over the ruts and potholes that were abundant in the ancient postfall highways. As I rode with George, my mind returned to Cherith and how I was forcefully torn away. I regretted it. I wished I'd had the chance to say a proper goodbye. Cherith might spend the rest of her life wondering what had happened to me. But then, something else came to mind.

As I thought back to Michael's journal, I remembered the time he'd met Cherith and Seth for the first time after he and Timothy weren't far from the silver mine. That was forty years ago. Give or take, as Michael had said. But forty years ago, Seth and Cherith were adults. That would've made them at least seventy years of age the last time I saw them. But Cherith was never in her seventies. She looked like she was still in the prime of her youth. The same went for Seth. As I thought it over in my mind, it just didn't make any sense. Then something else. I hadn't seen anybody at Newman that I considered elderly.

"Stop the truck!" I yelled. "I need to go back."

George shot me a sideways glare. "There's not enough time."

"Stop! Stop the truck! Right now!"

George shoved the brake pedal down hard. The truck lurched to a stop amid the sounds of rushing air. "What is it?" George asked.

"We need to go back. It's urgent!"

After a big sigh, George grabbed the mic and announced over the radio that we were turning around, and the rest of the convoy must continue straight on. "We'll catch up with them, but this had better be a good reason to go back. I'm just saying."

After George pulled up outside of Newman, my heart fell to my feet. My breath was wrenched away. There was nobody at Newman. It was as though ghosts had lived there. There were no crops of corn. No vegetables. No chicken and geese. Not even cattle. The buildings in Newman were like nobody had lived there in centuries. Everything was derelict and half fallen over. Through my shock, I wasn't able to feel my dismay. So, what, in the heck, had gone on in Newman? Was everything I went through all in my head?

George put his hand on my shoulder. "Come on. We need to go."

* * *

I remained silent for the rest of the journey north. Partly because I still couldn't figure Newman out. And partly because I was wearing a rad suit, and nobody could hear me if I didn't shout as loud as I could. And I was sick of the shouting.

As we got further north, I noticed the changes in the landscape, and I knew it was the radiation which had caused such ugliness on the planet. We went from flat colorless nothing to flat colorless deadly nothing. I could feel it on my skin how much deadlier things were getting with every mile we drove. I wondered if I'd be dead by now if I wasn't wearing any protection. Either way, it no longer mattered. The only thing I wished to do now was to finish my quest. Any moment spent alive after that was a bonus. Just as I had that thought, I coughed hard inside my rad suit. My face shield became an ugliness of phlegm mixed with spots of blood. I lifted my hand to take my hood down so I could at least clean it.

"No!" George responded just in time. "Don't take it off. Just deal with it. It's going to be worse by the time we get there."

For the next several hours, I sat there looking at my own blood sputum. But hey. Death was coming. What did I care?

* * *

We finally reached Amberton before the sun was due to rise. As George drove the tanker through the empty streets which were filled with the same post-fall debris, I'd seen everywhere else, we passed a huge aged and pockmarked sign that said, *'Welcome to Darwin. Estab. 1874.'*

It was obvious now. In recent years, the Darwin I'd once learned about had now become Amberton.

The truck wound its way around streets that got tighter and tighter—streets which had been modified or cleaned up or changed to suit the needs of the Ambers. When George pulled the tanker to a stop, the headlights briefly illuminated the convoy we'd left behind. George switched the engine off. "We're home!" he said smiling. "Come on. The faster we get underground, the faster we'll get you away from the radiation, and then you can take that suit off."

Getting out of the truck, an old cottage caught my eye with a sign that seemed even older. *'Charlotte Station.'* I wondered if there was a correlation between where I was and the angel in Michael's journal. But by the time we were at a steel doorway behind the cottage, I left that thought behind.

Chapter Thirty

Arrival

Peering down into the darkened stairwell, it beckoned as I stepped down. It was as though I was looking down into my own grave. Already, my breathing was heavy, and my throat felt like I'd swallowed a handful of sand. I did my best to ignore the sensation of fire in my extremities. I did my best to ignore all the symptoms. I had a job to get done. I *must* deliver the relics and see my journey at its end. I peered down into the darkened stairwell, and I stepped down.

George grabbed the lid of an electrical box to his left and flipped it up. After he'd flicked a few switches, the lights from below sprang to life and showed the stairwell going down even deeper. My tired and worn out boots clicked on the metal steps that went down for roughly a hundred hands and arrived at a couple of steel sliding doors.

George invited me to push the button with a simple hand gesture. "Go ahead," he said. "After this, you get to take off that rad suit."

After I'd pushed the button, the door slid open. At first, I thought it was an elevator like those I'd seen in movies. But after George stepped in front of me and entered the chamber, he showed me what to do. He put his arms out to his side. Immediately, he was awash with jets of water and air. After he was done and walked through to the other side, he gestured with a hand for me to enter the chamber and to do the same.

If anything, I was glad my rad suit was washed clean from the outside. But I was still looking through blood-snot after I'd been jet blasted. Nonetheless, the room on the other side of the decontamination chamber was an area to change into clean clothing. I took off that damn rad suit and tossed it aside. George passed me something fresh to put on. After changing into something that smelled fresh, I decided to leave my red bandana on my head, and I put my pistol back behind the small of my back. "I thought you guys were resistant to radiation," I said as I shouldered the bag containing the relics, and as George finished up putting on what he called his vault suit.

"We are. But our food won't grow if it's contaminated. Everything we need to survive is underground. The radiation can't get to it. It's imperative everything is clean, clean, clean. C'mon. Let's go."

It seemed a little odd to have animals underground. That was the height of cruelty. After I asked George about the Ambers' meat and protein supplies, things began to get a little weird.

"We're vegans," George said. "Our protein comes from the things we grow. We don't do animal meat of any kind. Unlike the Takers who'd eat their own given a chance."

As we walked the underground corridors that resembled a spider's web, my mind went back to Michael's journal. According to Michael, the reason the Ambers went to Newman was to drop off diesel and pick up meat. Now I'm finding out they're vegans? But nothing could've prepared me for what George said after I challenged him.

"The high priests sent us to Newman."

"Why?"

"To look for you, Richard Gabriel. The battle of Newman was prophesized by our high priests. And after the battle, the relics would find us. It was always said the relics would appear out of the hands of the white one. *You* are the white one. After all these years and decades, the prophecy of *The Angel of Bunjil* is about to come to fruition."

* * *

By the time we reached the main area of the underground commune, I was staggered by the size. I couldn't imagine how the Ambers had built such a massive structure underground. The span of the dome was enormous. The cathedral by itself reached as high as several hundred hands up. It was a place for all the Ambers to congregate and socialize. It was also the hub where all corridors connected. I stood high up on a landing and looked down to see the population of Amberton going about their business as though it was a day the same as any other. But one of the Ambers must've noticed me as I began my journey down the steps. Before I knew it, one by one, they began to stop what they were doing. One of them pointed. "The white one," she said loudly. Then everyone began to chant the words, "Bunjil, Bunjil, Bunjil."

Arriving at the bottom of the staircase, I began to move through them, and the crowd opened as I walked between them. It seemed an awkward time to begin a coughing fit, but I couldn't have helped it. This time as I coughed hard into my hand, I couldn't ignore the amount of blood. And I couldn't ignore what I was feeling. Someone had lit a fire underneath me. It was the first time I noticed the blood blisters all over my arms. I knew time was getting away.

In the center of the cathedral was a priestly structure. It was magnetic, pulling me toward it. I approached the center where two huge columns stood like obelisks reaching up roughly eighty hands. Standing beside the columns were five Ambers dressed in long gold garments which flowed out and dragged along the floor. The five turned to face me. I unshouldered the bag containing the relics, trying hard to stem another bout of coughing which I only just managed. Opening the bag, I gave over the contents; the crystal figurine and the human bone. My journey and my epic mission were over.

The high priests nodded before taking the relics and placing them down on a small altar. Immediately, bright blue light glowed between the huge obelisks, and a vibration pulsed deep into my body.

People behind me chanted. "Bunjil, Bunjil, Bunjil."

Louder and louder, they chanted. The light grew brighter. I shaded my eyes with the back of my hands and saw an outline of someone coming through. Then more appeared.

A woman with long flowing dark and greying hair, dressed in what appeared to be black rubber appeared through the blue light. She quickly studied the area, then turned to help others as they came through. By the time it was over, more than a hundred Ambers had passed through the light and appeared to be stunned with their new surroundings. The chanting from behind me had ceased. The high priests had stepped away. The woman dressed in black made her way toward me. Eyeing me intensely with her piercing eyes, she reached and took the red bandana off my head. "That doesn't belong to you. Where did you get it?"

I didn't know how to react. I did the best I could. "My gun was wrapped in it."

"Your gun? Show me."

I took the gun from behind my back and gave it to her. She read the inscription engraved on it. "Bosco . . ." she said with sadness. She swayed slightly before her legs collapsed from under her. I tried to reach out and grab her as she fell. The high priests immediately stopped me.

The woman bent her head forward and began to weep. Someone else of Amber appearance but much older stepped up behind the woman and placed his hand on her shoulder.

"I'm okay, Scotty. I just need a moment. It's a little more than I can handle."

"Angel. Take as much time as ya need, love. We've all been through this crap for a reason. Now, we're about to show 'em why, eh?"

* * *

The pain was such that I could no longer stand. They'd given me a soft and comfortable bed; and medication to help relieve the fire that raged in every corner of my body.

Despite everything, despite all the suffering and loss, despite the pain I was feeling; I was at peace.

Angel Bunjil reached out with her hand, lightly hovering it above my chest. Scotty-Blue reached and slowly took her hand away. "No, love. Let 'im go. After what 'es been through, 'e needs 'is rest, eh?"

Angel Bunjil and Scotty-Blue Thompson were at my side as I closed my eyes for the last time.

The Angel

and the

Mad Man

Shortly after I was shown a cushy-looking lounge that smelled of old leather, and looked as though it was recovered from a shipwreck, I sat slowly down, and I wondered how I would ever get myself back up. I was then told by someone more knowing than myself, that 'a child will process trauma in unique ways.' Young minds will either switch off painful happenings as though a section of mind poses as a guardian, almost as if it's detached from the being; almost as if it's duty-bound to protect little souls from damaging images. Or, memories won't be shut down. They will persist — memories, alive, and in vivid colour. Memories, which haunt and hurt; and will *not* go away. My memory of my father. My memory of my mother. And . . . of Charlotte.

* * *

Alice Springs, Central Australia, 1991

My mother had switched off everything that used electricity. The fridge. The dishwasher. The radio that she loved so much on Sunday afternoons while she sat in her easy chair and spun Merino wool into long curly skeins. The tall clock that demanded attention at the end of the hall stood proud but no longer ticked. There was no whirring of the Whirlpool from the laundry. There was no scent of freshly baked lamingtons or vanilla slices from the kitchen. There were no songs by Hi-Five from the television in the living room. There was no laughter. There was no happiness. There was nothing. And everything was dark.

After pulling down all the blinds, my mother scurried around the place, and with her hands visibly shaking, she reached with her trembling fingers, clawing at power points and switches. She raced methodically from one switch to another, muttering to herself as though somewhere in her mind there was a method in the things she was doing. But I could see it on her face. Her skin was sweaty. I was just old enough to recognise panic. I was old enough to feel brewing terror that made my skin feel incredibly hot. I remember as my mother scampered around the place; I kept telling myself it was just a game. It was, of course, no game at all. "Quickly, Angelique. We have to hide," my mother said with a voice that crackled and quivered.

My mother's eyes darted here and there. Was she trying to decide the best place in the house for us to hide? We had no basement or attic. There was only one place inside the house which had a lock behind the door — the bathroom. I recall as a child; there were so many times I got into trouble if I stayed in the shower for too long. The door was locked. Nobody could do anything about it. My mother decided to hide in there as soon as she grabbed me tightly by the top of my arm. She pulled me forcefully into the cold darkness behind the shower curtain. In the bathtub, we both quietly sat down facing each other. My mother's facial expression was steady as she appeared to listen for signs of movement from the outside of our house.

"Mum?"

"Shhh. We'll be safe in here," my mother told me while she held her finger up to her lips.

"But Mum, Dad will know we're home. Our car is at the end of the driveway. He'll come looking for us as soon as he gets inside."

"He can't get in. He doesn't have a key. I've changed all the locks. And he'll think we're at Maggie's house."

If my father knew we were at Maggie's house, he'd never go looking there. Maggie's husband was an Alice Springs police officer. And not only that, he was a sergeant, I recall thinking. My father and Theo were always at each other. Theo sometimes brought my drunken father home late at night and dumped him near our front door. My young mind began to put things together. What my mother was trying to achieve was to give my father a decoy. He'd turn up at our house and find he wasn't able to enter. He'd put his ear up to the door and listen for anything inside. My father would then most likely choose to meet with his mates at the pub. Or maybe an afternoon betting on horse races at the TAB. That's how my mother had explained it. She said it to me in plain words and sentences like I was already an adult. Then after she was done, she began to cry.

"Mum, you're scaring me."

My mother pulled me into her chest and wrapped her arms around me. I remember feeling nothing could ever hurt us. Any ten-year-old would be comforted. But I was also cautious. I was also vigilant. Why did Uncle Scotty have to show up and ruin everything?

* * *

As I sat in the cold and darkened bathroom with my mother, who seemed to be thinking of ways to get us out of danger, I reflected briefly on the horrible things that had happened. I remembered the blue, square, object that Uncle Scotty had given her after he arrived so urgently on our front porch. My uncle's tone of voice said he was hopelessly in a mad flap. "You need to get this to Maggie," I heard him say. "I'd do it, but I can't, love. You know I'm on the grid. If I approach Maggie, I'll blow my cover."

I recall as I stood and peered through the living room window, my Uncle Scotty gave my mother something else. It was something that looked like a handkerchief—a piece of cloth with something printed on it. He took it from his pocket and thrust it into my mother's hand. "These are the decryption codes for the computer disk," he said.

"So, what am I supposed to do with them?"

"Alisha. Get them to Maggie. Find a way. She'll know what to do next."

"And Franco? Any ideas where he is right now?"

Scotty immediately answered without a breath. "He's most likely down the pub gettin' plastered. Maybe . . . I'm not sure."

"You can't be sure? This place is so much better when you're both away on work. The two of you should've stayed at Pine Gap!" My mother sucked back a big gulp of air and paused a beat. "How much time do we have before he shows up?"

"You've got as much time as it takes to grab a few things and get out, I reckon. Grab your kit and go. Right-bloody-now."

After Scotty launched himself from the porch, ran to his car and drove away, my mother slowly closed the front door. She turned and looked down at me. I'll never forget her face. Her skin was paper white. Her eyes had become glassy like they were full of fear and sadness. I knew she tried her best to hide her true feelings from me. I could see straight through her. I knew what was *really* going on.

"Angelique, we have to pack a bag and get ready to go. Quickly now, kiddo."

I sprinted into my room, thinking about the things I needed to pack. I slid open my wardrobe door and grabbed my rucksack from the hanger. My mind immediately thought about my camera and photos. They were up on a high shelf. I often wondered why my mother had placed them up so high that it was difficult for me to get to them. My toes almost broke with my weight as I reached up to grab them. I jumped and missed. I jumped and missed again. It was no good. Then, I used the bed as a trampoline. That worked amazingly well, and I had my camera and all my photo albums, all at once.

After ramming my most precious items into my rucksack, I grabbed some of my clothes from my dresser and quickly formed them into a tight ball, shoving them in so hard I swore they were going to burst through the bottom. My mother stepped inside my room as I was finishing up. She brought the objects in that Scotty gave her. She showed them to me. "If anything bad happens, make sure Maggie gets these things." My mother then slipped the blue computer disk and codes into the top pocket of the rucksack.

As soon as she was done tightening the straps, she held out her hand to me. "Let's go," she said. "Fuck this place."

We were only five footsteps from my bedroom door when that sound of someone pushing a key into a keyhole, punched through the silence. My mother instantly crouched and pushed me down next to her. She put a finger up to her lips. I knew what it meant. Not a sound. Not a movement. Just like the game we used to play called 'quiet as a mouse.'

As we both crouched, whoever it was at the front door continued to scratch away at the lock. Then, the Mad Man made himself known.

"Alisha!"

My mother looked at me with terror sitting in her red-rimmed eyes. She again pushed her finger up to her lips. When she removed her finger, she tried to give me a comforting smile. But the corners of her mouth refused to cooperate.

"Alisha! Open the bloody door!" My father bashed the door a couple of times.

"Don't say anything," my mother said to me in a whisper so low, it was difficult to hear. But then she physically turned me around and gave me a gentle push toward my bedroom. "Go. Quietly," she whispered.

"Alisha. Open the door. My key won't fit the bloody lock!"

I couldn't be sure how many times my father had yelled out and demanded to be let inside. Each time he yelled out, his voice raised in obvious frustration. His bashing at the door became louder and heavier. Then, there was no sound at all. He was gone.

And my mother immediately began shutting things down and switching things off.

* * *

In the darkness of the bathroom from behind the shower curtain, we both waited in the cold silence. I could feel the steady beat of my mother's heart through her chest as she held me tightly in her arms. Sometimes her heartbeat picked up and raced race as soon as she heard sounds from outside. But through it all, it occurred to me; we could've easily used the time to exit through the back door and get far away. It might've worked out better than being boxed in. We could've already arrived at Maggie's house. And after having arrived there, we could've been safe from the rage of my drunken father. Things and events could have been drastically different than they turned out. It was a moment in time that has stayed with me for my entire life. I keep asking myself the same question. Why didn't we go? In that precise moment? Why? All through my twenties. All through my thirties. Even to this very minute, it still causes me heartache. It still causes nightmares and chills me awake. Why can't I go back and change anything? Why?

It was as though my mother had the same thought as me, and at the same time. She let go of me and looked down into my eyes. She seemed so much better without any panic. I was even able to breathe long breaths again. "Time to go, eh kiddo?"

I nodded my happiness, but my moment of joy shattered with the sound of someone scraping at the lock in the back door. My father was back from wherever he'd gone. He was angry. I could hear it in his tone. "Alisha! You've bloody-well changed the back-door lock too? What have you done? Are you doing this to make me angry? Alisha, this is my house too. Let-me-in!"

I shrunk from my father's rage. "Mum!"

My mother pulled me into her arms again. "It's okay kiddo. But I want you to understand something. Whatever happens, run. Run as fast as you can. Take the rucksack and run to Maggie's. Don't look back. Don't worry about me. Just run. Do you hear me? Just run."

I nodded, hoping my mother could feel my answer on her chest.

"That's good. You know what you need to do. That's good." It was as though my mother had said those final words to herself rather than to me. It was after she'd said it, I noticed for the first time how badly she was trembling.

But then, silence ensued once again. We both waited. We both listened out for the slightest of sounds. It was as though my father had finally left. Each moment felt more like hours, and we waited.

SMASH!

I heard a window somewhere near the back of the house, cave in and shatter.

"MUM!"

My mother pulled me in tighter. Much tighter than before.

I heard my father stomping with heavy footsteps around the house. "Alisha! Where are you? Are you home? Angelique?"

My mother immediately got out of the bathtub and went to the window. She used both her hands to push the ages-old window up, but it wouldn't budge. She put her entire weight behind it. It was no good.

"Smash it, Mum. Just smash it."

"No good, kiddo. The glass has got wire inside it."

Then, my father's footsteps stopped at the bathroom door. I could hear him breathing as though he'd pushed his face up close to the door jamb. My mother put her hand over my mouth. She placed her lips right next to my left ear and whispered, "Not a word, kiddo. Shhh."

"C'mon Alisha, I know you're in there. Angelique. I know you're both there. The car's outside, remember? I'm tired, and I need a lie-down. C'mon out and we'll chat a while. Maybe, I'll put a few snags on the barbie. What do ya reckon?"

For some reason, my mother took her hand away from my mouth. Perhaps it was a moment of weakness. Maybe she was about to get up and let my father inside. I couldn't let her do that. I had to stop her. I seized the opportunity, and I shouted, "Just go away and leave us alone!"

"Kiddo! What have you done? Didn't I say not a word?"

"Ya see? I knew you were both at home. Now, c'mon out, the two of ya. This is being silly; don't ya reckon?"

"Go away, Franco. Take the car keys; they're on the kitchen bench. Go away and leave us in peace."

"Peace? Do'ya want peace? I'll show ya fucking peace!" It was like my father's rage came rushing up from wherever he'd put it last. This time, he beat heavily on the door. "Don't make me break this door in, Alisha. I will break it if I need to. Come out! Come out now!"

I screamed as loud as I could. I hoped my high pitch squeal was enough to grab anybody's attention who might be in range. Perhaps the people from next door would hear. Maybe they'd call Theo Mack, and he'd rush down here with his siren blaring and his lights flashing. But even for someone as young as I was at the time, I knew it wasn't likely.

Then it was like a miracle. Suddenly, my father's footsteps walked away. I heard him walk through the kitchen, grabbing at the keys that my mother had told him were on the bench. I heard him a couple of minutes later start the car. The car reversed up the driveway, and my father was gone.

It was like a weight had lifted from my spirits. Even my mother looked happier than she was only a moment ago. We both cautiously exited the bathroom. I ran straight for my bedroom and picked up my rucksack. "Come on Mum; we need to get going to Maggie's. Let's go." I was happy that I could make a suggestion. My mother even laughed a little under her breath. "Oh, I see. You're making all the calls now, huh?"

"Let's go, Mum, let's go."

We were about to leave.

We were both about to exit our house of horrors, and I couldn't have cared less if it was for the last time in my young life. I was happy to be away and to be safe. But just as we were at the back door, my mother suddenly stopped her forward momentum. I grabbed her arm and pulled her. "What's wrong? C'mon Mum. We're running out of time."

"No, kiddo. We'll stay here. Your father already knows where we're going, and he'll be waiting for us somewhere."

I watched in dismay as my mother closed the back door, then grabbed a chair from the dining room. She brought the chair back with her and wedged the chair under the doorknob. "I'll make a phone call to Theo Mack, and he can sort this out; once and for all."

I couldn't believe what I was seeing. We had the chance to get away, and it was gone. Even if it were only to the house next door, even if that were the case, we'd still be away. But now . . . We were again trapped. There was only one thing left for me to do. And that was to get under my bed as far as I could get and hide. I ran there. I ran to my bedroom while my mother picked up the phone. I heard her jiggle the hanger a couple of times. "Hello?" Another jiggle. Another jiggle. "Hello!" I heard my mother draw an annoyed sigh before she banged the handset hard down. "Shit!"

As I lay hidden under my bed, my eyes began to fill with tears. I was now more scared than I can ever remember. I only hoped the chair at the back door was strong enough to keep my father out. Just as I had that thought, the back door exploded into what I thought must be more than a thousand pieces.

I hurried out from under my bed and raced to the back door to where my father was standing in the aperture; a gigantic sledgehammer dangled ominously from his grip. It occurred to me then that this was his solution to the locked bathroom door. I realised much later in life, had my mother and I still been in there; we would've been much more boxed in and vulnerable than we already were. Maybe my father would've killed us both.

As I stood, shocked, seeing my father with his face that told of nothing but hatred and anger, I managed to catch sight of my mother as she suddenly burst past me. "Get out! Get out! Get out!" my mother screamed with words that still chill me after all this time. She tried with all her weight to push my father back through the door. He grabbed my mother and spun her around. He locked his elbow around the base of her throat and squeezed. "Now, none of that," my father said in cold tone. "You don't have to be all pushy. I'll go. But you know what I want don't ya? I want those things my mate Scotty-Blue gave ya. I know you have the disk and codes. Give them to me, and I'm gone, Alisha."

My mother managed some words through her squeezed neck. "Franco . . . What're you talking about?"

"Don't play games with me. Don't-you-fucking-play-games-with-me!"

I picked up my rucksack and threw it at my father with all the strength I had in my body. "Leave my mother ALONE!"

"Angelique . . . run. Run, Angelique. RUN!"

My father laughed at me. He laughed hard, and sardonically like he'd seen something so very funny. He let my mother go. But only for a second. It was like he had all the power. He quickly gathered her up and choked her all over again.

"Angelique! RUN!"

"No Mum. I can't leave you!"

"Just . . . run . . . kiddo!"

My father squeezed his elbow around my mother's throat harder than before. Her face immediately went cherry red. Her eyes bulged, and I saw blood at the corners of her eyelids. She tried to say something, but it never came out. Her body went limp, and after my father let go of her, she slid slowly to the floor. Then, my father turned his attention on me. He reached and grabbed a handful of my hair. I remember the hot pain on my scalp as he picked me up and swung me. I floated only inches above the floor. "You're going in your bloody room, and you're gonna STAY THERE!"

After my father had thrown me through the doorway, I again slid under my bed as far as I could get. My cheeks felt raw and wet as I cried uncontrollably. But my father paused, laughing at me like my sobbing was one of the funniest things he'd ever seen. Before slamming my door closed, he shouted, "And don't come out!"

* * *

While I lay there, I listened as my father stomped around the house. I heard him rummage through drawers then slam them closed. I heard cupboard doors open, and I imagined the contents thrown across the room. I heard clanging of pots and pans. I heard the smashing of glass. I heard my father racing around the house. "Where is it? What have you done with it?"

"I don't know what you're talking about, Franco. You must be out of your mind. Go back to your mates at the pub. Maybe they know where it is what you're looking for."

I was glad I heard my mother's voice, but I was also terribly afraid for her. I heard my father's heavy footsteps rush across the floor. Then, the ugly sound of his fist connecting with flesh.

"NOOO!" I scampered madly from under my bed and ran out of my room. I saw my father standing over my mother. I launched myself onto my father's back, I began beating him as hard as I could.

My mother pleaded with me; her voice so dry. "Angelique. Stop. Please stop. I'm okay."

Before I had the opportunity to do more damage, my father peeled me off his back. He again lifted me by my hair and carried me to my bedroom. He tossed me like a pendulum with such force, I flew through the air and landed heavily on my bed. I grabbed my pillow and buried my face as I cried harder than I'd ever known.

Outside my room, I heard them arguing. The bickering went on and on and on. He wanted whatever he wanted, and she wasn't about to let him have it. Back and forth, they fought. Sometimes it was physical with the awful sounds of fleshy beatings. If I knew my mother, she'd give back just as much as what she was given. Maybe that would make things worse. She screamed at him. He yelled back at her. Hurtful and spiteful. Cruel and cutting. Words and sounds a child should never have to endure.

But suddenly, everything stopped.

I felt an urge rip up through my body. I felt as though there were eyes upon me. There was something outside of my bedroom window; I just knew it. Looking out, I saw an eagle had settled and had found a perch on the back fence. The moment the eagle's eyes made contact with mine, I knew it was not just any eagle, but it had to be *my* eagle. It was Charlotte.

It was at that moment that all my sadness and hurt had melted away. I felt strength take over the weakness in my body. I sprinted from my room and out through the back door. I cut a short distance across the back yard toward where Charlotte was busy, happily preening her feathers as though she was making herself beautiful just for me. I couldn't have been happier than in that moment. It was one of the most delightful times of my life. As I approached Charlotte, it was as though she beckoned me closer, and when I got there, she put her head down and flared out her huge wings in a warm gesture of hello.

I don't know how long I was there in Charlotte's company. It seemed like only minutes. But after Charlotte had lifted her head again, she appeared to become startled. She turned away from me and put her head down. She looked over her shoulder one last time before she launched into the sky; her huge wingspan compressing the air as she lifted herself into the sky.

I stood back and watched Charlotte disappear into the afternoon sun. And after she'd gone, my thoughts returned to the horrors of which I was given just a small amount of respite. Remembering my father's words to 'not come out of my room,' I slowly turned to get back into the house, but instantly, my legs stopped carrying me forward.

"Time to come in, love. It's gonna be tea time soon," my father said as he stood there on the back veranda, watching me.

But in my mind, a warning sounded, and somehow, I knew not to go to him. As he repeated the same sentence over, I noticed the sledgehammer in my father's grip. I noticed the thick dark coloured blood that dripped in steady drops from the shiny metal.

I noticed the red stains on his white singlet. I noticed the blood spatter all over his face and arms. He repeated his words slowly. "Come inside, Angelique. Tea time."

My legs were like pins that held me into place. Not forward. Not backward. I was frozen still. I felt coldness sweep up and over me, giving me goosebumps on my arms and neck as my father appeared to grow angrier with each passing second. "Get inside you little bitch!"

I moved one foot in front of the other. Then the other in front of that. Slowly, I gained speed, and in the next crucial second, I began sprinting across the back yard toward the gate. As I moved as fast as I could go, I caught sight of my father as he hitched the sledgehammer over his shoulder and launched himself off the veranda. "Get back here!" he screamed. I ran. I ran hard.

At the back gate, I jumped and cleared it with my father only inches behind me. I felt the breeze of his sledgehammer swish past me. I could hear his hard breathing as he struggled to get over. I ran on and paced away. Breathing. Running. Breathing. Running.

Out in the street, I turned and sprinted down the middle of the bitumen. If a car was coming, I could put up my arms and scream. Maybe whoever was driving might stop. As I ran, I saw a shadow on the road. The shadow of an eagle raced on ahead in front of me, and then suddenly, it disappeared. From behind, I heard an eagle screech with an ear-piercing cry and echoed through the suburbs. I stopped and spun around in time to see Charlotte's silhouette in the late afternoon sun. Her outline became backlit from the bright sunlight, as she tumbled and turned over high in the sky. I saw Charlotte as she tucked in her wings and became a bullet, head down, screeching her cry through the air as my father ran almost out of breath, panting, and still trying to shut me down.

With no warning, Charlotte came down from behind him and attached her giant talons around my father's neck. Screeching and squealing, she flared out her wings, and I saw her talons disappear deep into his flesh. Long red ribbons ripped away from my father's neck as Charlotte again took to the skies. My father screamed out then gurgled chillingly in a way I'd never heard before. He placed both his hands over his gaping open wounds but to no avail. The fountains of his blood reached high above him. Then, his body seemed to collapse from under his weight. I knew from that moment; there was no life left in him. The Mad Man was dead.

From a distance, I heard the sounds of sirens. Theo Mack would arrive, but by the time he reached the scene where blood was everywhere, the mandatory police 'guns drawn' approach was of no use. Theo exited his police vehicle exactly as I thought. "Get on the ground!" he shouted, pistol pointed at my lifeless father. When he got close enough, I saw his shoulders droop, and he put his gun away.

As I turned away from what I was seeing, Maggie was there, standing in front of me with her arms held out. "Come with me, love," she said, gathering me up and pulling me into her arms. Maggie smelled of lavender. After that moment, lavender took on a new meaning for me. Whenever I smell lavender, it transports me back to the time I was orphaned and left without my parents.

My Angel saved me from the Mad Man, but now, I must somehow live with the memory.

* * *

I am Angel Bunjil. I am leader of The Breakers. I am destined; hear my voice. Those who are righteous shall have their vengeance. And those who stand for evil shall have their day of reckoning.

ABOUT THE AUTHOR

Carl Lakeland lives with his wife in the sleepy town of Snake Valley, 36 kilometres south west of Ballarat in Australia. Lakeland grew up during the early seventies in the western suburbs of Sydney. Having enlisted into the military at the age of seventeen, he draws on his experience to create powerful and engaging speculative fiction.

"Sometimes, I can't let things be," says Lakeland. "I write stories with passion that others might see as being obsessive. I live and breathe it. I dream it when I sleep. But I never write down my dreams. If I can't remember those things I've dreamt, they're not important enough."

Lakeland's stories revolve around the element of 'what if?' He pushes the boundaries of his stories to the edge of the *Official Secrets Act*, which will leave the reader wondering about the aspect of creative license, or the possibility of fact in his writing. Either way, the reader will be left to make up their own mind. His books are fast paced, edge of your seat thrillers that are distinctively written in a way that will have the reader guessing which way the story is about to head.

"As a writer, unpredictability is the key essence. If I write something that can be foreseen in coming chapters, it's not good enough. I will scrap it. My goal is to keep the reader wondering, even sometimes to the detriment of my good guys!"

WEBSITE: carllakeland.com EMAIL carl@carllakeland.com

ALSO BY CARL LAKELAND

COMING IN 2020